Aztec Gold

(Alicia Myles #1)

By

David Leadbeater

Thriller, adventure, action, mystery, suspense, archaeological,
military

Other Books by David Leadbeater:

Connect with the author on Twitter: @dleadbeater2011
Visit the author's website: **www.davidleadbeater.com**
Follow the author's Blog
http://davidleadbeaternovels.blogspot.co.uk/

All helpful, genuine comments are welcome. I would love to hear
from you.
davidleadbeater2011@hotmail.co.uk

This one's for Amber and Jade.

Aztec Gold

PROLOGUE

The City of Tenochtitlan,
Mexica,
June, 1520 AD

The boy perched on the highest point of the highest hill, watching. His name was Acalan, meaning 'canoe'. He had no idea why a boy named so would fare particularly badly at watery pursuits nor why his parents, artisans both, had named him after a water going vessel. Even the *tiacotin,* the slaves of his household, questioned it though not knowingly within earshot.

His eyes swept the gleaming city below. The Spanish were everywhere, their conquistadors prancing in full armor atop their horses, already conquerors in mind if not in reality. And though their leader, the one called Cortés, had departed days ago, it was later said, to fight off fellow Spaniards that were coming to arrest him, there was still another in charge tonight—one they called Alvarado.

This preening deputy governor had finally consented to the Aztecs' many requests to allow them to celebrate the festival of Toxcatl, granted after the imprisoned leader of the Aztecs, Montezuma himself, made an impassioned plea. They were all down there now, almost a thousand men gathering in the Patio of the Gods, mostly lords and nobles, naked except for their glittering jewels and feathered headdresses, surrounded by singers and drummers, readying themselves for the festival's beginning.

The Spaniards watched dispassionately.

Acalan squinted harder, trying to distinguish the familiar figure of his father making ready in the square. The men all looked very much alike from this distance, the women—he was starting to realize as he progressed in years—not so much. One in particular, Chimalma, meaning shield-bearer, had already caught his eye, her sparkling flirtatious gaze the core of his dreams. He looked away from the area of the main temple, seeking her dwelling, but the white pathways were full to bursting with so many dark-haired people on this early eve that it was impossible to tell one from another.

The sun was starting to set, a fiery blaze on the horizon. Some would say a portent of bad things to come. Others—warriors and priests—would say death and slaughter were never far away from a culture that practiced human sacrifice.

The festival would soon begin. Acalan, in his curious way, was looking forward to it. This night always produced a fine spectacle. Maybe even the sly, stoic Spaniards would be impressed. The boy sat back and sniffed the air, allowing his senses to wander, the smoky reek of fire vying with the natural heady scent of fresh air. The grass rustled and the soil scraped into ruts beneath his bare feet as he dug them in hard, enjoying the sensation.

Let the men have their ceremony. All Acalan needed was this sense of freedom. The arrival of the Spanish, though at first welcomed by Montezuma and many other lords, had instilled within the community an underlying, multifaceted sense of dread. If the Spanish were indeed returning gods, then why didn't they act so and why were they insatiably greedy? If they were conquerors why didn't they fight? And where was their leader now?

Acalan stretched as the noise coming from below intensified. A caterwauling of religious admiration spread its passionate voice across the heavens, rising up on a self-centered cloud, the nobles engrossed in their worship. Acalan watched with a kind of fascinated disinterest. He saw the men whirling in their fancy garb; saw the musicians around the outside playing furiously, the great noise beginning to swell yet again. Acalan flicked a glance over the watching Spaniards—their faces rarely changed expression and tonight was no exception. From his vantage point he could see further afield and it was he that first saw the disturbance.

Nothing major—just a change in pace and raised voices. It came from over by the Spanish compound, impacting Acalan's awareness more than if it had come from anyplace else. The conquistadors were forming together, amassing into a unit and their captain, Alvarado, was shouting at them.

Acalan wanted to smile. Perhaps a thief existed in their midst, or a rebel. It could be that they were getting a dressing down, but Acalan's parents had taught him to always be wary and trust very little, and thus he wasn't surprised, just alarmed when the men formed into lines and began to march out of the compound's gates.

Having no concept of politics, but knowing violence when he saw it in the set of a man's shoulders and the way of his walk, Acalan bounced to his feet and set off down the hill like a bolt of lightning. His parents were at the Patio of the Gods, as was most everyone else. On this night they would have no warning of the approaching menace.

Acalan's feet whispered through the tall grass, swishing their way through the clumps like scythes with the speed of his passage. At one point he lost his balance, falling head over heels for a few moments, and the scene vibrating up from the square below assailed his vision like a tumbling kaleidoscope. He fancied he could hear the march of the men, the dull clunk of their weapons, even the sly sibilance of their murderous breaths. He fancied he could hear the tuneful lilt of his mother's voice, the intonations remembered from a happy childhood of sweet songs, and the thudding in his heart rose until he could no longer bear it.

He caught himself, arrested the fall, then stood and screamed.

"They are coming! Beware. They are coming!"

But of course the chanting and the music drowned him out. The people were ear-splittingly ecstatic in their celebration of the festival of *Toxcatl,* oblivious to all else.

Acalan despaired.

He ran on. The soldiers approached the square, their leader taking point. Acalan expected them to stop and shout, to halt proceedings, to gesture and accuse and march somebody off to captivity. He expected a dangerous stand-off, the Aztecs outraged at the interruption and the Spaniards forcibly trying to drive their collective will home.

What he didn't expect was the heart-stopping suddenness with which the Spaniards drew their swords, the violent vigor with which they charged forward, the happy abandon with which they began to chop down his people.

Acalan cried out as he ran, an entreaty to the gods. Even from this distance he could see the blood flow, the bodies collapse as they were hacked apart. A cry went up from the square, a cry to arms, but the Aztec warriors would not arrive in time to save their brethren.

A mass of people poured away from the massacre. The Spaniards let them go, concentrating their murderous efforts against the Patio as if seeking some kind of retribution. Several townsfolk went to the aid of their lords, but were treated none the less ruthlessly.

Now it seemed, only now, the Spaniards were showing their true colors. They laughed as they slaughtered, stabbed helpless men time and again in a form of torture, chopped a man's head clean off and then kicked it around between them. They did worse to the women, leaving none alive.

Acalan sped down beyond the bottom of the slope, mercifully losing sight of the massacre and threading the streets toward his parents' abode, heart heavy and pounding, desperately, staggeringly hopeful that they'd made it out alive. Screams and the sounds of death and dreadful laughter now infused the night air.

Acalan came around the final corner.

His mother's arms were open, her face the epitome of relief. His father's face was grim.

"This is the first night of their destruction," he said. "If Montezuma won't help us, we will help ourselves."

Following the events referenced during the night above, the Aztecs laid siege to the Spanish compound until Cortés returned and even elected a new leader. Following the Spanish captain's triumphant reappearance, having subdued and indeed gained even more followers during his time away, the imprisoned king, Montezuma himself, was killed and Cortés decided the Spaniards' best chance was to break out of the city at night.

During this night—later called 'La Noche Triste', the Night of the Long Sorrows, the Spaniards, under cover of a rainstorm, broke out along a narrow causeway. A battle of ferocious intensity ensued. Hundreds of canoes appeared alongside the causeway, filled with warriors. Weighed down by plundered gold and equipment, the Spaniards stumbled along, some losing their footing and drowning, sinking into the mud below so burdened were they with treasure that was not theirs to take.

Thousands died that night. Even native women, cooks and housekeepers that had been given to the Spaniards, died amidst the rage of battle.

Unknown to the Spaniards, and little documented since, were the actions of the Aztecs during the weeks following the original massacre at the Patio of the Gods and the return of Cortés. They took firm action. Whilst the Spaniards under Alvarado were besieged in their compound, the Aztecs amassed the majority of their remaining wealth—a great treasure trove of jewels and gold coins, the largest monetary treasure ever assembled. Even the buildings were stripped of their gold and gems.

It is said that seven caravans set out, following a northern course.

Writings tell of the caravans traveling for a long time, but no one knows where they ended up or the actual treasure location . . .

ONE

Alicia Myles gripped the monster between her thighs, holding on tight as it bucked and weaved under her.

Damn British roads aren't made for bikes, she thought. *Too many unrepaired potholes.*

The Ducati rumbled as she laid it down around the next curve, engine growling like a restrained predator.

Its rider, the same kind of animal, allowed her mind to wander as the road finally straightened out. Her new boss, Michael Crouch, had gathered a new team together after the devastation of his old unit, the Ninth Division, and his subsequent exit from the British Army. Objectives changed, but loyal contacts didn't, and Crouch already knew he could rely on dozens of well-placed, well-financed, highly-influential connections to help him succeed in his new venture.

But first he needed a world class team.

Hence the recruitment of Alicia.

Crouch's new HQ was situated somewhere in Windsor, UK, and it had taken her many hours of confined air travel from Washington DC to get here. The Ducati was an indulgence; rented near to Heathrow airport it was a tribute to a former friend.

The road unfolded before her, a blank empty canvas, an endless journey with hazards around every corner, the way her life was lived.

At that moment a raucous noise interrupting her thoughts. The shrill, cantankerous tones had become more than a constant companion, more a never ending nightmare since they'd left DC, and filtered through her Bluetooth headset even now whilst they rode on separate bikes.

"This *ain't* how I remember London. Goddamn trees and shit.

And *tractors*. Every bloody bend—always another tractor."

"Quit yer whining," Alicia breathed back. "Before I leave you twitching in a hedgerow."

"Yeah, yeah," the voice said. "Y'know, I'm starting to think with you it's bark worse than bite."

Alicia raised her eyebrows, unseen beneath the helmet. Her companion was known as Laid Back Lex and was a member of the biker gang Alicia had briefly joined several months ago. Following the gang's near-annihilation at the hands of the dreaded Blood King and the death of Lomas, its leader and Alicia's boyfriend, the gang had drifted apart. Lex remained the only member that had clung to Alicia, heart-warming at first, not so much many months later when his incessant droning had begun to flay her nerves like a leather-jacketed hunting knife.

"Is that what you think?" she breathed. "Man, do you have a lot to learn about me."

The place Crouch had described was approaching on the right, confirmed by a beep from the satnav. Black iron gates stood open. Alicia slowed her bike, allowing the machine to drift to a stop right outside the entrance, and stared down the long, winding path that led to the house.

Another unknown road. From leaving home she had followed some kind of road, content to let it lead her wherever it so chose. From the Army to questionable military allegiances to Matt Drake and his SPEAR team; then to Lomas and the Slayers, back to SPEAR and now here. The path wound ever on. It meandered, it twisted harshly, but it never brought her any kind of solace.

She sighed. Lex was at her side, staring. "What the fuck are you doing?"

She took her helmet off and gestured that he should do the same. She shook out her blond hair. "How old are you, Lex?"

"Thirty. Ish."

"Any regrets?"

"Course not. Life's too short for that shit."

"And the future? What does it hold for you?"

Lex appeared confused. "Are you asking me out on a date?"

Alicia slapped her forehead with her hand. "Of course not! All I'm saying is this—we can't keep on running forever." She gunned her bike, opening the throttle, and roared down the path.

Trees swayed and rustled around her, the wind whipping through them before striking her face. Ahead, the path curved and a stately house appeared, large enough to house an army. Alicia pulled up in between a Mini Cooper S and a blue Mitsubishi Evo. Not the best sign. The Mini was okay and probably belonged to Crouch but the Evo no doubt belonged to some young upstart.

She hadn't joined a new team to be the resident babysitter.

Lex pulled in beside her. "Shit, man, move over. Can't get a goddamn space."

Alicia had had enough. With all the recent traumas and the long trip her patience was wearing thin. She rounded on the biker. "Christ, Lex, give it a rest. Do I look like a man to you?"

Lex eyed her leathers. "Dunno. Be happy to take a look though."

Alicia struck faster than the biker could blink. One minute he was sitting, a grin of mischief beginning to stretch across his face, the next he was sprawled in the dirt, bleeding from the mouth, his bike held upright courtesy of Alicia's lightning-quick right hand.

Lex grunted.

Alicia shook her head at him. "Show a little goddamn respect," she said and walked off, letting the bike fall.

The resulting high-pitched squeal followed her to the door of the house where Michael Crouch stood waiting. Her ex-boss's boss's eyes held more than a glint of amusement.

"Haven't changed, I see." He squinted past her. "Are you sure we really need the biker?"

Alicia shrugged. "I'm beginning to wonder. If nothing else he'll be good cannon fodder."

"Agreed." Crouch smiled at her. Though Crouch was in his

fifties there wasn't an ounce of fat on him; the man was solid, possessed of short-cropped black hair, a sculpted jawline and a pair of twinkly eyes. When he held a hand out to welcome her, Alicia felt almost proud to shake it.

Crouch had previously headed up the British Ninth Division, a covert agency that looked after Her Majesty's interests abroad, its agenda blank, its brief to do whatever was necessary. Able to call upon all entities from the local police to the SAS, Crouch had run the department with astonishing success right up until the day it was closed down. After that, then a freelancer, Crouch decided to indulge his other major life-interest—the search for archaeological treasures—by setting up a new team. His countless contacts, garnered previously through countless years as a respected leader, would bend over backwards to help him.

Now, Crouch waved a hand inside. "The team's all here. Would you like to meet them?"

TWO

Alicia followed Crouch through the door, memorizing the layout and judging the security as she went. Crouch laid it out for her quickly, clearly eager to get to the meat of the matter.

"Eight bedrooms upstairs. We're fully stocked, the grounds are private, and we're on our own. No maids. No room service. No mail man. If something moves outside," he nodded back toward the open door where Lex had just arrived, "it really has no place being there."

"Good. I like to know where I stand."

"Cook your own food, make your own bed, clean your own dishes. But, having said that, I don't expect you to be cluttering the place up for too long."

Alicia eyed him. "Good to hear because, darling, I don't do dishes. Are you saying that you have a mission in place already?"

Crouch couldn't keep the smile off his face. "We do." He laughed. "This change of life has rejuvenated me. I truly feel like a man with a new lease on life, Alicia. This is my dream: chasing down long lost treasures, the dream I've nurtured for fifty years."

"Not Catwoman? Lamborghinis? Chris Evert?"

"Do fifty-year-olds do that?"

"Wow, fifty? You're old, man," Lex piped up as he approached. "Where's the refrigerator?"

Crouch pointed toward the end of the hall and watched the biker creak away. He appeared lost in thought for a moment, but then turned to Alicia. "Shall we?"

Alicia allowed him to lead her through a nearby door, hiding her anger. Lex's current attitude wouldn't do. Crouch deserved respect, he'd earned it and he was now their boss. Again Alicia wondered if bringing the biker along hadn't been a bad, self-absorbed idea. With thoughts and solutions half-formed she entered a vast room populated by leather easy chairs, low coffee tables and fronted by a deep pair of bay windows. Two figures lounged in the chairs.

Crouch pointed. "Alicia Myles, meet the other members of our team. This is Rob Russo, of the Ninth Division, a man I have trained and worked with for twenty years. And Zack Healey, also of the Ninth. I can vouch for both of them."

Alicia sized the two newcomers up with a soldier's eyes. Russo was big and craggy, with a face like a windblown escarpment and bone structure that could deflect bullets. He sat in a kind of wary ease, confident in his environment but always alert. He regarded Alicia with blank eyes that could have held suspicion, hatred or amusement—the man was unreadable. Healey on the other hand was almost bursting with excitement, eyes darting from side to side in exuberance and already leaping out of his seat with a hand outstretched.

"Zack. Call me Zack," he said. "Or Healey," he added in answer to her impassive gaze. "Whatever works."

Alicia raised a brow toward Crouch. "Don't remember you sayin' we were running a crèche here too."

Crouch sat down. "Healey's young but he's good. Loyal. Vital. Hands-on. Reminds me of myself forty years ago."

"Reminds me of a puppy," Alicia said. "And Michael, forty years ago you were *ten.*"

Crouch just shrugged.

At that moment Laid Back Lex entered the room, nursing a Bud and what appeared to be a fully-loaded ham and pickle sandwich. As all eyes turned to him he made a face. "What? Riding makes me hungry."

"Everything makes you hungry," Alicia said before turning her attention back to her new boss. "Is this it? No mad professor? No geography whizz or Internet geek?"

"This is everyone, Myles, though I dare say the door will never be off limits to the right person. I can run any Web traffic from our HQ and all the research gets done in the field. We're well funded, but it's not a bottomless pit."

Alicia took her own seat across from Russo. "So tell me, who exactly *is* funding this little venture?"

Russo didn't respond. Crouch shifted a little, a creak of old leather accompanying his movement. "A moderately wealthy man by the name of Rolland Sadler. To cut a long, tragic story necessarily short I assisted him once. Saved his family through the Ninth, against the wishes of the eggheads. Once he heard I'd finally decided to go my own way I could barely stop him doling out the cash. He's funding us, and he's on the level."

"But he'll want results." Russo finally spoke up with an eye on Alicia.

She thought she now understood the craggy-faced soldier. "I see. He'll want to see some kind of return, yes? And Russo thinks he's big enough to be field captain. Am I right?"

"I follow orders," Russo said immediately with a little glance toward Crouch.

"Good. Then follow mine. That way, big boy, we won't have to test the solidity of those magnificent cheekbones of yours."

"All right." Crouch stood up at just the right time, averting a confrontation. "This team's solid. Made up of the very best, hand-picked by me. I run it. I say how it goes. If anyone doesn't like that they can leave right now."

No one moved. Alicia held Russo's gaze.

Crouch nodded. "Good. If we do this right we might even make a name for ourselves. The *Gold* Team. How do you like that?" He didn't stop for an answer. "Consequently, it's vitally important that our first mission is a success. That's what makes its topic a little unfortunate."

Now Alicia blinked. "In what way?"

And Zack Healey leaned forward, cheeks flushed with excitement. "We're heading to Mexico in search of gold. Lost *Aztec* gold."

THREE

Alicia settled back in her seat. "Tell me."

"Well . . ." Crouch rubbed the bridge of his nose as if pondering where to begin. "Make yourself comfortable. I guess the story begins with the Spanish conquistador, Cortés, whose expedition in the sixteenth century led directly to the fall of the Aztec empire. Tales tell us that the man was in fact a fairly controversial character, ignoring direct orders to carry out his sea voyages—acts of mutiny in effect—even having to return to Spain on occasion to answer charges. Cortés was once quoted as saying 'it is more difficult to contend against my own countrymen than it is the Aztecs'. At one point he was even suspected of poisoning the Ponce de Léon."

Healey joined in. "So with a boss like that you can imagine what his men were like."

Alicia ignored the young upstart.

Crouch went on, "Well, after he ordered the scuttling of almost his entire fleet in order to minimize any potential retreat, the captain marched toward the Aztec capital, Tenochtitlan, gathering an even larger army as he went. Natives joined him— warriors of the Nahua in particular. His men massacred thousands even before they reached the great Aztec city. When they arrived, the city's king, Montezuma, allowed Cortés and his men to enter the island city, perhaps hoping to learn their weaknesses."

"Enemies closer," Healey put in.

Crouch nodded. "And despite the locals' offer of gold and jewels the Spaniards were driven to more frantic acts of greed and plunder. The more gold they saw the more they wanted—"

"Huh," Russo spat in a deep voice. "Nothing changes."

"Cortés believed the Aztecs thought him a god, the feathered serpent god Quetzalcoatl, or at least an emissary of his, and perhaps they did. He wrote as much in a letter to the king of Spain. But Cortés remained a harsh ruler. When he learned that several of his soldiers had been slain along the coast by Aztecs he took Montezuma prisoner in his own palace and, without the population's knowledge, ruled through him."

"A nice history lesson." Alicia tried not to yawn. "But I'm not hearing anything relating to the treasure yet. Hey, are you going bald?"

Crouch blinked twice, caught off guard. While he struggled for something to say the rugged Russo came to his rescue.

"Try to concentrate on one thing at a time, Myles. Attention span a problem for you, is it?"

Alicia turned in her seat. "Are *we* gonna have a problem, Robster? Cos my pit bull here, he really wants a piece of you."

Laid Back Lex was practically seething in his seat, an animal straining at its leash.

"Calm down," Alicia directed Lex and turned to Crouch. "Continue."

"Well, you have the Aztecs on one side, living in a city of gold, with more jewels and precious gems than any other race on the continent. The Spanish conquistadors on the other, who seemed to hold the ideal of riches and wealth above even their own lives. Everything soon fell apart. Following the terrible massacre of thousands of Aztec nobles at the Patio of the Gods near the main temple, which triggered a rebellion, Cortés and his men saw that the game was up. They escaped during what later became known as the Noche Triste, fleeing across the Tlacopan causeway while their rearguard was massacred by Aztec warriors. The gold they stole weighed so much it actually killed half the Spaniards, drowning them in the mud of the river. Now, the time gap between the murder of the nobles and the Spaniards' escape was about two months. What do you suppose the Aztecs were doing during that time?"

"Sharpening their swords?"

"Maybe. But they were also safeguarding their valuables as any nation would. For instance, remember all the Romanian gold that was sent to Russia during the First World War? Every nation wants to protect their assets and the Aztecs were no different. And of course, this is where the stories differ and we get the thoughts and opinions of a thousand treasure hunters from the last five hundred years. Where did all that wealth go?"

"You're saying they transported it out of there?"

"It certainly didn't stay in Tenochtitlan. Cortés returned soon after he fled, now with reinforcements from Cuba, and laid siege, cutting off supplies and subduing the Aztecs allies. He ended up destroying the city. On 13 August 1521 the city fell and the Aztec empire disappeared, crushed. Cortés claimed it for Spain and renamed it Mexico City. He governed it for three years."

"No mention of the gold," Alicia said. "The golden city, the jewels."

"No mention." Crouch smiled.

"So what *did* happen to it?" Laid Back Lex chomped at the bit.

"And what exactly did it consist of?" Alicia wondered.

"The mystery begins with the night of the first massacre at the Patio of the Gods," Crouch said, taking time to drink from a bottle of water before continuing. "Now, how about we continue this over dinner?"

Alicia coughed. "I thought the directive was that we had to fend for ourselves? I sure hope you have a microwave."

Crouch smiled. "For this first night I'm sure I could knock together a pretty mean chili."

Alicia looked genuinely impressed. "Wow, I hope I can do that by the time I'm fifty."

Soon, with steaming bowls of chili laid out before them and glasses of red wine and bottles of beer positioned around the table like strategically placed chess pieces, Crouch continued his story.

"With so many nobles murdered and such utter brutality shown for the locals, the Aztecs must have started to panic. Who was this crazed beast their leader had invited to live among them? Their king was a mere captive in his own palace. What could they do?"

"Elect a new king?" Alicia ventured.

"Exactly. Enter Cuauhtémoc, the new king. Following his order and under his guidance it is believed that the Aztecs hatched a great plan. Through the nights following the massacre, with the Spaniards beaten back and under siege inside their compound, surrounded by warriors, Tenochtitlan's main horde of gold was systematically stripped away, its jewels packed into crates. It was a great undertaking, so much so that seven entire caravans were filled—"

"And Cortés never noticed?" Russo's eyes widened skeptically.

"They left the surface gold where it was," Crouch said. "Which was all the Spaniards had ever seen and quite plentiful. It was the far more spectacular *vaults* they emptied."

"Seven caravans worth?" Lex whistled. "That's a shit-ton of money, man."

"Treasure," Crouch corrected him. "There's a very significant difference between the two. It's what separates our team, the one that will display and donate it to the world, from the thieves and villains that might try to stop us."

Lex nodded quickly. "Okay."

Alicia snorted. "He doesn't get it. He's more of a 'hands-on' kinda leatherhead. But he will."

Crouch continued, "In answer to one of your earlier questions, Alicia, apart from the copious amounts of gold and jewels, several items of major historical importance to the Aztecs were loaded onto the caravans. Our main focus will be on the legendary cartwheel treasure."

Alicia shook her head. "The what?"

"A large wheel of gold decorated with glyphs in the shape of the sun. As big as a cartwheel. It's where the phrase 'pieces of eight' originally comes from."

"So something that spawns a legend powerful enough to live down the centuries has to be considered a huge find."

"It quite possibly was a symbol of the entire foundation of Aztec belief."

Alicia chewed her lip. "Impressive. What else?"

"Cortés described gigantic idols of beaten gold, masks of silver and turquoise, and piles of gleaming emeralds, rubies and garnets. These were just the treasures he was allowed to see. It's a safe bet that the *real* treasures were aboard those caravans."

"But what of the people that guarded the caravan?" Healey asked perceptively. "Wherever they ended up, wouldn't they speak of this treasure they carried for so many miles? And if they were killed then their murderers would shout it to the rooftops."

"I know I would," Lex added drily.

Crouch scratched his chin. "Then you know nothing of warrior loyalty. Take Attila the Hun for example. When his thousand-strong personal bodyguard, the greatest warriors in his army, diverted a river and buried his tomb they then allowed themselves to be massacred to protect the secret of its location. It has never been found."

He turned back to the group. "It's thought that once the treasure arrived at its destination, all the slaves that helped transport it were killed. Half of the Aztec warriors remained to guard it whilst the other half returned to Tenochtitlan. The plan was probably to retrieve the treasure once the Spaniards had been eradicated from their shores. However, for those that remained near the treasure months and years will have passed without word. Tenochtitlan, if you remember, was first besieged then destroyed. Any survivors and returning warriors will have drifted away, joining other tribes like the Nahua, and will have eventually intermarried with local tribes, now equipped only with

19

stories of the great empire to the south."

"*So where is it?*" Alicia hissed, laying down her fork and glancing around at the assembled team. "Do we know?"

Crouch smiled grimly. "I've lost count of the number of legends relating to the fabled lost Aztec gold. It's purported to be anywhere from the bottom of the sea to Texas. The *true* story, however, lies in the rich history of Tenochtitlan itself. That's where we'll start."

"You're talking about traveling to Mexico City, the old Aztec capital?"

"I want to start from scratch and see what we unearth. A good treasure hunt always starts at the very beginning and there's good reason for that. It helps shake off any presupposed ideas we may have about the treasure's location. We have plenty of tech stuff and state-of-the-art equipment thanks to Sadler's generosity." Crouch looked around the room. "If we do this, we do it right."

"Speaking of your contacts," Alicia said. "Who else do we have on board?"

"Too many to mention." Crouch shrugged. He had major contacts in virtually every region of the world. "But our main source of operational Intel will be Armand Argento. Do you know him?"

"Not as well as I'd like." Alicia grinned. "I heard he's a looker."

Russo grunted. "I guess *your* reputation is well deserved."

Alicia looked over with an air of innocence. "What reputation?"

Crouch broke in quickly before the confrontation could escalate. "He's the very best at what he does. And whilst Interpol aren't particularly happy to be committing resources in our direction they aren't forbidding it either. It's all about the payoff."

"I thought you said we'd be 'donating' the treasure."

"That's true. But the monetary proposals from various

organizations will still be tremendous. And we don't need any of that. Hence—"

"Interpol gets a slice of the pie."

"Technically." Crouch waved his hand carefully. "Not officially of course. But they would certainly get a say as to where the treasure ended up, and if it was all kept together or separated. In addition to that we've drafted a very careful official policy relating to what happens if and when we locate any treasure, now or in the future. The policy is a public document, forwarded to all the relevant governmental and historical organizations, and must be adhered to. It helps to validate our efforts, adds sincerity and seriousness to our roles, and covers our asses in case anything gets out of hand. Generally, a treasure found belongs to the country whose land it was found on . . . but whilst not definitive we have set in place an international strategy." He sighed. "Of course, time will only tell if each nation follows it."

Russo grunted. "Huh, time and the worth of the treasure, I'm guessing."

Alicia nodded, impressed and relieved Crouch had delved so deeply into the real-world politics and laws of treasure hunting. "So the same goes for whoever helps us along the way? I get it. The scratching-of-the-back scenario. Preserve your contacts. You listening to this part, Russo? It pays to be nice."

The man's face remained rock solid.

Crouch pushed his plate away and studied her. "So what do you think? Can this team pull it off?" He didn't need to say—*can you even work together?*

Alicia studied them one by one, sipping wine. The Gold Team was a mismatch and that wasn't necessarily a bad thing. Healey was young and inexperienced but lively and willing to learn. If handled right he could become a major asset. Lex was feisty but loyal to the point of torture, a fearless bodyguard. And Russo? Well, the ex-soldier looked seasoned and capable and was just going to have to learn to follow her orders. There were two ways that particular scenario could go, and Alicia preferred the tough one.

She shrugged. "What can I say? It's the perfect team."

FOUR

As the small jet bumped and grumbled its way through waves of turbulence in its descent into Mexico City, Alicia thought about the irrational follies of men. Cortés, when he set out from Spain, surely hadn't harbored the desire to raze a nation, but he'd ended up doing just that. For Spain. For glory and wealth. Tenochtitlan had been destroyed and a new city built in order to erase all traces of the old. A two-hundred-year-old culture shattered and expunged for the advancement of another.

Did the world ever change?

Not in my lifetime, she thought. Whilst old religions still clashed there would be no respite from bloodshed and mayhem. Whilst greed and envy still existed there would be no reprieve from the actions of bitter and twisted men.

Through the small window she watched the unfolding sprawl of the country's largest city. The gray and white mass of thousands of dwellings stretched for untold miles, swelling over hills and down into valleys, an unending, dreary expanse of concrete. Even the higher hills, untouched as yet, appeared to be brown, almost lifeless blots in the landscape. In the center the high rises rose like towering stalagmites, carved from the heart of the city. Roads were dark, straight slashes, their occupants contributing by the minute to an air pollution rate that had earned the city the moniker 'the most polluted city on the planet'.

The plane dropped fast, aiming for Benito Juarez International, the landing point only about eight kilometers away from their first prearranged appointment. Carlos Rivera, a local Aztec historian that had worked on many exhibitions and dig sites, had agreed to meet them at his place of work—the renowned museum Templo Mayor, which had been built to house and assist in the excavation of one of the most famous Aztec temples of the same name in 1987. The excavation continues to this day, so with the history and the kind of people it attracted, Crouch theorized that it might be a good place to start.

Alicia put up with the landing and immigration procedure, finding solace in the fact that she was back on the road, on the trail where new experiences and encounters helped focus her mind on the way ahead, not on the past. With careful, well-trained eyes she studied every face, every man and woman standing at a newsstand or queuing up for coffee. Training of the kind she'd been subjected to never allowed you to let your guard down. It was all and everything, an extension of your body as much as your right arm and far more important. Without it she'd have died a thousand times by now.

They exited into what for Mexico City was the warm period with temperatures roaming around seventy one degrees. A man wearing a chauffeur's uniform caught Crouch's attention and led him to a parked limo.

"So," Alicia said as they climbed into their seats. "Who do we have to fuck to get hold of some guns around here?"

Healey made a shocked noise. Alicia turned on him. "Stop squeaking, Zack. Feels like I'm part of a Mouseketeer parade."

Crouch smiled reassuringly at the driver who had also raised disbelieving eyebrows. "She's kidding." He turned away.

"If we need them I'll find a supplier," he mouthed quietly close to Alicia's left ear.

"I prefer to have them close at hand from the kick-off," she returned. "They tend to work better that way."

Russo cracked big knuckles, the sound almost as loud as a gunshot itself. "Do you actually expect to use them, Myles? This mission ain't exactly Iraq."

"I've been to Iraq. More than once. They have those big bloody sand spiders there. Got legs on 'em that're bigger than anything you've got and no mistake."

Russo shrugged and turned away. "Sure."

The taxi peeled out onto a black-topped highway clogged with traffic, slamming almost instantly to a stop. Alicia sighed, still happy to be moving but feeling a little like she was missing out on the action, and leaned forward to study the limo's half-hearted array of goodies. Boiled sweets and sticks of gum filled one cup-holder, whilst fresh, cold bottled water and Pepsi sat in the rest. Although the tops were clearly sealed, Alicia didn't feel confident enough with her surroundings to try one. Her companions were similarly reticent, Healey to the point of taking a short nap.

Alicia shook her head at him. "Kids. Don't make 'em like they used to."

Russo was also gazing at the young man. "Kid's been through a lot," he rumbled. "He needs all the R&R he can get. Zack may look fresh and young but he sees this world through an old man's eyes."

Alicia could have responded sharply, hinting at her own turbulent past, at the drunken father that regularly beat up her mother, making Alicia run away for the first time in her life, at all the chaotic years since, but chose only to say, "Kid looks even younger when he's sleeping."

Russo seemed happy with that, offering a slight smile.

Crouch filled a long silence. "Carlos Rivera is a civilian, so be nice. He's offered to help simply because he's a nice guy. He's cut from the old cloth—wanting to believe in the treasure, but due to the nature of his job is forced to be a skeptic. There will be no sudden revelations here, people, merely hard detective work."

The traffic thundered and growled along to left and right of them, horns honking, and hot, angry Mexicans gesturing out of their half-open windows. Alicia looked ahead to the approaching high-rises, wondering briefly what manner of mayhem Matt Drake and the SPEAR team might be up to their necks in by now. Her old team . . . if those guys ever stayed out of trouble for more than three days she'd happily moon a vicar. Although that was a distinct possibility on any given day.

25

When they arrived at the Templo Mayor Museum, Alicia was surprised. The dig was ongoing, taking place in the middle of a sprawling, busy city, but it looked like it was being carved out of the center of the industrious masses whilst they still worked. Several buildings stood right up against the dig site, their rear facades pitted and broken as if an adjoining building had been torn down to make way for the museum. Alicia wondered how many caverns extended underneath the surrounding buildings and how fragile the infrastructure was around here. Mexico City had been the epicenter of several terrible earthquakes including one in 1985 that took thousands of lives.

Crouch stepped out of the limo, gesturing for them to follow. Alicia left Russo to wake the youngster, joining their boss beside a bleak gray façade—the side of the building. Though she hadn't visited many museums, Alicia had seen her fair share and wasn't impressed by this one.

"Seems . . . uninviting," she said. "Like Birmingham in the seventies."

Crouch nodded. "They're desperately short of money. Every dollar they make goes toward the dig. And the government's bogged down with the cartels." He blinked and added cryptically, "One way or another."

Alicia caught on instantly. "Mexico never changes either, huh?"

At that moment a figure approached them. Alicia, always hyper-aware, turned quickly to see an older man wearing jeans and a faded brown leather jacket, his wrinkled face scrunched up as he faced the sun.

"Michael." He smiled. "So good to see you."

"And you, Carlos." Crouch gripped his hand warmly. "How's the life in la Capital?"

"As she says," Rivera nodded toward Alicia. "It never changes."

She gestured behind the historian. "So this is the dig? The great pyramid?"

Rivera turned. "You're looking at the eastern side of the great twin temple of the Aztecs, the Templo Mayor, or what's left of it. Called the Huei Teocalli in the Nahuatl language, which was the language of the Aztecs, and dedicated to not one but two gods— the god of war and the god of rain and agriculture. Each had a shrine at the top with separate staircases. Construction began around 1325." He sighed heavily. "Destroyed by the Spanish in 1521."

Alicia walked across to the black railing and leaned over. "All I see is a great big pile of rocks. And a few snakes."

Rivera and the rest of them joined her, staring over the ruins of the once great temple. "The Aztecs and most other religions around the world held the serpent as a double-headed symbol. One head seduces you, the other gives you self-control. Or it could have merely symbolized rebirth—the shedding of the skin. As for the pile of rocks, well, Cortés thought so too."

Alicia said nothing, the wind catching her hair as it swept across the open space. Crouch stepped in.

"What can you tell us, Carlos? What can you tell us about the seven caravans that left here on that June night five hundred years ago?"

"What I *want* to believe," Rivera took a self-conscious glance around, "is that seven caravans left this place loaded with the most precious of all the Aztec treasures. I want to believe that they were transported safely, hidden away, and that Cortés never got his hands on them. Skepticism though . . . it is drilled into us from the very beginning."

"We're open to anything," Alicia told him. "Always have been."

"My heart says that these treasures—the ones authentically verified through study of letters sent by Hernán Cortés to the king of Spain—were not destroyed by the Spaniards nor stolen and spirited away to who knows where. It tells me that the Aztecs were as clever as we all believe and managed to save their riches, expecting them to be returned at a later date."

"So the caravan left," Healey broke in. "Secreted itself for a few months, and then returned?"

"If that only were the case." Rivera pursed his lips, unhappy. "But again history and the head tells us that only half of the warriors would have returned immediately, bringing directions to the treasure. The problem is that what they returned to wasn't at all what they left behind. Their capital, Tenochtitlan, was under siege, then razed, destroyed. Demoralized and beaten, what would they do? Make the long journey back to the treasure yet again? No, most would have stayed close to their birthplace and assimilated into the local tribes, the ones Cortés didn't massacre to the last man."

"Keeping the location of the treasure close to them." Crouch squinted across the ruins. "And as they died . . ."

"The treasure's existence passed into legend. Folklore. Those that stayed behind to guard it would have faced a similar dilemma, eventually dying also but with no knowledge of what had happened." Rivera shrugged. "Unless some kind soul actually made the journey back. Who knows?"

"So do we know what happened specifically to those that returned?" Alicia picked up on the thread. "Where did they go?"

"We do, yes." Rivera nodded. "Mostly, one group of people, a single large tribe in Mexico retain Aztec DNA in their blood to this very day—"

Healey cleared his throat. "Now that's cool. Damn cool."

"You'd like to have Aztec blood in you?" Russo wondered.

"Christ, yeah. Wouldn't everyone?"

Alicia rolled her eyes and held Rivera's gaze. "Which people?"

"The Nahua. Once a great rival tribe to the Aztecs, the Nahua largely survived the Spanish invasion. It is generally believed that the returning and any other surviving Aztecs would have joined them. And of course, authentic DNA tests now prove that they did."

"Sounds like a starting point," Crouch said. "But you

mentioned the Nahua were a large tribe. That's going to make it tough to find any descendants."

"Not any more. The Nahuatl-speaking people are the largest Indian group in Mexico, forming almost a quarter of the native population of our country. They still reside around the periphery of what was once the Aztec empire. One of these peoples, those living in La Huasteca—such a beautiful area—are the oldest living relatives of the Aztecs. They would not dilute their heritage. For good or bad those particular Nahua are now a small tribe living in northern Mexico. You would need a guide to take you there, though. The landscape, though stunning, can be treacherous."

"Not a problem," Crouch said. "If you have any recommendations . . ."

Rivera nodded. "Follow me into the museum."

The odd group turned around and made their way to the entrance. As they walked Alicia spoke into Crouch's ear. "I get that a tribal group may keep secrets down the generations," she said. "I understand the likelihood that they have some kind of knowledge. But why would they now reveal it to us? Surely this has been tried before?"

"Not necessarily in this way," Crouch said. "The Aztec treasure has always been considered mere legend, even a joke much like fool's gold. Sought by crazy men and idiots. If any of these men took the time to visit the Nahua they'd have been laughed out of there."

"And we won't?"

"I'm guessing not," Crouch said as Rivera led them past a high gray stone façade and under a shiny black entrance sign. Entering the lobby a row of exhibitions lined one wall, enabling a stream of colorfully clad visitors to file past. Backpacks were strapped to almost every back and constant chatter reverberated around the high walls. A large glass case showed how the site would have looked in the Aztec era.

Rivera paused before the case, staring reflectively. "Firstly, to help prove your case and your sincerity, I will appoint to you a guide the Nahua trust. I know several- this kind of introduction is invaluable. Second, you need to prove to them how serious you are—as you say most of the previous hunters have been nothing more than loons. Also, rather importantly, you have to convince them that the treasure, if found, will become an obligation of the World Heritage Committee, ensuring them it will belong to a particular historical institution and not be dispersed or sold for profit. Believe me, the descendants of the Aztecs want their treasure returned more than anything in the world. If they deem you're worthy and if they *can* help, they will."

Alicia listened as she studied the impressive model. "The Aztecs had all this and still they fell."

Rivera nodded. "Staggering isn't it? This museum, as I said, stands beside and over the old site. You can visit the catacombs below and walk straight to Montezuma's temple and his meditation chamber and office if you like. Remember that Cortés only tore the temple down in anger when no further treasure was found. He knew the Aztecs had misled him then and reacted accordingly. Who knows, perhaps Montezuma's chamber holds a clue."

Alicia listened intently right up until the end. Her eyes, still staring through the glass, fixed onto the reflections of the large dark figures moving purposefully toward them from behind.

Museum visitors stumbled out of the way. Guards sprang into action.

Alicia whirled.

"Hello boys. About time our team got to kick some ass."

FIVE

Mayhem and chaos ruled inside the museum.

When the first punch was thrown, screams and surprised shouts ignited panic across the lobby. When the first antagonist smashed head-first into a display case, people began to run. When Alicia moved onto her second opponent, lifting him off the ground and throwing him bodily against a wall, the entire space exploded into chaos.

Alicia raised her head, seeing Russo cut in before her to get a load of the action, taking the next man. She took a moment to her assess her new colleague; saw him deliver a one-two-cross with a good mix of power and dexterity and decided she wouldn't want to be on the receiving end of one of those bad boys. She moved around the grunting mountain, only to find Healey already facing up to the next adversary. This was good; Crouch had trained his men well as a team, something she should have taken for granted. Crouch himself was standing apart, also assessing the team with Lex at his side as bodyguard.

And me, she thought. *Crouch is assessing me too.*

She skipped around Healey. With three men down their unknown attackers still had five men remaining. Alicia front-kicked the knee of the leading man. He went down, crying out and holding his leg. Alicia paused for a moment.

"What is this? The local hockey team?"

Russo only grunted, hit by two at once. Healey traded punches with another. Crouch, behind her, said, "Good question. I wasn't aware anyone knew we were here."

Alicia stepped around the fallen, mindful of their speedy recovery times. At least these guys had had *some* training. The first head raised met a bootful of muddy, rubber sole—a nice new tattoo for his face.

"We should go." Crouch was keeping an eye out for security. "The last thing we need here is some kind of major incident."

Alicia heard him say a quick farewell and offer an apology to Rivera, although by his tone it was clear he didn't have a clue as to what was going on. Quickly then, Alicia pressed forward, clearing the path. Healey and Russo squeezed in behind her with Crouch taking the rear. They raced for the exit, pushing through the throng. Crouch, looking back, shouted a warning.

"They're not giving up."

The crowd spilled out onto the concrete path outside the museum, still running, still raucous. Alicia and her team ran with them. When they reached the roadside more paths opened up and the mass started to dissipate. A horde swarmed across the road, stopping traffic and causing even more noise and chaos. Alicia turned back.

"I don't see why we're still running."

Their adversaries, eight-strong, plowed into them, bloody and bruised but eager for more. Crouch stepped back again, searching around. He was looking for a reason, a motive, a face he might recognize. So far, nothing presented itself.

Alicia wanted to end this fast. A throat punch and a kick to the groin took two permanently out of the fight. Twisting off the back of that she stiff-armed a third in the face, breaking his nose. Blood spurted. The piglike squeal was muted as he hit the ground hard on his back, all the breath smashed out of him. Russo lifted a man, slamming him down onto the front of a parked car. The next attacker he grabbed around the waist and flung into the road. Healey sought to be more clinical, trading swift punches and strikes before neutralizing his target with a blow to a nerve cluster. Laid Back Lex, though slow to start, soon warmed up to his task and began smashing heads together.

Crouch moved away as sirens sounded down the street. "Finish it," he told them. "Time to go."

But their attackers, though lacking skills, were certainly

tenacious. No sooner did one go down, groaning, than another got back up. Alicia felled yet another, certain that it was the third time she'd put him down.

"No guns," she said again, reminding the boss. "Takes more time this way."

Russo glanced over at her. "They are unarmed," he said. "It wouldn't be fair."

"Fair?" she repeated, taking an ineffective punch as she turned to stare. "Who said it should be bloody fair?"

"Get in the damn car!" Crouch shouted as they backed up to where the limo was still parked. "Let's get out of here."

Crouch held the door open as Healey slid in. Russo was there next, gesturing that Crouch should go first. The boss just grimaced and shoved the big man ahead, then signaled Alicia. "Hurry!"

The sirens were almost on top of them.

The engine roared. Alicia slipped past Crouch and jumped inside, ending up on Russo's lap which caused the big man to let out an animal-like squeal. Crouch dealt easily with Alicia's two pursuers, tripping and pushing them into a tangle as he took one last look around.

And saw a face . . .

"There," he muttered. "Son of a bloody bitch."

Crouch slid into his seat. Alicia untangled herself from Russo, slamming the man's left bicep as she went for good measure. Didn't hurt to let the new guy know you could injure him when you chose to.

The limo raced away from the curb, swerving into traffic amidst a noisy flurry of honking horns. One of their adversaries rather ambitiously threw himself onto the car, didn't get a grip on the windshield, and went bouncing across the remainder of the carriageway, narrowly missing a braking bus. Crouch shook his head at the display of idiocy.

Alicia grimaced. "He's just gotta know he ain't that good.

There's people I've worked with *are* that good. Drake. Mai. Dahl. I mean, the whole damn team. But these guys? Talk about amateur hour."

"And now I know why," Crouch said. "Greg Coker."

"An old friend of yours?" Alicia wondered. "What's he doing here?"

But before Crouch could even open his mouth the sound of squealing tires shattered the peaceful cocoon around them, and three black shapes swerved in close.

"You gotta be kidding!" Russo cried. "We just kicked their asses twice and they're *still* coming?"

Alicia surveyed their surroundings. Three black Nissan Qashqais were running alongside and behind them. "Christ," she said. "Even their cars are slow."

As if in retaliation for the slur the nearest Qashqai veered toward them, connecting with a solid impact of metal. For a moment both cars ran side by side, connected. Alicia glared into the crazed eyes of the guy she'd already decked three times. The Qashqai leaned in hard, trying to force the limo into a line of parked cars, but their driver was no slouch. Accelerating and twisting the wheel at the same time, he swung in front of the other car, leaving it to sway under its own momentum. The limo surged ahead, instantly blocked by another black Nissan.

Crouch turned to look through the back window. "What on earth is Coker doing here?"

Russo also turned around. "Greg Coker. I've heard the name. Can't place the man."

"A heavy rival, all my life in the Army. Coker and I used to work together—" Crouch let out a lengthy sigh. "Such a long time ago I can barely remember the dates. Jesus. He was always a competitive one, but sly about it. Pleasant on top, a cauldron of rivalry underneath. Not deceitful, just contentious. Funny thing was, he didn't mean to be so challenging. He just couldn't help himself. Like a small child, Coker always had to come out on top.

Anyway, after a few years he left the service, became privately employed. We kind of lost touch after that, but—"

"But!" Lex blurted, unable to keep a lid on his impatience.

"The name keeps cropping up. Time after time. This job, that job, another job. Coker always on my tail or just in front. It always felt a little strange, but I put it down to the job and the tight circles we all run in. You know the score. Sooner or later, we all come across the same bunch of men and names time and time again."

"But Coker was different?" Healey asked as the next Qashqai decelerated in front of them.

"Hard to say," Crouch mused. "I'm wondering now if he hasn't been flying along on my shirttails the whole time."

The limo narrowly missed ramming the lead Nissan, but the evasive maneuver allowed the other two cars to catch up. Boxed in on three sides they had nowhere to go. Alicia decided enough was enough. She grabbed hold of the front headrest and pulled herself forward. "Hey, driver, this is Mexico City. Don't you carry a gun in the glovebox?"

The driver didn't look back. "No guns. I do have a riot stick."

Alicia narrowed her eyes. "That'll do the trick. Pass it here. Time to end this fiasco."

She climbed across Healey who blushed, then Russo who gave her a stony stare, and jammed her finger on the electric window button. As soon as it lowered sufficiently she leaned out and up so that her face practically pressed against the other car's rear window.

"How ya doing' shitheels?"

Surprised faces glared at her, lips forming big 'O's. But that was nothing compared to what came next. Alicia brought the riot stick around with great force, shattering the glass, sending splintered shards spinning across the rear interior of the Qashqai. Her knees were braced and she was all ready to leap through the new gap, but at the last moment the Nissan swung away and entered the oncoming flow of traffic, slewing broadside.

"Next!" Alicia cried, waving the baton feverishly.

Again the driver stamped on the gas, making the limo lurch forward. Within seconds they were coming up alongside the next Nissan. Crouch shouted that he could see Coker in the front passenger seat.

"Get alongside him," Crouch cried. "Alicia, wait!"

The Englishwoman grunted. "Hmm. That sounded suspiciously like *Alicia, heel!*"

Healey sniggered. Even Russo grunted. "Move over, big guy," she said. "You've got twenty seconds, boss."

Crouch waved frantically as the limo pulled alongside the lead Nissan. Coker's face was already turned toward them, stony, forehead a creased canvas of worry lines and eyes as deep as ancient mysteries. Crouch gestured for the man to lower his window.

"Greg! What the hell's going on?"

In answer, Coker spun toward his driver. Their car instantly changed direction to smash into the limo's front end, sending it swerving into a parked car. The impact jolted everybody and left their side mirror lying on the road.

Alicia coughed loudly. "That went well."

Russo glanced back. "No sign of the cops."

"Won't be long," Crouch said. "I don't think he wants to talk to me."

"Ya think?" Alicia pointed ahead. Coker's car had pulled away, pulling off some dangerous maneuvers to melt into the traffic ahead. Only one Qashqai now remained and it was practically glued to their rear.

"On my shout," Alicia addressed the driver, "swing sharp left."

"Shiiiiiit," Lex said. "Girl's gone mad."

Alicia half-turned. "Says who? *You?*"

The following Qashqai nudged their rear, its occupants

laughing. Slower cars flashed by to the left and right. A crazy motorcycle delivery driver tried to squeeze by them both and lost his pizzas in the crush. Alicia leaned out as far as she dared, which meant only her knees held by Russo remained in the car, and held up the riot stick.

"Hold on to yer balls, guys!"

She flung it hard, end over end, straight at the windshield and though the glass didn't shatter this time it did crack at the impact point and cause the driver to react instantly. The Qashqai squealed to a sudden halt.

Alicia grabbed hold of the door handle. "Stop the fucking car. Let's go!"

The limo ground to a halt as the black car shuddered in place. Alicia was first out, hitting the ground at a run just as the Nissan's doors were flung open. She grabbed the first man around the neck and hurled him into decelerating traffic. Cars, vans and buses braked all around, and the high-pitched sound of stressed metal stung the air. Passersby lined the sidewalk, some scrabbling for cellphones. Alicia flung the next man onto the Qashqai's front end, holding his shoulders in a vice-like grip to stop him falling off.

"What the hell do you want with us, asshole?"

"Just checkin' your passports, love," the man said in a decidedly British accent.

"Funny." Alicia saw two more men exiting the car but sensed Russo and Healey coming around her flanks. She gripped her prisoner around the throat. "Maybe you should rethink that answer."

The sun blazed down. Pedestrians screamed or watched excitedly. Angry motorists shouted from safe distances. Coming closer now, Alicia heard the approaching whine of the local constabulary.

"Damn it."

Time for one last squeeze. One final connection. "Tell me or you won't talk for a week."

The guy spluttered, flailing weakly. "Dunno, love. Really I don't. I'm just a relocated local. Coker spread the pesos around and told us to rough you lot up. Give you a few black eyes."

Alicia snorted. "Didn't really work out for you, did it? What's he want with that kind of intimidation?"

"Lady, the man's our boss. Tells us eff all. Only thing I know is he's working for somebody else and he's scared." The guy's eyes widened. "*Very* scared."

Alicia let him fall to the ground and shouted at Russo and Healey to get back in the car. Crouch, who'd been listening from a few paces away, also climbed back in.

"Go," he said to the driver once they were inside. "We have a lot of work to do."

"Yeah," Alicia murmured. "Like getting us some goddamn guns."

"And . . ." Crouch deliberated. "This episode has taught me one thing if nothing else. It seems we need a pair of eyes and ears beyond our team. Somebody to watch from afar and help. We need one more."

SIX

Once they were safely ensconced, Crouch started putting his connection machine into gear. Through Interpol he acquired a new associate in Texas that had a good friend in the Mexican police. So far it was easy for him, friends helping friends, working on goodwill. The Mexican policeman knew various unsavory sorts and agreed to send out several feelers to identify the team Coker had been working with. The understanding from Alicia was that at least some of them had to be local.

Alicia took a shower, then returned to the main room. Their accommodation was spacious and clean and by the time she'd tuned back into Crouch's cajoling phone conversations she understood he was close to securing a new member of their team.

"She's English too? She sounds perfect, Armand. An ex-MI6 operative would work for us and I trust your judgment. Put her in touch directly if you would, and thanks for reaching out."

Alicia stalked over. "Thank God she's a woman, but *ex*-MI6?"

Crouch shrugged. "Wouldn't do to poach their serving staff now, would it?"

"That's not what I meant."

"I realize that and you'll have to trust Armand and me. Now, whilst we're waiting for the Mexicans, I'll have to get hold of Rolland and rustle up some clever technology."

Alicia drifted away. If a young MI6 operative no longer worked for MI6 but was still available for intelligence work then it usually meant they'd burned out or hit an insurmountable personal problem. Either way they were damaged.

But then aren't we all? Alicia shrugged it off, padding over to the window.

"So what's the plan?" Russo asked of her, somewhat

39

challengingly. In reality, he had to know it would all depend on the worth of what the Mexicans came back with.

Alicia kept her eyes on the view outside. "Gold's still out there, Russo. Goons or not. If we have to, we'll go straight through 'em."

"Isn't that always your style?"

"Yeah. I don't fuck around. That's for pussies. Are you a pussy, Russo?" Now she turned, throwing down the gauntlet.

The big man rose to his feet, simply because this wasn't a moment to be the only one sitting down. "I'm a team player, Myles, and if I have to I'll lay it all on the line for my men."

Alicia nodded. "Then quit yer whining and buckle up. This ride's gonna get a hell of a lot bumpier before we reach the end. I'm guessing the guy pulling Coker's strings ain't just offering us a guided tour."

Russo turned reflective. "Yeah, I wonder what's going on with Coker, and how the hell they found us."

At that moment Crouch put the phone down from Rolland Sadler. "All right. We have computer tech and surveillance equipment en route. Some if it mobile, tweeters and comms and such, most of it fixed for hard-wiring, so now we'll need to scout a secure HQ set-up wherever we go."

"If that means mobile transport," Lex spoke up. "I can drive anything with wheels. And most things without."

"I'll bear that in mind."

Alicia took the quiet time to carefully assess her new team. Settling in took time, she understood that, but already several concerns were playing ping-pong in her head. Crouch himself was highly skilled but, lost in the excitement of living his dream, appeared not to have thought all the logistics through. If he'd missed one angle maybe he'd missed another. She didn't want to be ass-up in a gunfight when she found out. Moving on, Russo was belligerent and Healey was green, but the action they'd just shared had proven that both were dependable and possessed potential. Lex, her own little addition, hadn't stepped up yet but Alicia knew it was within him to do so. Despite what she said, if she hadn't already seen a latent ability within him she'd have cut loose back in DC. Crouch's benefactor, Sadler, was an unknown quantity, and Alicia didn't like to judge a man she'd never met. Hopefully, the guy was in it for all the good reasons.

As her mind wandered Crouch turned toward his laptop screen. A new message had flashed up, catching his attention. As he reached out to open it Alicia moved closer. The message read: *Contact made with locals. Have asked them to have leader call you.*

Crouch raised an eyebrow and turned toward Alicia. "Fast work."

"I don't doubt that the Mexican authorities have their contacts."

"Down here, the currency is money, drugs and people. My concern is how much of that currency exchanged hands to facilitate this phone call."

Alicia grimaced. "Maybe it's best not to think too hard on that one."

"Yeah, that's what the cops say."

Before Alicia could respond, Crouch's cell rang. He held the screen up. The word *Unknown* flashed in red letters. Alicia stepped back.

"Crouch here." The ex-Ninth Division boss hit the speaker button.

"Michael," a deep, self-assured tone drawled. "Didn't hurt your head back there, I hope? I noticed you stayed clear of the action."

Crouch wasn't one to be bated into an argument. "What's going on, Coker? What do you want with us?"

"If you hadn't run away so fast you would know by now."

Crouch looked genuinely puzzled. "Greg." He said. "Last time I checked we were friends. Rivals, yes, but gracious ones. What changed?"

Crouch covered the speaker and, looking to Alicia, mouthed, "I used to like this guy."

A silence stretched on the other end. When he ended it, Coker did so with resignation in his voice. "Needs must, Michael. Needs must. I'm in a jam. Lately, the world has worked in ways not often to my liking."

Crouch hesitated. "It does and always has. It always will. That doesn't mean burning bridges."

"Ah, is that what I'm doing? Well, I highlight an earlier comment. *Needs must.*"

Crouch knitted his eyebrows in thought. Was Coker trying to tell him something? He tried a different tack. "What are you looking for?"

"Oh, gold. Treasure. Tombs. The usual. I'd say Quetzalcoatl, but hasn't he been found already?"

"Then why attack us?" To Crouch, the attack meant only one thing. It was a sign that Greg Coker was being cruelly controlled by someone. An operative like Coker would never ordinarily draw attention to himself unless the opportunity was textbook or desperate. The museum debacle had been neither and it had been senseless, especially if, as Crouch suspected, Coker was attempting to fly along on their shirttails in the hope of pipping them at the post when the treasure was located.

Coker again took his time to formulate an answer. "It's complicated, I'm afraid. Very fucking complicated. But look, please carry on. I've no doubt our paths will cross again soon."

Crouch held the cell tighter. "I can help you, Greg. Look, my friend, this is not you. I get that. But you have to—"

"Goodbye, Michael." Coker's long-suffering tones rang out. "Goodbye, and good luck."

Crouch swore as the connection ended. Alicia turned as, immediately, the laptop pinged again and a new message opened up.

All the locals we have reached out to suggest your man is not the crew's true leader. He is a field captain, no more. Locals suggest true leader is very bad news, some kind of criminal kingpin. I'd say back away from this one while you still can.

Crouch sat down hard. If nothing else, Coker was clearly in trouble and despite the guy's inept attempt at hurting them, needed help.

"What could make a man like Coker work for a criminal kingpin?" Healey wondered.

"That," Crouch said, "is the loaded question. Along with why would a crime boss be interested in a five-hundred-year-old treasure? And how the hell did he find out about it?"

"Information's everywhere." Lex spoke in a challenging tone. "Anyone could find out."

"Agreed," Crouch said. "But not like this. Not at the exact same time that we arrive."

"I know one man that knows," Alicia said with a slight smile. "Coker. When we see him again we'll ask him." She made a wringing motion with her hands. "Hard."

"That won't be necessary," Crouch said. "Coker is, or was, a good man. Clumsy, but likeable. I've never had a problem with him, despite consistently having to feed him false information to stop him following my every move. I've had my fill of violence, Alicia." He held her gaze. "Haven't you?"

Alicia shrugged. "Hey, I never start it. Usually though, I do finish it, and often with a smile on my face."

Russo spoke up from his position near the window. "So what's the plan, boss?"

"Time to start the real treasure hunt." Crouch couldn't keep the smile from lighting his face. "Time to seek out the Nahua."

SEVEN

The journey to the north did not start out as long or as arduous as Alicia imagined it might. The treasure hunters rented two four-wheel-drive vehicles, stowed their gear and their new guide, and headed out. The skies above were perfect blue, the clouds pure white and cotton-tailed. Alicia made sure the air-con was cranked up high before settling back into her seat.

"So," she said to their guide who was seated behind her, alongside Lex. "How far?"

"Ten to twelve hours, depending on the roads," Jose Cruz told her in perfect English. "You didn't want to take the airplane, so it takes longer."

"I get that," Alicia said. "Planes attract too much attention. At least this way we can spot a tail."

"Speaking of which," Crouch said from the driver's seat. "All well so far."

"Are you expecting trouble?" Cruz asked with a touch of fear.

Alicia shrugged. "None more than usual." Her mind flicked over the stash of old weapons they'd purchased before setting out. Nothing outstanding, but still nothing short of much-needed added protection.

She caught Crouch's twitch of a smile. *Yeah, he's thinking 'none more than usual' could mean anything from a fist fight to an apocalypse. Shit, what a crazy legend I'm becoming part of.*

The hours passed slowly, eased along by the incredible unfolding landscape. Jagged, vertical rock faces rose straight up out of the earth, the haunt of climbers from all over the world, and dark mountains towered in the distance. Turquoise blue rivers ran fast, circling toward the road and then away toward some distant ravine or cavern. Cruz spoke of great waterfalls and tremendous flocks of birds, stunning cave systems and great canyons. The highway became small and winding, occasionally perilous as they started to climb. The group stopped where they could to take on food and water, seeing no advantage in arriving at their destination worn out.

Alicia quizzed their guide as the hours ticked by. "Rivera mentioned that you would be known to these people. A friend? What is it that you do, Cruz?"

Their guide, a thin man with a shock of black hair and a tendency to sweat, tore his eyes away from the road ahead. "It's not just a conventional job that I do. It is . . . moderation. I usually act as a go-between for the more secluded tribes and their supposed government. A referee at times. At others simply an intermediary. They trust me." He shrugged. "I trust Carlos Rivera, who has taught me much of the Aztec legend, good and bad. Do not let either of us down."

Crouch inclined his own head. "You have my word. You say he's taught you much?"

"To help me in my work. To help me understand the people, yes. Now, I'd like to know what makes you qualified to find a mythical treasure where everyone else has failed."

"Us?" Alicia smiled. "Nothing. Short of, we're the real deal. Serious as a bullet. We don't have time to waste. People like us, we're normally off fighting bad guys and keeping the world safe. You're actually very lucky we're here."

Cruz didn't look convinced. "Okay."

More climbing and they passed a group of life-jacketed people manhandling a kayak onto a stretch of water. Another clearing revealed several youths scrambling small ATVs across a shallow stream bed.

Cruz cleared his throat. "Before we arrive I want to give you a clearer picture of what you will find. The Nahua people living here are a simple race. If they want to earn and work for money they walk or take a bus to the nearest town—which takes sixty minutes in one direction. No more than sixty families live in this small mountainous village. An insignificant race, you might think, but then consider that the words *avocado, chili, coyote* and even *chocolate* and *tomato* have Nahua roots. You will see many coffee trees, amazing vistas, and even clouds filling the valley below. This is their life and it is enough. The wives try to support their families the traditional way—through weaving and stitching—but it is often a road to nowhere. Their husbands grow crops, potatoes, mushrooms and peppers. They are surrounded by old ruins and green hills with altars carved into their sides. A very religious people, their festivals are normally loud and colorful. They can, literally, dance for days."

Crouch slowed as the road narrowed. "I think we're close."

Cruz pointed ahead. "Pull in over there. I hope you guys are ready for this."

Cruz directed them through the small, clean village, all the time heading for a huddle of dwellings that sat on the outskirts, built up against a high stepped hill. Above the roofs of the dwellings and dotted up the hillside, Alicia made out the altars Cruz had mentioned—small niches carved out of the rock and adorned with colorful ribbons. Her eyes followed a sandy path that led all the way to the top.

She spoke quietly to Russo, who had been driving the second vehicle. "Any problems?"

"All clear," he reported back. "Haven't seen another car for hours."

As they walked, the village quieted. Strangers were not unknown to these parts but were still rare enough to attract a little pall of uneasiness. Remembering Cruz's words Alicia fought to keep her silence even when a small group of men started pointing at her. The path continued through numerous small dwellings and past well-ordered fields where men and children worked, even though the sun had begun to set to the west. Alicia kept a sharp eye in all directions, even as far as the tree line high above, but nothing untoward occurred.

Cruz chatted to the locals as he passed through. Everyone seemed to know him. The guy probably spent half his life visiting villages and townships such as this, but perhaps not for today's unusual reason. Crouch followed and stored away his every move as if learning the ropes for some later visit. The man was nothing if not meticulous.

Cruz stopped before the huddle of dwellings. The rough poured concrete construction didn't fit well out here where the new world hadn't penetrated, but Alicia chose to see it as a verification of the wisdom of the village elders. As they waited, three men emerged into the sunlit evening.

Alicia stared. With only a small stretch of her imagination she could easily see them at that aforementioned battle of Tenochtitlan, fighting the conquistadors. Cruz approached reverentially and spoke for a while. Alicia understood none of it and kept her eyes sweeping the area, always alert.

After five minutes Cruz finally turned to Crouch. "It's up to you now. I have done all I can and expressed Rivera's wishes that they help. But you must convince them that you mean well, that you are the real deal. Otherwise," he shrugged, "they will give you nothing."

Crouch nodded, stepping forward. It wasn't lost on him that the language barrier would severely dent the impact of his speech, but he hoped the sincerity in his voice would shine through in any dialect. He started out by explaining a little of his background, then quickly moved on.

"Carlos Rivera trusts us to do the right thing," he continued as Cruz translated. "As does Mr. Cruz here. They would not help us if they didn't believe in us. I have pulled together this entire team, professionals all, to help and we are funded by a man with major contacts inside the World Heritage Committee. Your priceless treasures, if found, would be displayed in a museum in their entirety, not sold off or smuggled away to a private collector as so many are these days."

Crouch paused to let Cruz catch up, then continued.

"I realize most everyone that has approached you so far were not exactly . . . genuine, honest people. I can't prove that we are any different save for the tone of my voice and my choice of words, but I *can* offer something that you already inherently know—your ancestors were not fools. They will not suffer fools to find their gold. Only a highly professional outfit, richly underwritten, can hope to stand any chance of succeeding. And then only with your help. Do you want your heritage back?"

Cruz's voice persisted for a minute then fell silent. Alicia gazed into the faces of the elders, seeing nothing there. Not a flicker of expression. Not once did they turn to each other, as if conversing through mental telepathy. But after a while the tallest man with the most weather-beaten skin and deeply crinkled eyes started to talk.

Cruz translated. "Your words are welcome, but strangers are not. Any man can lie, and most very well. There is nothing for you here." The guide looked a little crestfallen.

Crouch leaned forward. "Carlos Rivera, my friend, said that you might."

The elder made no move, instead staring at Crouch without let up. Eventually Cruz said, "To me you are still a stranger."

Alicia scanned the valley once more. It wasn't that she was expecting trouble, it was that trouble was never far away during operations like this. Truth be told, trouble seemed to cling to her like a besotted high-school senior. In the twilight of her SAS days, and because it was new and cultish at the time, the guys had taken to calling her Veronica, after Kristen Bell in the TV series, because the two women looked so much alike and were beset with misfortune. But that was where the similarities ended. Alicia had escaped the hell of her home before college and even then she could have incapacitated a man with a double strike. It could be said that her formative years had shaped her for war.

The elder expressed himself again. "We have long accepted that our heritage is lost. Perhaps it is better staying where it is."

Alicia picked up on the charged statement as quickly as Crouch. "Then it *does* exist? You have proof. Your people and certainly your ancestors would not have wanted it to stay lost. The plan was to return it, yes? Bring the caravans back after the Spanish left. They could not have foreseen what happened. Think carefully, my friend, because *this* is your chance. Maybe your best chance."

The elders retreated then stopped in sync. Alicia thought their simultaneous movements a little unsettling. The crowd of villagers at her back continued to grow, men returning from the fields and women and children leaving their houses to examine the newcomers. A light breeze blew through the modest valley.

The elder finally betrayed an emotion, that of weariness, and turned to his fellows. Some rapid-fire conversation ensued which Crouch didn't look to Cruz to provide a translation for. It would only show bad manners. At last the main elder turned his attention back toward Cruz.

"They speak of the great journey. Seven caravans leaving the capital during that ageless night, heading north." Cruz's eyes widened at that as he passed on the information. Crouch fancied the tribe had never imparted so much before. "With prodigious treasures aboard. They speak of the cartwheel, what many call the original pieces of eight, the pre-eminent Aztec treasure of all time and the main item the elders might really want returned. Primarily they speak of each building's jewels, because as you know every structure was stripped of its underlying gold and jewels and packed separately. The horde, the *value,* must be immense."

Crouch betrayed no emotion. "What else do they say?"

"They want us to wait. Wait here."

Alicia glanced sideways at her team. Russo was as observant as she, constantly scanning the terrain. Healey bore a look of wonder on his face and the glow of fire in his eyes. *That'll do,* she thought. Lex shifted his weight from foot to foot as if uncomfortable and no doubt bottling up some kind of complaint. She watched the elders retreat into their cluster of houses.

Crouch didn't turn around. "Stay alert, people. One way or another we'll be out of here shortly."

Sometime later the elders reappeared, shuffling at a slow march, one after the other. The leader grasped something in his right hand, a metal box of the modern world, somehow seeming incongruous out here. With an odd kind of reverence he placed it on the ground at his feet and then knelt before it.

He looked up. Cruz translated as he spoke. "If you know your Aztec history then you will know what a codex is." He added, "It's a book written by the ancient Aztecs, largely pictorial but they can contain a version of the Nahuatl language too. The old pictograms can be translated into writing now that the Nahuatl language has evolved." He smiled at the elder. "There are very few surviving codices from the pre-conquest era."

"Any that describe their capital's destruction?" Crouch wondered.

"No. But there are over half a dozen bound manuscripts in existence. The Codex Aubin, Codex Mendoza and Florentine to name a few. If this is a codex" —he indicated the box— "it represents a great treasure in itself."

The elder opened the box very slowly, reached in and pulled out a sheaf of papers. Cruz's sharp intake of breath was enough to confirm the man's suspicions. Now, however, the elder again started to talk, this time with a gravity to his tones.

Cruz blinked, suddenly looking shocked. "What? Are you kidding?" he said in English, forgetting himself before reverting to the elders' language.

Alicia frowned. "What did he say?"

But Cruz was shaking his head, clearly upset, disagreeing with the elder. After a moment the man put his hand onto the top of the box and threatened to shove the papers back inside.

Crouch raised a hand. "What's the problem, Jose? Perhaps I can help."

"I doubt it," Cruz muttered. "I'm the problem, it seems. *Me.*"

"You? How on earth—"

Alicia patted a pocket. "I have a gun. I could take you out if needs be."

Cruz looked alarmed then resigned. "I don't know what to say, sir. The elder won't let you take a look at the codex unless you agree to take me with you on this . . . odd quest of yours."

"What?"

"They don't fully trust you. After all you still remain a stranger to them. But me and my mentor, Rivera, they do trust. It is the only way forward, I'm afraid."

Crouch clicked his tongue, frowning hard. Alicia watched the elder and the elder watched Crouch. Everything depended on their leader's next few words and the whole village knew it.

"Of course we will take you, Jose. It's not a problem. But will you come?"

Cruz signaled an affirmative to the elder. "If you're asking me to join a legitimate quest to find a five-hundred-year-old legendary, priceless treasure then my answer is—damn, yeah!"

The leader held up the sheaf of papers. Alicia saw that they were very old and bound on one side. The man didn't open the book, but indicated them as he spoke.

"This is the Codex Azcapotzalco as written in the sixteenth century. It is a pictographic, that is a writing system that consists mostly of logograms and syllabic signs. It is written on deer hide and is this village's most valuable artefact, more valuable even than these elder's lives." Cruz bowed deeply. "Please respect that."

Crouch bowed too. "Thank you for bringing it forward."

Cruz went on. "Azcapotzalco is the name of the Aztec that wrote the codex, the one that returned. The Nahuatl have studied its meaning for many years and, at least this learned generation, can now decipher the pictures and translate them into words. It is . . ." Cruz paused, creasing his brows. "A poem, I think."

He clarified with the elder. "Yes, a poem. I think the word has been corrupted though. Either through the ages or by their literal translation. Poem could mean story or even *map*."

Healey's face lit up. "As in a *treasure* map?"

Alicia pressed on his shoulders. "Down boy."

"Azcapotzalco returned many years after the first warriors. Most of the codex is an account of the subsequent lives of the Aztec warriors that decided to stay with the hidden caravan," Cruz said. "And still more tells of those warriors that mixed with the local braves after the caravan was safe and the ones that returned. There is, however, deep within its pages, a *passage* that points to the place where the treasure was hidden."

Crouch felt the corners of his mouth twitching and fought to keep them straight. "Go on."

Cruz listened twice before repeating the elder's words. "It's a poem, I think, it has a kind of rhythm. Listen:

"Through the great, endless river you must travel,

"Past canyons and rocks of waves,

"The Shield Arch shows the way,

"But heed our warnings to the mushroom rock,

"Then beyond the known territory of the braves,

"Look between Hummingbird and the ritual for your final guidance,

"And betray the sacrifices of your loyal warriors not."

Crouch blinked, digesting the information. "It sounds exactly like an original series of pictures translated into modern words, as the elder said. Fantastic."

Alicia nudged Healey. "You wanna write that down."

The young solider grunted. "Damn, if only I had one of those eidetic memories."

"Oh yeah," Alicia murmured. "Now there's a thought I have every day."

Healey caught the sarcasm and asked Cruz to repeat slowly as he jotted it down. Crouch was clearly mulling through the text. "But there's no starting point," he said. "It's all very well to follow those directions, but where from?"

"North," Cruz said. "The caravans traveled north. And the elder says the ancient Aztecs used to have a method of counting days. They indicated quantities using the requisite number of dots. A flag represented twenty, repeated up to four hundred, and then a sign like a fir tree signified four hundred. They can give us an accurate dateline for the entire march."

Crouch smiled. "Then it looks like we're ready to get started."

EIGHT

It seemed the fates were aligned with them that day. The return trip to Mexico City passed without a hitch, the whole team newly energized by the thought of finally being able to pursue a real treasure. Slumped down in the passenger seat, Alicia allowed the team's exuberance to enliven her whilst staying razor-sharp and objective in her head. The molten sunset gave way to pure, impenetrable black. Not even the stars proved their silent shimmer tonight.

As the journey continued, she tried to stay awake.

Crouch noticed her predicament. "You have to trust your team sometime, Alicia."

Another reminder of how astute her boss was. "Doesn't have to be tonight though."

"Well look at it this way. My guess is that between now and when we find the treasure this is the *least* danger we'll be in."

"*When* we find the treasure?"

Crouch grinned in the gloom. "I've always been a pretty confident kinda guy."

"Yeah. Combine that with your sentimentalism and you're a hard act to keep up with."

"You mean 'get along with'?"

Alicia pursed her lips. "No, but if that's what you like to think . . ."

Crouch drove in silence for a while. As they breached the outskirts of Mexico City, Alicia thumbed the walkie that connected their car with the one ahead.

"Stay alert, you guys. No slacking. This ain't the time to be missing something."

No let up.

Back in their temporary HQ, they found a surprise waiting for them.

Caitlyn Nash.

With short black hair and piercing blue eyes, Caitlyn had a body created through regular visits to the gym and the quick, nervous smile of a geek. She was twenty one years old, completely untrained in combat, but one of MI6's best real-time analysts. Part of her job had also included collecting any historical data relevant to the task at hand—an undertaking she had excelled at.

After meeting her Alicia wondered just one thing. *Why the hell is she here with us?* Not in a bad way, not because she doubted the woman's skill, but quite the opposite. Twenty one was a damn young age to have burned out.

Still, Caitlyn was here and eager to prove her worth.

Alicia put Healey on watch and listened as Caitlyn outfitted the team with some new gadgets. There were Bluetooth comms, to be inserted in the ear, which worked full time unless you double-tapped to close the gadget.

"Just make sure you switch them off before you start doing anything umm . . . private," Caitlyn said with a little blush.

Alicia turned to Healey. "Shit, the kid will de double-tapping every three hours."

Even Russo laughed. Healey turned as red as Caitlyn. The new analyst continued in a hurry, "Once we have the new mini wireless cameras fitted into all your equipment we'll have full-time, always-on documentation and analysis between site and base. Essential for proving providence and ownership, trust and true intentions. Those are the priority features for now, guys. Don't worry, it won't take long to set up."

Alicia nodded, pleased. The idea of documenting everything they discovered through video link was sound as far as it went. She wondered how capable the link signal was but didn't query it at this point. Crouch would have thought of pretty much everything. Even their new reluctant addition, Jose Cruz, accepted a comms system, clutching his hands together as he did so as if praying for good fortune. Once she'd outfitted all the earphones and connected them to the main network, Caitlyn set about installing the micro cameras.

Alicia watched her work. The young girl fairly whistled as her dexterous fingers flew between chores. Bent to her task she seemed happy, content. Perhaps she felt safe in her own world, surrounded by another world of highly trained men and women, insulated. Alicia thought that her pasty complexion might attest that she never got out much, but then remembered that she lived in England. *Either way,* Alicia thought, *Caitlyn's an odd package and worth keeping a close eye on.*

Christ, she thought. *Listen to me. Since when did I decide to take on these kind of responsibilities?* Was it since she'd started running with Matt Drake and his team, each member's deep sense of accountability to the crew rubbing off on her? Was it since the man she thought she might love died in a wild, legendary battle on a windswept bridge late at night? Harleys and Ducatis versus cars and machine guns. Or had this quality been merely overlooked ever since she returned home to save her mother from her father's bruising hands only to find the two of them dead, her mother from an overdose and her father from alcohol poisoning four months earlier.

Caitlyn smiled at her, fresh face lighting up and reminding her uncomfortably of Healey's. "Almost done."

Alicia just thought, *Shit, I'm a fucking child minder here.*

Russo rose to his feet, mumbling about turning in to get some sleep. Maybe the mountain was having similar thoughts to her. Crouch was riveted to his laptop whilst following Healey's hastily scribbled notes about the codex. The poem had been jotted down along with the calendar that the elders had translated from the original text. Crouch was trying to make sense of it all and, judging by the set of his shoulders, not doing too well. Cruz was seated alongside, reminding him about the numerous Aztec inscriptions found in several areas of North America.

A voice at her shoulder snapped her attention around. "I thought those guys might've jumped us again," Lex said with a malicious little grin. "Y'know, when we were on the road. Was hoping for it actually."

"Don't get ahead of yourself," Alicia told him. "Coker's boss is the real danger here. There's plenty of action to come before we ride home holding the winner's trophy aloft."

As if in corroboration of her statement the entire front window of their rented ground floor apartment lit up. It was a picture window, wide and arguably vulnerable, but equipped with remote control smart glass that turned opaque or transparent blue at the touch of a button. Thus, the team had turned up the juice and considered it safe. Now, Healey's squawk wailed through the various walkie-talkie handsets discarded around the room.

"Christ, they're coming in hard and tooled up. Get the hell outta there!"

Alicia responded without a moment's pause. Her lifestyle demanded that she be ready to react instantly at any time of the day. Before anyone moved Alicia was already racing over to snatch up her weapon and motioning people toward the rear door.

"Get down!" Healey hissed through the new comms. "*Get down now!*"

Alert and fired up, the team dived headlong, Caitlyn the only one that looked a little ungainly. Instantly the entire picture window exploded behind them, gunfire ripping it to bits. Glass chunks scythed through the air, embedding deep into furniture and appliances, and cascading down from the wide frame in a razor-edged torrent. Alicia swiveled on the floor and fired between her heels, a spray and pray, hoping the return fire might slow their enemy's advance. Healey was tracking them and screaming through the comms.

"Climbing outta four big trucks. Semi-autos and handguns

everywhere, no attempt at concealment. I don't see Coker. These guys look and act like pros, not like the goons we fought before . . ."

As Healey provided the running commentary, Alicia urged her team to crawl forward. Crouch and Cruz were in front, using elbows and knees to slide along the polished floor in the direction of the kitchen. Caitlyn came next, barely moving, her head almost buried into the laminate.

Alicia scooted next to her. "Grab my arm," she hissed. "Now."

As soon as the young woman reached out, Alicia took hold of her elbow and dragged her across the floor. The two slithered fast, smashing into a set of chair legs, but staying low as another salvo of bullets raked the air. Alicia heard the girl whimper.

"You're gonna be okay," she said a little prematurely. "Don't worry. It's the map they want not you."

Despite the reassurance Caitlyn barely looked up. Alicia's mind turned to how well the analyst might be able to cope with the forthcoming mission and wondered if Crouch may have made another mistake. Carefully, she placed a hand on Caitlyn's blond hair.

"I'll look after you," she said, hardly believing her own words and the inherent responsibility in them. "Stick with me."

She'd refrained from saying *trust me.* Because that was inviting disaster and just never worked out.

Russo took his turn to lace the air with lead. Through the shattered glass Alicia could now make out three sets of large round headlights, all blazing on full beam and clearly illuminating the apartment's interior. Crouch was already at the kitchen, Cruz a quick shuffle behind. Lex was next. Alicia hauled Caitlyn along whilst firing backward and keeping an eye to their flanks. Their prospects weren't good.

"Healey." She tapped her comms. "Make sure you keep our right side clear. We'll be coming fast."

"Already on it."

Alicia dragged her charge again, but now Caitlyn was helping and moving under her own steam. As they passed Crouch's laptop still open and switched on atop the table—and miraculously untouched—Alicia noted that Crouch had already pocketed their interpretations of the Aztec poem along with whatever their boss had been working on.

Great move.

As if in response, the laptop suddenly whirled and danced under fire and blew apart. Alicia saw a shadow cross one of the headlights. Bad mistake. She squeezed her trigger and heard a gratifying scream. When an enemy started taking casualties it always slowed them down—assuming they were relatively sane that was.

Russo scuttled behind her, now the last man. Alicia took the opportunity to help Caitlyn along, practically flinging her into the kitchen. Crouch had upended the tall refrigerator and pulled out the oven, and was now standing over it.

"What?" Alicia stared. "You cooking bacon and eggs? You really think that'll help slow 'em down?"

"No," Crouch answered quietly. "I'm turning it on and disengaging the gas pipe. Even the smell should make them think twice."

Cruz was approaching the back door. Alicia yelled, "Wait!" and contacted Healey.

"Where are you?"

"Out back. I can see Cruz, the idiot. Go now. The coast is clear."

"Move!"

Alicia leaped forward, guiding Caitlyn by the arm. Bullets again slammed into the walls behind them and now came the crunch of broken glass as booted men stepped over the devastated sill. Bloodthirsty shouts followed them.

Alicia stepped it up. Russo breathed down her neck. Cruz slammed open the rear door and dashed out into the dark, closely followed by Crouch with pistol drawn and poised. Lex came next, moving like a TV caricature of a special-forces soldier, and then she cradled Caitlyn through the door.

Cool air greeted her. The apartment's rear was a small grassy yard, bounded on two sides by a scraggly hedge and open to the back. A short wall and rusted gate led to a narrow alley. Healey was already beckoning them toward it.

"Keep it moving, guys. I have no eyes to your right."

Cruz raced straight for the young soldier. Crouch angled right, staying low. Two pops from his handgun told Alicia the enemy were too close. And why the hell weren't police sirens braying at the night skies? In any other country the cops would be all over this by now. But here in Mexico City . . . business as usual, she imagined.

Behind her Russo unleashed a burst of fire. A stray bullet passed through his coat, making him grunt, then lightly grazed Alicia's arm—the touch barely registering—before continuing its flight down the alley. That, as much as anything, told Alicia a fact that she'd assumed from the start—they were being hunted tonight, not warned.

Caitlyn yelped as if sensing the nearness of the bullet. Alicia sympathized for the girl's utter bad luck—she had only just arrived after all—but now wasn't the time. Crouch was engaged ahead, struggling with an opponent. Alicia pushed Caitlyn toward Healey and branched off to help her boss. When the man struggling with him registered her presence, momentarily taking his attention off the battle, Crouch felled him with a jab to the throat.

Two more adversaries took his place.

Crouch brought his gun up, but found his arm wrenched sideways. He took a blow to the gut. Alicia stepped in, sidekicking Crouch's opponent whilst pulling her own into an arm-breaking waltz. The arm was quickly followed by a knee. Crouch swung his weapon up and fired. The two pulled away.

Healey was already sheltering Caitlyn in the alley. Russo was ahead of them. The sound of breaking glass told her he'd smashed a window, the shape he stood next to, towering over him, told her that it was a van. Both she and Crouch ran for the head of the alley, firing back toward the house to deter their pursuers.

But by now, several enemy combatants had secured good positions. Bullets blasted through the dark, the position of the shooters clear because of the unsilenced weapons. For Alicia it was a mad, surreal moment; caught out in the pitch black with deadly fire strafing to left and right of her, Crouch at her side, unable to take cover or offer any kind of defense. It was blind luck that they escaped.

But down the alley they ran, unscathed. Shouts of anger went up from behind. Alicia gave it a three count, then turned and loosed her weapon, emptying it before ramming in another mag. Two men lay screaming.

Russo fired up the van, throwing open the side doors. Everyone piled in unceremoniously and then became even more tangled as the big man revved the engine. The van spurted forward, roaring. Alicia heard strangled shouts into radios but couldn't make out the words. A quick look through the smeared rear window showed their pursuers hotfooting it after them. She tried to rise but found her knees were inexplicably locked with Cruz's.

"What the hell, man?"

Then she saw his eyes. Their guide was barely holding it together. Christ, this wasn't as easy as the Drake set-up, where every member of the team was pretty much a super hero. This was hard work.

"Take a breath," she said. "You're okay. Now ease up with the creepy boa-constrictor stuff."

Cruz shuffled back. Healey grabbed his shoulders, giving him a winning if slightly blood-crazed smile.

"We all in one piece?" Crouch asked from underneath both Lex and Caitlyn.

61

The whole group slid around the back of the van as Russo slung the vehicle through a sharp right-hander. Alicia found herself having to fend off Cruz yet again.

"Feeling like I'm gonna throw up is all," Lex gargled. "You want me to drive this fucker, big man?"

Russo only grunted. Alicia took it as a refusal.

Bullets clanged off the back doors. Both rear windows shattered. Russo slowed for a junction ahead and then floored it on seeing the road was clear. Unlit shops and bars flashed by to either side. The only lights were the dimly glowing streetlamps. Even the moon was having no part of this mayhem.

A gust of wind blustered in through the jagged rear windows. Alicia saw that they were pulling away from the runners now, but that three vehicles were already in fast pursuit. They appeared to be faster than the van. It was only a matter of time.

"They're determined bastards," she said. "We have to find a defensible position, Russo. Fast."

The grunt came again, seemingly one of those replies that worked for every occasion. Alicia was shocked to see how fast their followers closed the gap.

"Shit!"

From out of nowhere a battered white truck crossed their path. Alicia caught the logo *Swift* before her face almost merged with it. Russo slung the van sideways, again forcing its occupants to crash into each other; coming to a jarring stop only when both vehicles smashed together.

The van wobbled, suddenly still. Alicia, though suffering from a bruised forehead, didn't miss a beat. She scrambled furiously down to the back end, flung the doors open and jumped down. The chasing vehicles were already in view, not yet slowing. A conservative spraying of their front ends made them slew to the right, one smashing into a storefront. Men piled out, taking cover behind bins and railings, concrete posts and parked cars.

Alicia herded everyone around the closest corner. "Run like hell!"

An immediate problem snagged her attention. The area they were headed toward was severely lacking in buildings. A relatively small patch of open land with a dilapidated, rusted child's playground set at the center, but the entire area was open plan.

"Of all the bloody luck," she muttered. Maybe this was payback for not getting shot to death earlier.

Russo ground to a halt three feet away. "What's the plan?"

"Remain unventilated." Alicia pointed to the widest car parked behind them. "Think we could roll that over? Then, if we're forced to retreat, at least it'll offer us some protection."

Russo nodded, called Healey over and motioned at the others to keep hurrying across the playground. "Be right behind you."

Alicia moved to help the giant but Russo had the car turned over in seconds. Healey grinned at her surprised reaction.

"Don't worry. He used to do it to my little Astra all the time."

"You ever do that to my Ducati and the chances of you reproducing will be cut by at least a half. You get me?"

Russo made the grunt.

Healey grinned. "Oh, he'd just throw the bike onto the nearest roof."

Alicia lined up with the far corner. When the fastest of their enemy showed his face she took aim, waited a few seconds, then opened fire. The man folded, blood spraying the wall at his back and the man to his right, whom Alicia also took out. There followed a momentary lull before a new weapon appeared, clasped in the hands of a man wearing full body armor.

"Shit. Are you kidding me? Is that a fucking Steyr?"

"Start running." Russo rumbled and began to turn.

Alicia dived on top of him, dragging him to the ground. "It's a tactical machine pistol, you idiot. Stay down or it'll shred you to pieces."

The Steyr burst into action, ripping through the car in a matter of moments, bullets passing straight through the torn metal. Their enemies ran hard under cover of the Steyr, crossing the road and approaching the area where Alicia, Healey and Russo were pinned down. The three twisted and covered up as best they could, rolling a short way down a sharp incline away from the side of the road and onto the grass-covered playing field.

But, prone as they were, when the well-armed pursuers flowed around both sides of the dead vehicle, Alicia and her two comrades didn't stand a chance.

It was utter mayhem, utter devastation. Bullets chewed up the concrete and the soil and grass near the car. Lines of lethal lead stitched several haphazard paths of random death. Their only savior was that they had rolled out of the way, but now their enemies had seen them. Alicia fired back with Russo and Healey at her side, all three on their knees and with weapons held to their shoulders.

Men collapsed, tripping others; some were slammed back into the already devastated car. But there were too many; the stream kept coming. In another two seconds Alicia guessed the bullets would reach her.

Then another sound joined forces with the nightmare cacophony. Different caliber pistols, fresh gunfire. It came from behind Alicia. Without being able to turn she saw the oncoming men fall even harder and silently threw a grateful prayer toward Michael Crouch. The extra firepower deterred those attackers who hadn't already committed themselves, giving Alicia the chance to scramble away.

The ditch was deeper than anyone anticipated. She flew ass over head, all the way down to the bottom, tangling with Healey and only just managing to get her head up at the bottom before seeing the mass of bodies rolling down toward her.

"Oh fu—"

NINE

Alicia ducked as the bodies slammed into her, forcing them over her lowered back and away. Still more came, some dead, some dying, tangled with others that were very much alive. Alicia fought to keep her balance, to keep her head above the growing jumble of arms and legs, whilst dodging out of the way of even more heavy, tumbling bodies.

At last the flow came to an end. Russo stood to her left, a man withstanding a tide, using the considerable strength in his arms and legs to divide the waters. In the end Alicia almost expected him to start beating his chest.

She fought to pull herself free, kicking with her legs, all efforts at grace or skill put aside. She used the cargo vest of a dead man to haul herself free, balancing on top of his body. Where the hell was Healey?

Russo was also searching the mass. Bullets still flew from Crouch's position behind them, where they used the kids' slide for cover. Alicia knew it was only a matter of moments before their enemies brought the guy with the Steyr forward.

One man rose before her. She headbutted him back down among his brethren. Another challenged Russo and found himself launched into the air, arms and legs flapping as if trying to fly. Alicia hopped from man to man, using their backs and chests as purchase.

"Healey!" Russo's bellow surely woke half of Mexico City.

Alicia saw hands waving as a disabled soldier managed to untangle his limbs just enough to swivel a rifle at her. With the speed of a striking viper she reached down and tore the gun from his hands, upended it and blasted a hole through his forehead. She wouldn't indiscriminately kill these men in their helplessness even now, as they clearly fought to kill her, but if they didn't learn their place at her feet it was game over.

Alicia bounced her way over toward Healey's hands. The young man was caught beneath a lifeless slab of meat, someone approaching Russo's size, but lacking the hard lines and craggy exterior in favor of scars and black tattoos.

"Looks like you were enjoying that," she said as she pulled him free.

Healey breathed hard, unable to retort between gasps. Russo joined them. Healey took a second to dig out his cellphone and take a picture of the big soldier's neck tattoo.

Alicia wished she had a moment to comment. The possibilities were endless. But now was most certainly not the time.

"What do you say we get the fuck outta here?"

Alicia jumped down the struggling pile, running the instant her feet hit hard ground. By the time her eyes registered the terrible scene ahead she was too far to turn back and hunt for a new weapon.

A second team had clearly ambushed Crouch's position. Crouch himself was pinned down underneath the slide, his arm around Cruz, keeping the attackers at bay, but Lex and Caitlyn were anything but safe. The uncommon feeling of terror gripped Alicia's chest as she saw both Lex and Caitlyn being dragged away by a group of armed men.

"No!" Not after her promise. Not after Caitlyn had trusted her. And not after she'd brought Lex all this way.

To die.

Alicia increased her pace, outdistancing Russo with ease. The enemy soldiers continued to drag Caitlyn and Lex along, struggling up the ditch's incline at the other end of the playing field. If Alicia had a rifle she could have started to pick them off, but it was lost under the groaning mass back there. A man turned, saw her, and took a potshot. Alicia didn't flinch as the bullet droned past her face.

She was closing the gap.

Then more men saw her. Shouts went up. Guns were snapped in her direction and aimed. The moment they fired she anticipated and rolled forward, tucking her arms and legs in, passing under the deadly flight, and hit the incline at speed. The men vented their alarm. One of them suddenly spun Lex and shoved him hard down the hill toward her. Alicia, at full speed, couldn't dodge out of the way. She hit the biker head on, the impact causing an explosion inside her head. Falling, plummeting to the ground, she tried one last time to correct her balance.

Above them, at the top of the slope, Caitlyn's despairing eyes were more like an accusation than a statement of hope.

TEN

Licking their wounds, Crouch's team melted into the night before finding a vehicle and using it to take them to a hotel. Alicia wondered if their escape hadn't ended up being a little too easy in the end. Maybe all the enemy had wanted were kills and a kidnap. Clearly, they thought Caitlyn had been a part of the team since the beginning.

The worst part was, she hadn't been. She didn't have the whole picture, not by a long shot. Alicia knew the type of pressures their enemy would exert on her and it was driving her crazy.

"C'mon," she said as the remainder of the team unloaded their belongings into the new hotel room. "We have to track down these bastards before they start hurting her."

"Can't believe they took Caitlyn." Healey's face was despondent. "Poor girl's only just joined the frickin' team."

"At least she won't be able to tell 'em anything," Lex said gruffly.

"That's part of the point," Alicia explained. "It will be worse for her."

Crouch said nothing, but opened and booted up a laptop as soon as he found a seat. Alicia herded Healey straight over to him. "The tattoo. Show him."

Crouch took the cellphone from the young soldier. "This is good. Gives us a fair starting point at least."

"One thing worries me—" Russo began.

"Only one?" Alicia shook her head.

Russo ignored the comment. "Greg Coker. From what we know about the man this doesn't come even close to his modus operandi. What are we missing?"

Crouch was busy downloading the tattoo from Healey's phone onto the laptop. "We have to assume Greg's merely a pawn, part of something that goes way deeper. Greg Coker would not do this to our team. It's the criminal organization behind him that's the concern."

"But what could they do to Coker to make him cooperate in such a way?" Healey asked with an air of innocence.

Alicia eyed him but saved her comment. If the kid stayed in this game he would learn soon enough.

"You get any other pictures down there?" she asked, thinking a little ribbing might help take his mind off Caitlyn. "Tangled up with so many men?"

"Umm, no I—" Healey suddenly looked sheepish. "Oh, I see."

Russo jumped to his rescue. "Did *you?* Seemed kinda at home underneath all those men."

"They were throwing themselves at me." Alicia spread her hands. "What's a girl s'posed to do?"

Crouch made a noise as he finished uploading the data. Once he was happy with the picture he turned to his phone. "Let's see who we can find."

"Hope you never lose that thing," Russo pointed out.

"Oh yes, the contacts on here are a treasure themselves. Cleverly though I've saved everything to the Cloud."

"Really? From what I hear the Cloud ain't exactly unhackable these days."

Alicia nodded. "Yeah. Thank God I take all my nudes by Polaroid."

Healey, unable to help himself, glanced over. Lex barked out a laugh. "She's not serious, man."

Alicia kept her face straight. "Aren't I, Lex? How would you know?"

The biker shrugged indifferently. "Whatever."

"That sounded a bit like 'fuck you'."

Lex almost smiled. "Whatever."

Crouch waved them to silence as his first call connected. "Healey. Get on the database and start trying to match that tattoo. Russo, go for a recce and set up a watch. The clock is ticking, people. If we want to find Caitlyn in one piece we have to find her *now.*"

ELEVEN

As far back as she could remember Caitlyn Nash had always been burdened with a nervous disposition. If anything remotely outside her comfort zone presented, the uncertainty began to creep in, the barriers went up, and she crept back into herself. It was one of the reasons she'd learned her craft so extensively—at least in her field of expertise she would never feel ill at ease.

Joining Crouch's team had seemed to be a perfect opportunity. The offer came at the right time, in the right way, through Armand Argento, one of the few men she could now trust. A change was what she needed and, not having had a boyfriend since high school, pets, or indeed parents she could look in the eye of late, she counted her lucky stars and jumped at the chance.

A dream job.

Now a nightmare. Caitlyn recalled the shock she felt when men started storming the apartment and shooting at them. She remembered the only respite being Alicia Myles, the woman that had promised to take care of her. Then, when chaos took the night in its grip and everyone became separated the only eyes she could see were the hard, flinty eyes of her enemy. The ones that forced her along with them and strapped her arms together.

Now, tied to a chair, arms behind her and ankles secured, she could only wait for the inevitable. Nobody had visited her yet. The room where she waited was a simple concrete box, empty, windowless, with water dripping somewhere she couldn't see. No other noise interrupted her isolation. It was as if the end of the world had come and left her behind.

Caitlyn fought the anxiety. It wouldn't be good to let them see it. Her field training had been brief, perfunctory, and of little use. They said the training would kick in. They told her she would have untapped reserves. That she would be fine.

Clearly they'd never expected her to be kidnapped by lethal treasure hunters.

Caitlyn wondered about that too. Beyond setting up advanced comms and eyes-on equipment she had participated in nothing. All she knew was what she'd overheard and that was very little.

Would these men believe her?

Sure, a cynical voice spoke up. *And then they'll let you take a shower, prepare you a nice meal and send you on your way. Because that's what killers and mercenaries always did.*

The sound of a key rattling in the door snapped her to attention. Adrenalin surged through her body and she sought to moderate it. She could feel how wild her eyes suddenly looked. So much for keeping it under wraps.

A man entered, dressed conservatively in jeans and a faded leather jacket. Graying at the temples he wore his worry lines with dignity, with pride. Handsome, Caitlyn would have called him given a different venue, but here—menacing.

"I'm Greg Coker," he said quickly. "I'm sure you've heard of me."

Caitlyn hadn't. The fear choked her voice but Coker read the answer in her eyes.

"When did you join the little crew? I don't recall you being there at the museum."

"Yesterday," she said finally, proud the word came out without a stammer. "After they returned from the north. I'm just a techie."

"Yesterday?" Coker repeated. "Man, that's some flat out bad luck, little lady. Not the best start to your new career. Letting yourself get abducted so easy. They won't come for you, you know."

Caitlyn was unable to hide her worry. "What?"

"It's not Crouch's style. Do you know him at all?"

"Through reputation. He sounds better—"

"Ah, but how did he *earn* that reputation? By taking the glory, the kudos. Not by wasting his time rescuing *techies.* You're ours now to . . . do with as we please."

Coker's hard smile speared her heart. An icy flush washed through her veins, making her forehead clammy. As if to prove his point Coker came forward and laid a hand on top of her head, stroking the short black hair. Caitlyn felt the breath catch in her throat.

"Please . . ."

"Tell me what you know." Coker backed off a few steps, gauging her reaction. "It will go easier for you."

Caitlyn balked. The fear overruled her, making every muscle tremble. For a few seconds she was out of control, then managed to slip inside herself and gain a little outward dignity. In the deeper confines of her mind she delved into the dreadful, unprecedented event that had devastated her world only weeks ago. She sought its ugliness, its vile evil. What could be worse? Certainly not her present predicament.

And all made even crueler by the knowledge that it was her parents. Or more precisely her—

"That's better." Coker interrupted her nightmare. "Speak now."

"I . . . I joined yesterday. I don't know anything."

Coker's face turned nasty, but his eyes appealed to her. "Not good enough. You must tell me something. You must have heard *something.*"

Caitlyn stared at him. This scenario suddenly didn't seem right. She'd never been the best at reading people, but Coker was acting as if he was playing a scene. Performing for some hidden watcher.

She turned hard in her chair, managed to glance quickly over her shoulder. Sure enough a small silver camera with a black lens was mounted on the rear wall, overlooking the scene. She turned back to Coker with new eyes.

"You asked to interrogate me first?"

Coker immediately rubbed his nose, using his closed hand to hide his lips. "They can't hear us. But they see everything. Please . . . I'm your only chance. I can't stand what they'll do to you weighing on my conscience." He finished with a snarl, shouting "Now!" at her for the benefit of the hidden watchers.

"All I know is their names and the treasure they're chasing." Caitlyn found her anxiety lessening now as Coker presented himself more as a covert ally. "And that they have a map."

Coker bit his lips. "We know about that. It's what they were told to look for."

"Look. You're clearly not with them. Why are you doing this?"

Coker's face took on a stressed expression and all the light left his eyes. He carefully placed a hand on each of her knees and crouched down between them so that he could look up at her. "The camera can't see me down here. Pretend I'm hurting you somehow. Throw your head back."

Caitlyn performed admirably as Coker continued.

"In short, I'm also a prisoner and have to do whatever the boss wants. I hated attacking Michael, doing everything in my power to botch the operation whilst still appearing to implement their plan. I hate everything about this entire operation. But I'm also the one to blame for it. Solomon, he's a parasite but a rich one."

"Solomon's your boss?"

"Yeah. Underworld bottom crawler. Leeches onto people's mistakes and makes them pay big time." Coker paused, stricken for a second as if dredging up a terrible memory, then shook it off. "Look, we don't have much time. If I don't get my ass out there soon with something juicy they're gonna send the worst of the worst in here. Please tell me you've got something you can tell me."

"Get me out then. Get yourself out."

"Don't you think I've thought of that?" Coker hissed. "Shit, I used to be a field agent, lady. But even if I could take them out" —he shook his head, tears fighting to spill from his eyes— "they have me in other ways. There's nothing I can do."

Caitlyn stared at him. Coker was a defeated man. How, she didn't know. But he was an utter wreck, barely hanging on. Christ, she was in deep shit now.

The door suddenly flew open. A man walked in, seeing Coker's position and ordered him up. "Does girl know anything?" The man's accent was thick, guttural and halting. Calling her 'girl' was depersonalizing to the extreme and a bad sign.

"I haven't finished yet."

"Get out, Coker. I will finish."

"Just give me a bit—"

"Now." The man came forward, spitting on the floor at Coker's feet, his dark face twisted with hate; fists bunched. Caitlyn felt a spike of fear, of desperation. Unrealized dreams and visions swept before her eyes.

I'm dead.

Coker, to his credit, stood his ground. "I am in charge here, Dingo. Let me do my fucking job."

Dingo snarled, practically shaking with anger. The body armor he wore vibrated along with him, its many pockets and knives quivering too. He grasped a baton that sat in his holster like a short sword. "You have till I find cow prod," he said with an emotionless glance at Caitlyn. "Then, I don't care. We do it my way." The sudden calm demeanor was scarier than the anger.

Coker watched him leave. "That guy's unmanageable. Any man in my unit would've buried him by now."

"Please." Caitlyn felt the fear spreading through her once again, a cold deluge of anticipated horror. "What can we do?"

Coker turned to her, body closed and expression as cold as arctic ice. "I can't help you now. It's a fucked up, last chance world, lady. Tell me something before that madman returns."

TWELVE

Crouch knew exactly what was at stake. Wasting no time he placed a fast call to Armand Argento, the Interpol agent.

"We have a major problem." Crouch quickly outlined the situation, unaware of the hour where Argento was and knowing it would not be an issue. "We don't know the name of the South African. But we do know he's employing local muscle, one part highly mediocre and the other part highly skilled. That many men, someone's gotta know something. Plus," he described the tattoo and attached it to an e-mail. "On its way."

Argento, speaking through an open line, said, "Got it, amico mio. Ah, but you owe me yet again. That is five is it not? Or six? No mind. What it is, is what it is. No?"

Crouch thought it best not to interrupt the man known as the Jabbering Venetian in full flow.

"So again we go off the book. You and your friends. You would not win so well without me, no?" Thankfully Argento always worked as he talked, which was one of the reasons he got an awful lot done. "But Caitlyn, you must help her, Michael. I feel guilty, mortified, even dirty to have sent her into the hands of the enemy."

"It's not your fault, Armand. If any it's mine."

Alicia stopped herself from chiming in. They could sort out the blame game later. Right now, both men needed to concentrate on what they were doing.

Argento renewed his flow. "So fair, so English. I felt sorry for her after what happened between her parents. The whole of MI6 found out—somehow, but we will say no more on that, eh? Shocking. Shocking."

Crouch fielded a return call from the Mexican police. "Thank you," he said after a minute, hanging up. "Armand, listen. The Mexicans know of this tattoo, but more importantly they know the scars that surround it."

Alicia leaned forward, now seeing an array of tiny white scars surrounding the distinctive inking of a green dragon wrapped around the turret of a castle, spitting fire. "Knife wounds?"

"Something like that." Crouch pointed at the screen. "Has to be self-inflicted. There's too many and they're too small for anything else to make sense."

"Could be what gets him and his girl off," Alicia proposed.

Healey turned to her. "Now that sounds sick."

"Takes all sorts, kiddo."

Crouch addressed Argento. "The man is locally known as Dragon Teeth. He's some kind of ex-military enforcer, paid by the hour. Real name—"

"I have it." Argento was fast. "Rodriguez. Major war dog. Visited all the worst places you can name and many you can't. Commonly runs with a local gang they call the banda, which I believe is the Spanish word for gang. So, not very imaginative. But they are feared because of their skills. Their military background. It could be the group you are seeking, Michael."

Crouch paused and called the Mexicans back. "Please run a check on a local gang, the banda. I realize it's probably unusual, but we're wondering if they have recently been contracted to anyone."

Argento's voice sprang from another phone. "When Caitlyn returns you tell her Armand helped. You tell her that or we will speak no more. And inform me. The moment you know."

"I will." Crouch thanked Argento and hung up. The room fell into silence as they waited for the Mexicans to call back. Alicia checked her guns again, not liking the old weaponry but knowing it was better suited to her proficient hands than most others. Thinking that way made her slip out to check Russo's surveillance net, just to double-check they were safe, but the gnarled, watchful warrior was in full control.

When she returned Crouch was talking to the Mexicans. He covered the speaker, looking up at her. "The banda are working for an outside contractor. We're just waiting for Intel updates."

Alicia eyed Healey and Lex. "You ready?"

"Can't wait."

"Damn stupid question."

Alicia could have matched the answers to the men with her eyes and ears covered.

Crouch pursed his lips, listening. "Is that it? That's all you've got?"

Alicia swallowed. "Don't leave me hanging, Crouchy. What the hell?"

The ex-soldier looked up. "The banda have a hideout. A place of business. Of course, like any gang's HQ it's extremely well known to all and sundry. The authorities can give us no confirmed sightings of gang members in the last two days but say there *is* activity inside the HQ right now."

"Then let's go get 'em." Alicia picked up her guns.

THIRTEEN

Caitlyn's heart stopped when Dingo reappeared in the doorway, a cattle prod in one hand and a machete in the other. Coker's first reaction was one of outrage, playing a dangerous angle.

"Boss ain't gonna like this, Ding. Nobody said anything about this kind of torture."

"Boss say get answers." Dingo brandished the machete. "This work before. Will work again. Now leave, unless you want to join her in the chair."

Coker hung his head, gradually moving aside. "Wait until I talk to Solomon. You piss him off, not you nor any of your gang buddies are going to be safe. Don't forget, you're only working for this guy, not goddamn family."

"You talk." Dingo jerked his head toward the door. "Out there. Me and this woman gotta talk 'bout knives and guns. Mmm."

Caitlyn stared, transfixed, by the blade. Its edges looked dull, almost a burnished orange. It was only when the blade came closer that she understood why.

Blood. Congealed, dried blood clung to the edges. She jumped when Dingo juiced the cattle prod.

"You speak for me, woman? Let me hear you speak. Be free, say your words. Nothing else in life is free, eh?"

Caitlyn struggled against her bonds. The chair was shaky, but the ropes were tight. In this moment, at this point in her life, raw emotion and a passion to survive could have thrust her into any action. A person never knows how they will react to a severe or desperate incident until they're faced with it, with life or death, unexpected pleasure or terrible pain. All bets are then off.

"I want to be saved," she said. "We all want to be saved in

some way. Even you, Dingo. You mind me calling you that? What's your real name?"

"You want saving? Ah, but only one thing saves. You know what that is, woman?"

Caitlyn shook her head, trying desperately to hold the man's eyes.

"An altar," he said seriously, then burst out laughing. "Altar full of gold. And diamonds. A pit of money. All the rest," he shrugged, "is our living hell."

"It doesn't have to be."

Dingo brought the cattle prod around until its fizzling prongs were an inch from her nose. "You gonna save us? You figure I ain't heard all that before? I heard it from the mouths of cops. Childcarers. Even priests. Most truth I ever got from a priest was the one told me the best use he ever got outta the Bible was that he used it to bash a mugger's head in. That's real. That's our world, woman. We were born with one foot in Hell."

Calmly, he laid the machete on the floor and lit a cigarette. "How 'bout we get to the point. Boss wants answers. Let's start with the map."

Caitlyn felt a sudden rush of annoyance, unprecedented. "I don't have any answers! I joined the fucking group just yesterday!"

Their inability to believe her, their unending distrust, irritated the hell out of her. This guy was never going to believe her no matter what she said. But deep, deep inside her memory lay a fact that might give them pause. Her eyes had slipped innocently over Crouch's work yesterday as he sweated over the map and its translation. She had noticed a destination and sentence that stuck with her.

First treasure of Tenochtitlan is in Utah!

First treasure? What the hell did that mean?

If she told them . . . she would be betraying the team and her new boss. Truth was, they would hurt her anyway. Still, she

80

fought a testing inner battle to keep her silence.

That was when the prod touched her left knee. White hot pain stabbed hard through every nerve and she threw her head back for real this time, unable to stop the scream.

"No! I'm just an analyst and a techie. You can't—"

The agony came again, the prongs fizzling briefly against her right knee this time. "I can," Dingo muttered. "You're in my world now, woman. There ain't no heroes coming for you."

Caitlyn gasped in agony. "You might . . . be surprised."

"Not in ten years. Life just wears you out around here. Jades you. By the age of ten—" Dingo spread his arms. "World weary. Seen everything."

"Believe me, you've seen nothing like what my friends will do to you when they get here."

Dingo laughed. "Friends? What friends? Nobody follow us here. Nobody know we here. Cops won't help. That kinda hope gonna get you nothin' but dead."

Caitlyn tried again to connect with Dingo through eye contact. "My friends are coming right now. I'd recommend you treat me well."

If there was one thing a hardened criminal worried about it was any kind of threat to his business. Dingo was no exception. The first thing he did was to stare at Caitlyn as if gauging her sincerity; the second was to dig a cellphone out and press speed dial.

"Marco? What you got out there? Anything around the shop?"

Dingo listened carefully. Caitlyn watched him without expression, shocked by her own coolness under pressure. Hard to believe that she was a wreck inside. Maybe it was the training kicking in or the faith she put in Alicia and Crouch. Maybe it was denial. The reasons didn't really matter. Dingo listened for a while, waving the cellphone about beside his left ear.

"Don't worry," he said to Caitlyn. "Marco find them if they around."

Caitlyn flinched when Dingo suddenly hung up. "All right." He tucked the phone out of sight and came forward. "This time I ain't fuckin' around, lady. I don't care if you tell me or not but I'm gonna have me some fun."

He thrust the prod forward into her stomach. Caitlyn screamed as fifty thousand volts entered her body from the point of impact. She struggled against her bonds, the ropes abrading flesh. Caitlyn felt her muscles stretched in a rictus of agony, taut until Dingo pulled the prongs away.

"So what you got for me, bitch? You wan' some more, 'cause y'know I'm happy to serve it up."

Caitlyn shuddered. Before she had a chance to catch a breath Dingo was pressing the prod forward again, this time into her ribs. Again she screamed, convulsed against her bonds. Spittle flew from between her lips.

"Fuck you!" she yelled, amazed by her own defiance. "Fuck you and the whore that shat you out!"

Dingo looked a little startled, but then a crafty leer crept across his features. "So." He smiled. "You trained? The choir girl was all an act. Good!"

Again he zapped her. Again Caitlyn juddered and jerked against the ropes, wishing it were indeed all an act. Her wrists bled, her ankles were bruised. The chair trembled with every movement. An involuntary twitch began in her left cheek and wouldn't let up.

Dingo slowly brought the prod up until it sparked before her eyes. "Think you've felt the worse? Nothing near. How 'bout the face? Ears? Eyes? Or maybe I'll just jam this baby into your mouth." The sneer told her he would be good to his word.

"The treasure." She panted. "I know. I know where it is."

Dingo leaned toward her, the sparking prongs between his eyes and her own. "I thought so. Tell me. I'll go easy on you."

Caitlyn forced out a tear. "It's . . ." The rest was lost in a murmur.

Dingo tilted his body another few degrees. The instant he was at full stretch Caitlyn jerked forward, headbutting the cattle prod and forcing it against Dingo's own forehead. The pain was immense, making her see blackness and stars but the shocked squeal that came from Dingo's mouth almost made it worthwhile.

Almost.

Dingo was suddenly enraged. "Bitch! Fuck, fuckin' bitch! I'll kill you. C'mere!"

He grabbed her left hand, leaned on it, and brought the cattle prod around until it was level with her right eye. Without a word he pushed it forward. Caitlyn struggled hard. Using the leeway she had created in her bonds, she threw her head from side to side. Dingo grabbed her throat, trying to keep her still.

"Goddamn it!"

Caitlyn spat at him, then started to rock the chair from side to side. The moment Dingo attempted to arrest the pitching by perching on the arm, the entire flimsy seat collapsed. Both Caitlyn and Dingo crumpled to the floor amidst a pile of shattered timber.

Dingo was beside himself, scrambling around in the pieces, swearing uncontrollably. Caitlyn rolled to the side of the room, still attached to the arms of the chair but at least able to hold the broken wedges up before her face.

"Stop fighting, dammit!" Dingo muttered. "I've seen meeker pit fighters and cops sat in that chair."

Caitlyn prepared herself for his next attack. He was concentrating on the prod but she knew exactly where the machete was, over the other side of the room where it had been discarded. If she could—

Dingo's cell chimed. The sudden interruption almost sent him over the edge. Veins stood out in his forehead, a tapestry of unhinged madness that might have made a great abstract painting. With hands curled into fists he sought to calm himself down. Caitlyn took the brief respite to regain her balance.

"*What?*" Dingo's anger was becoming infectious.

Caitlyn tried to listen but could hear only one side of the conversation.

"Now? I thought you said—"

A quick rush of hope swept through her. Could it be? But she quelled it; her situation was dire beyond belief. Even if someone had come to save her could they find her in time?

Dingo spat onto the floor. "Deal with them! Give me time to finish this bitch off!"

Alicia kept her head down as Crouch drove their car through the locked warehouse door. The outside was a gaudy canvas of altered signage, one new name painted atop the other, and constructed of solid blocks. But the entry doors were wooden, held together by a thick iron strap, and crumpled at the first impact. The doors crashed onto the front of the car, then slid away. The car itself slewed to the left, turning almost a full circle before coming to a complete stop.

Alicia cracked one door open and Russo did the same to the other side. With no immediate retaliation forthcoming they piled out and headed for the nearest cover—several chopped apart cars were scattered around the inside, some stacked on top of each other. Tall, brightly colored toolboxes with dozens of open drawers stood around the place like sleeping robots. A dilapidated table and dozens of plastic chairs sat in one corner, the remains of food and soda cans left around the dirty surface and the floor. An open pit lay in the center of the warehouse, a car lift at the far end.

Alicia took it all in without stopping to look. The banda were well equipped, their chop shop business was no doubt lucrative. The current crop of cars weren't exactly high-end, but they were no rust-buckets either—an old Lotus Eclat, several Volkswagens and aging Mercedes, other marques that she didn't recognize but looked middle of the range. Harder to pick out, at the rear of the space were the back ends and front ends of cars, side panels and stacks of wheels. At full muster, Alicia dreaded to think how many men the banda employed here.

Presumably, all on call right now.

She pressed on quickly into the warehouse, flanked on the far side by Russo and Healey, followed by Crouch and Lex. She ducked behind a deep blue Volkswagen as men began to flood the place from the far end. *Don't give them a target until you're ready.* She slipped around the edge of the Volkswagen, keeping to the shadows cast at the side of the warehouse, gaining even more precious ground.

One man saw her. He was dead before uttering a word, but the gunshot sent the chop shop into chaos. The Mexicans opened fire indiscriminately and without clear targets, spraying out of fear and ignorance. Alicia hopped up onto the next car, using the broken window frame to gain the roof, and fired down at them. The line of Mexicans suddenly parted as men darted for cover. Alicia picked them off where she could, leaping down before anyone could draw a bead on her.

Men screamed and ran straight for her, brandishing knives and axes. She lowered her machine gun. Crouch and Lex knelt to her either side. This sure as hell wasn't going to be pretty.

Caitlyn swung as Dingo approached her. The wooden planks attached to her arms caught his shinbone, making him hop.

"Oh man," he breathed. "This is gonna be so much fun."

Caitlyn's brow dripped sweat. Her fear made her hunch up into a ball as Dingo jabbed the prod forward. Luckily the prongs slipped past her left ear and struck the wall. Caitlyn immediately scolded herself. Sitting there and turning into a terrified ball of sweat wasn't going to keep her alive. When Dingo poked again she swatted the prod aside with her arms, protected by the timber. Dingo surprised her by kicking her hard in the thigh. When she cried out he thrust the prod toward her again, catching her in the sternum.

Caitlyn cried out. She kicked frantically at his legs again and again, her movements powered by strength born of terror, anger and pure old-fashioned stubbornness. Dingo skipped away. Caitlyn knew the game was almost up.

Last chance. No more options.

With a heave that took most of her strength she used the side wall to lever herself upright and then launched herself straight at Dingo, in mid-flight, striking his upper body with her own and taking him to the ground. The two of them crashed together, the cattle prod skidding away.

Caitlyn bore down hard.

Dingo grabbed her throat. "Bad mistake."

Alicia took out the first few men, quickly aware even in the midst of battle that there were no offices within the confines of the warehouse. Caitlyn wasn't in here. That meant they needed a hostage. The banda were a fearsome opposition, screaming and shouting as they poured forward, weapons brandished above their heads in the way of warrior tribesmen. The bullets tore them to pieces, but that recourse soon proved tricky when armed opponents began to find superior firing positions.

Alicia moved constantly, slipping between cars and toolboxes. After sheltering behind one six-foot-high, bright-red unit for a minute she began rolling it toward her enemy, still hiding behind it. To both sides she thrust out her gun and fired alternate shots. Before she reached the far end she dived behind an old Mercedes S-Class, letting the roller box continue. By the time it crashed into the far wall it was riddled with holes and so were the men shooting at it, their focus destroyed. Alicia managed to disarm one of the Mexicans and take a good grip of his shoulders whilst aiming her gun at his midriff.

"Talk," she said amidst the sound of shouting and gunfire. "Where's the girl?"

"No speak! No speak!"

Alicia fired a bullet into his stomach. "Then you're no good to me."

She tripped another who poked his head around the side of the car, eyes opened wide when he saw the fate of his friend, groaning and slowly dying. Alicia quickly put him in the same position.

"The girl?"

"I . . . I . . ."

"Be careful what you say, asshole."

"Out back. Through the stacks. There is an office."

Alicia spoke through the team's Bluetooth connection. "I have a location. Back me up now!"

Caitlyn would not die today.

A sudden eruption of gunfire stunned the air as Alicia ducked out of hiding and ran full tilt toward a rear exit. At first the Mexicans concentrated their fire on her; bullets fizzed and ripped up the concrete and metal hulks all around her; her sprint was a dash through a barrage of death. She ran hard, not stopping nor even flinching when a hard tug signified hot lead piercing her jacket and again when a searing flash scorched her upper thigh.

Caitlyn will not die today.

Then her colleagues drew the bulk of their enemy's attention, shooting volley after volley. Mexicans flew backward amidst sprays of blood and cracked bone, decimated flesh. But this was not a weak band of mercenaries, this was a Mexican gang, born and raised in fire with expectations to die young. Instead of retreating and regrouping they forged forward. Russo and Healey were forced down. Crouch barely kept his head. Only Lex showed a certain foolhardy mettle, copying Alicia's example and standing strong through the fusillade.

Alicia rolled near the end. Bullets struck all around her. A broken shell, an old giant, rocked and shuddered and fell apart in front of her. She picked her way through, feet barely touching the floor. Something smashed into her back, sending her into a second roll and when she came up she found the back entrance right before her.

She slipped outside. A graveyard scene met her eyes. Piles of chopped cars, each stacked atop the other; five rows of rusted wrecks, ruined carcasses.

Alicia sprinted down the first row. A man stepped out in front of her, machete swinging at her head. Alicia ducked and slammed into his chest, sending him cartwheeling back into one of the piles, gratified when the entire mass started to topple slowly onto him. Another man charged her, head down. She stopped for a second, caught his neck and twisted him right off his feet, the spinning body broken and lifeless before it hit the ground.

The office lay ahead, built against the rear of the property. Alicia aimed for the door. She didn't slow down.

Caitlyn looked up as the door smashed inward. Dingo's hands were still around her throat, making the whole scene swim before her eyes but the crazy beautiful figure of Alicia Myles was unmistakable. She was Kristen Bell and the Terminator all rolled into one but twice as deadly. Blood soaked her jacket, tears in her jeans indicated knife wounds or even grazes from bullets. Dingo's instant reaction was to let go of Caitlyn and defend himself.

Alicia's voice crept through Caitlyn's haze. "Don't bother, asshole. You were dead the moment you touched her."

Dingo flew at her. Alicia stepped clear of his range, then came back in, somehow aiming an elbow to the back of his neck even as she tripped him. Dingo flew headlong, but managed to catch himself, no slouch from his years on the streets. He came in again, this time with more care, fists positioned like a boxer. Alicia backed toward Caitlyn.

"You ready for some fun?"

Caitlyn shook her head, not in rejection but in amazement. How could she stay calm at a time like this? She watched the woman's body, the way she held herself and adjusted to Dingo's every move. She sensed the power that flowed through every poised sinew, the pure skill that permeated her every thought.

God, I so wanna be as good as her.

Determination and pride spurred her on. With a last glance her way, Alicia met Dingo's attack head on, easily matching him blow for blow. Not only that, Alicia caused damage even when defending herself. Dingo's face grew bloody, his arms heavy. Caitlyn saw the fight go out of him as Alicia broke his nose and left arm in a single maneuver.

"He's all yours." Alicia flung the weakened man so that he fell at Caitlyn's knees. Even then he struggled, hate in his face, bringing an arm around.

Caitlyn thrust the cattle prod into his face.

The fizzling sound of flesh filled the room. Caitlyn pressed on, holding the prongs in place until the man passed out and then began to gingerly press her own throat.

"A few bruises." Alicia peered closely. "Nothing worse than you'd get from a heavy night out with the boys. You'll be fine."

"Thanks." Caitlyn's voice sounded deep and husky due to the damage.

"Oh, and perfect that tone and they'll be eating outta your hand at least, if not your—"

"Thank you!" Caitlyn enthused, almost ready to grab the Englishwoman and start hugging her. "You saved me."

"We don't hug in the military," Alicia said a little gruffly. "Maybe a pat on the back. A smack on the ass if you're really lucky. You coming?"

Caitlyn rose; battered, bruised and shocked but feeling better than ever. Was this how it felt to have a real family?

She'd almost forgotten.

FOURTEEN

Alicia dabbed her thigh and left arm with water then antiseptic before applying a bandage, bemused that the only person in the room trying not to stare at her was Michael Crouch.

"I realize they're a nice pair of pins," she said in annoyance. "But at the end of the day they're just legs. Healey, you ever see this far up a woman's leg before?"

She was sitting on a couch in their new communal hotel room, jeans resting on the arm beside her as she fixed her wounds.

Russo didn't try to hide his eyes. "Can't you do that in one of the bedrooms?"

"Sorry, this ain't one of the two things I do in a bedroom."

Caitlyn was also staring, but with admiration. Alicia was the single most confident, powerful woman she had ever encountered. "I have a pair like that, but they can't do half as much as yours can."

Alicia grinned rudely. Caitlyn realized what she'd said a second later and blushed. "I didn't mean—"

Alicia saw Healey gawping between Caitlyn and her. "Ole Zack here's wondering if you could try, though."

"I . . . I . . ." Healey didn't know where to put himself so ended up staring hard out the window.

"He did help save you," Alicia pressed on. "Maybe a little reward?"

Now Caitlyn was reddening even further. "The only thing I know," she said after a short pause. "Is that if I'm fighting with you guys I want to be able to fight *like* you guys. That's all."

Now Crouch turned his head from where he'd been in conversation with Jose Cruz. "I like that kind of thinking."

Alicia nodded, still dabbing her wounds. "And I like a girl that doesn't quit at the first obstacle. Good for you."

Healey spoke directly to the window. "I could help to train you if you like."

Caitlyn nodded. "That would be great."

They team had been together, resting, recovering and seeking to determine the impact of what Caitlyn had revealed to the enemy, for a few hours. Caitlyn felt the room swell with respect when she revealed that she'd kept their secret even under deadly pressure. It was a moment of comradeship, of new belonging, earned on the front lines and treated with respect.

At last, Crouch had taken the map and the notes out and they'd sat down to figure out a plan of action. Cruz, tired of waiting for the action to be over, had joined him. As Healey put it, the Aztec treasure was out there but where would it lead them next?

Crouch addressed the room. "Working from our notes I've managed to calculate that if the Aztec warriors walked roughly north, as the map states, for fifteen to twenty days, which is the closest approximation I can make using their calendar, their detailed, almost perfectly straight route would take them into Arizona."

"Big place," Cruz said.

"Sure. And there's another problem. You remember the accurate dateline they gave us for the *entire* march?"

Healey finally tore his gaze away from the window. "I do."

"If it's right," Crouch mused. "It means that the caravan traveled beyond Arizona, probably to Utah judging by the timeline, then doubled back before arriving at the point where the poem takes over and starts giving us directions like a treasure map." He stared around the room for suggestions.

"Misdirection?" Caitlyn submitted. "Now we have two locations."

"Or they split it up," Russo said. "Two treasure troves."

"Or maybe they just scouted Utah, didn't like it, and went

back to Arizona," Cruz told them. "We can't second guess them five hundred years later."

"What's not to like about Utah?" Russo wondered. "It's a perfect location for any traveling caravan."

"I agree with Jose," Crouch said. "We don't know. But it has to be checked out. As I mentioned previously the timeline is very accurate. The Aztecs were advanced in almost every aspect of building, guidance and travel. I studied the map itself, using the ancient calendar, and have also fed it into a simple modern geographical program. Both the physical and tech results point to one thing—the area around the Grand Canyon for the second location."

Caitlyn walked over to Crouch and stared at the computer screen. "Aztec writing has been found far into the US. Utah is what, three thousand kilometers from Mexico City? That would take a fit man fifteen to twenty days to walk, I reckon."

Crouch nodded. "And in answer to another suggestion, why would the warriors add any kind of misdirection to a map they were taking back to their elders? Doesn't make sense. Utah, the furthest location, means something, and so does the second, Arizona."

"How close . . ." Alicia waved toward the screen as she stood up and shrugged her jeans back on. "Can you get? I mean, does it point to the right cave?" Her features took on a bemused expression. "That would be nice."

Crouch made a face. "It's accurate, but both Utah and Arizona are big places. The poem should help with the Arizona location, another reason to go there second. With Utah, although the timeline gets us fairly close, I think we need boots on the ground and see what pops."

Caitlyn waved a hand at the screen. "The map Healey copied has several markings. I guess they're landmarks, and pretty distinctive even in Utah. How closely did you copy the map, Zack?"

The young man shrugged. "I'm a field agent that occasionally relies on being able to read and make sense of a map to save lives, including my own," he said. "Pretty closely."

"Then we have a starting point," Crouch said. "If you guys are ready to try Utah I'll make the arrangements."

"One thing's for sure," Caitlyn said, glancing around the room. "It can't be more dangerous than where we are now."

Alicia winced. "Damn. Now you jinxed it."

"Story of my life." Russo snorted.

"Ah, so you're our jinx?" Alicia shot back. "And here's me thinking that sunny disposition might qualify you for being our mascot."

"Life's a bitch," Russo murmured. "And so's our boss."

"You say that like it's a bad thing."

"Nah. It's glowing praise."

"Thought so."

Crouch closed his laptop. "You ready?"

Healey bounced to his feet, shining with enthusiasm. "Let's go track it down!"

FIFTEEN

Kanab, a city of Kane County, Utah, is located a tad north of the Arizona state line. Founded in the 1800s there are now over three thousand people living there. Arguably best known as a location for many old westerns, including *Stagecoach*, *The Lone Ranger* and *The Outlaw Josey Wales*, its attractions also include much of the Grand Circle—the Vermillion Cliffs and Bryce Canyon, Zion National Park and Lake Powell.

After several hours of research, Crouch called the others to full alert in the cramped confines of the small private plane.

"It seems in 1914 a man arrived in Kanab saying that in his research he found that the great treasure of Montezuma was hidden in the mountains around the town. After much searching and digging, a plan was formed to drain the lake in the hope that the treasure lay in an underwater cave. This plan was later blocked by the government because it was one of the few refuges of the ambersnail."

"Underwater cave?" Alicia raised her voice. "I'm about as happy in water as I am in the desert. Which means—not."

Russo grunted. "I have a little training, not so much experience."

"I think we'll cross that bridge when we come to it," Crouch said. "The map we have doesn't even show a lake."

The plane landed with a bump and a squeal, taxiing speedily to the hangar. When Crouch and the team had cleared customs they headed into downtown Kanab. Alicia stared at the single-story hotels, the wide streets, pawn shops, western-themed restaurants and photo shops; the tall, lush green trees and the mountainous, red-hued backdrop, the Utah monuments towering over all, and came to a single conclusion.

"In this town," she said. "A secret's gonna be hard to keep."

"Wow," Healey said. "The closer you get to that mountain the more impressive it becomes."

"You sound like my last girlfriend," Russo said with a rare outburst of humor.

Alicia soon quashed it. "They found a female Sasquatch then?"

Caitlyn laid a hand on Healey's arm. "Fantastic country. I know exactly what you mean."

Healey beamed at her. Alicia thought back to the long plane journey from Mexico. Healey had taken it upon himself to begin Caitlyn's induction into the art of self-defense. Nothing major at first, he'd told her.

"I'm a fast learner," she'd said.

Healey had nodded. "Yes, but I don't want to overwhelm you."

Caitlyn had pointed to the raw cuts and bruises around her wrist. "Overwhelm me."

Alicia knew there was a vast difference between being taught by a civilian instructor and a special-forces soldier, just as there was a vast difference between the actual knowledge they gave you to start with. Preservation of life and helpfulness to the team was of major import. With the Army there were no colored belts.

Alicia had watched Healey train Caitlyn and had offered her own advice. Lex had watched proceedings closely and even Russo came up with a trick or two. Lex had leaned over the back of his chair, saying, "When *he's* shown you the soldier's way *I'll* show you the biker's. It's quicker."

Alicia saw Healey as the kind of guy that could achieve big time, but needed the security of more experienced people around him. The skills were there, the willingness was unquestionable, but the true man would never break out unless it was nurtured properly. In the brief time she'd had to glean his file she'd put this down to a warring family. Back home, Healey had been the youngest in a three-sibling family, mother, father and siblings always at each other's throats with Zack usually the scapegoat. This affected his behavior at school, which led to worse grades and more reprimands; more humiliating abuse from his older brothers. The Army had offered a way out, a chance to learn from greater, responsible figures. It had given him his life back.

Alicia compared Healey's story to that of her own. It wasn't the same, but it had many parallels and offered up those same two fundamental questions: Why were some parents so blind to their own children's difficulties and why weren't they more aware of and responsive to the situations they themselves created?

Alicia didn't dwell. Zack had won, in her mind. And so had she. The pain she lived with every day could be shrugged off, the old anxieties buried beneath unending action. It was at uneasy moments like this that she piped up and offered her own sarcastic slant to almost any conversation.

Kanab lay sun-blasted beneath an azure sky. Huge old American cars prowled the wide streets, Buicks and Chryslers and Cadillacs; the relatively short trees and towering backdrops gave the place a wide-open, insecure kind of feel, offering little shelter. Straight roads bisected the place, leading from the main street to the many houses.

Crouch aimed their car toward the largest restaurant. "Let's get some food," he said. "And start asking questions."

"Think that's a good idea? Won't Coker and his South African widowmaker be on the chase?" Russo asked.

"We cut out of there kinda sharpish." Crouch shrugged. "Flight plan was bogus. It'll take them a few days. I hate to leave Coker in that situation," he added as he parked. "But we don't have the resources to take on a criminal kingpin just yet."

Alicia slipped out of the car. "Coker will show his head again. If I don't have to blow it off I'll find out why someone's controlling it."

Cruz followed the conversation in silence, his thoughts

seemingly lost in the surrounding wonders.

The restaurant was almost empty, the waitresses standing around bored. As the team took their seats a smiling woman sporting schoolteacher glasses and pigtails ambled over to them.

"Help ya?"

Crouch reeled off a set of drinks, then waited expectantly for her to write it all down. The waitress grinned and tapped at the side of her head. "Memory like Microsoft. Drinks will be right up. Name's Rosie by the way."

She ambled off, taking her time. Crouch looked from face to face. "Maybe we should have ordered food at the same time."

"Cheer up," Caitlyn said. "It's not like we have anywhere to go."

"Not yet. Do you have everything you need to install those cameras into our new gear?"

They had lost some of their gear in the hurry to leave Mexico.

"Sure. I can make do. Plus, they're bound to have some kind of electrical supply store around here."

Rosie returned with their drinks. Crouch immediately slid Healey's map before her. "Do you live in Kanab, Rosie? Do you recognize any of these landmarks?"

The waitress looked a little bewildered. "You guys don't look the treasure hunter types."

Crouch grimaced. "You get asked that a lot?"

"Three hundred sixty days a year, honey. Though I can't recall seeing something quite like this." She squinted at the drawings. "That one looks like the Tower of Babel, a long way from here but quite distinctive, whilst that one looks like the Fiery Furnace, quite close to the Tower. Can't be sure though. Oh, and that one could be a view of Grandview Peak and Little Black Mountain together. You live around here long enough you see all the famous views time after time. Pretty close, I'd say, but don't quote me on it." She reeled off several more landmark sites. "Some can look pretty much like another. You get these from a children's book?" Her eyes twinkled.

Alicia snorted at Healey. "Kind of."

Crouch spoke again before Rosie could turn and leave. "I guess we won't stand out in Kanab as being any different?"

Rosie grinned. "Tourists. If I had a dime for every would-be gold digger that drifted through here I'd be a millionaire." She nodded toward the shiny counter. "And several more o' them gold diggers are back there, honey. Watch yourself."

She spun and walked off, hips swaying, leaving Crouch staring after her in surprise. Alicia leaned across the table and held his hands.

"Calm down, Michael. You look like you've never been hit on before."

Crouch blinked. "It's been a while."

"Maybe we could ask her to be our guide?"

Crouch collected himself and threw her a look that clearly said, 'behave'. "Let's move on. Caitlyn—the laptop."

The tech was already on it, tapping at the keys to bring up Google Maps. Once she'd enlarged a map of Utah she located the geographical map and started to scrutinize the topography. Rosie returned, took their menu order, and made a point of offering the group slices of free apple pie.

Crouch jumped at the suggestion, hooked by Rosie's twinkling eyes. Healey and Caitlyn were snagged too, but Alicia and Lex managed to decline.

Russo only grumped. "Huh, I'm allergic to cake."

Alicia squinted through one eye. "To *cake?*"

"It gives me a sore throat," Russo declared.

Rosie winked and wandered away to start tapping their order into a terminal. Caitlyn looked up from the computer screen.

"I have the three landmarks that Rosie mentioned and others. They're all pretty accurate if I'm being honest. Of course, this is a land of crags and hoodoos, odd shaped formations and weather-beaten rocks. My guess is there could be even more similarities."

Crouch took a swallow of coffee. "Find them."

Alicia watched the girl work, thinking that one of the obvious things they now needed was more laptops. But she was enjoying it, this learn-as-you-go adventuring with the new team. This new venture was nothing short of building an entire unit from the ground up, discovering mistakes and correcting them for the next go round, determining what worked and what didn't, and adapting in mid-stride. It was a busy, engaging creation, peppered with danger and troublemakers and if this was their first run out—she couldn't wait for the second.

Rosie placed their meals on the table and noticed what Caitlyn was doing. She placed her hands on her hips. "Y'know, I have to say. A lot of them prospectors come through here lookin' for gold, they don't come back. End up finding their bodies weeks or even months later, picked at by coyotes and crows. This can be a harsh part o' the world for the unprepared."

Crouch looked up at her. "Thanks for the advice. We've been in worse places."

"Just sayin'. Some folks put it down to the land. Some put it down to the militia. Only thing I know is most that come lookin' for a heap of gold get a heap of dead. Stories been around these parts for hundreds of years." She fixed Crouch with a hard gaze. "There ain't no damn gold."

"Wait." Crouch had stopped eating a while back. "Wait. Back up. *What* militia?"

"Some of the land out there ain't all national park y'know. Some's considered to be privately owned, at least by those that dwell on it. They call themselves the High Desert Militia; peculiar lot. Come into town sometimes spouting their beliefs and waving their guns. Plain jealous and plain bitter they are. All as straight as a three dollar note."

Healey's face creased in thought. Alicia twirled her finger around her ear. "She means they aren't. Tell me, Rosie, where do these boys hang out?"

Rosie waved a hand in a northerly direction. "Across that way. You can't miss 'em. Got a fence around their property, but if you ask around we got plenty of guides in town. Most of 'em will be happy to show you around for a fee."

"Maybe we'll do that. Thanks for your help, Rosie."

"Anytime."

"Wait." Russo spoke up. "This militia. What's the worst thing they've done?"

An odd question, but Alicia knew why the big man was asking it. Simply to determine the threat level. For the first time since they entered the restaurant Rosie's face grew guarded, her movements cautious.

"I dunno. Folks don't talk overmuch 'bout the militia."

"You said earlier—"

"You heard that? So what you asking for when you have an answer? I wouldn't want to wander into their compound, put it that way."

Crouch thanked Rosie again and then addressed Caitlyn. "What have you found?"

"The many formations unique to Utah are in fact mostly one of a kind. The weather has molded them, shaped them. It does so differently with each part of the landscape and even each rock. The Tower of Babel is highly distinctive and incomparable. The Fiery Furnace is special too. Now, if either Grandview Peak or Little Black Mountain were formations on their own you couldn't tell them apart from a hundred other landmarks, but put them together, and again they're exceptional."

"And the Aztecs relied on this." Crouch nodded.

"Sure. They believed they would be following the map back within months, I would think. And though there are many escarpments and stepped monuments and odd towers, each one is an individual. I see only five matching objects to the ones on the map—and only three follow its actual lines."

Alicia smiled. "Like having your cake and eating it too." She clapped Caitlyn on the back, then shot a look over toward Russo. "Except in your case, Rob. Don't wanna get those allergies going now, do we?"

Healey tapped on the table. "I feel like saying—saddle up!"

Caitlyn gave a gleeful little laugh. "Me too!"

Now Cruz grinned.

Alicia groaned. "Shit, why do I keep feeling like a Friday night babysitter?"

Crouch did nothing to dissuade the sudden upsurge of excitement. "The gold's out there, guys. I'm sure of it. Imagine—my first venture into treasure hunting yields Montezuma's famous gold. Damn, I've dreamed of this my whole life."

"Is that why you collect old things?" Alicia wondered, remembering Crouch's affectation for past-history souvenirs and relics. He had a reputation as a sentimentalist and, when not working, often pulled out a photo album packed with snaps as wide-ranging as his Corgi Ferrari Daytona 365 GTB/4, his Lee and Ditko Amazing Spiderman #4 special edition, his working Betamax and Honda CBX motorcycle. Other favorites included desk ornaments, paintings and restaurant keepsakes—the older within his own lifetime the better.

"Maybe," Crouch acknowledged. "There was a time, quite recently actually, when I never thought I'd get to live my dream. Now, everything has changed. We can blame life for that, or fate, but it is what it is. And it will never change. In the military it's like—here's the new threat, same as the old threat. The Taliban and Al-Qaeda we helped snuff out of Afghanistan and Iraq have returned as IS. The Wall Street thieves the world saw disgraced returned as high-frequency traders without spending a single day behind bars." He shrugged. "There will always be another war."

"So we're better off doing this?" Alicia finished clearing her plate and sat back. "At least until the next apocalypse."

Crouch grinned warmly at her. "Yeah. Until then."

SIXTEEN

Within an hour the team had secured a local guide and directed him to take them to the first location—Grandview Peak and Little Black Mountain. The entire route had been mapped out to over three hundred miles, but the group wanted to follow the map precisely rather than skip straight to the last location. Crouch in particular wanted their first expedition to be defined rather than ballpark, specific rather than nebulous.

Alicia hesitated at the idea of employing a guide. Did they need one? Surely finding these locations was a pretty painless exercise. After all, people had been finding them for years.

Caitlyn made sense of it. "He wants the drama, not to mention the added credibility. It will help make the find unquestionably authentic and even more appealing to our friends at the World Heritage Committee. It's another reason he didn't complain too much about having Cruz here tagging along."

Cruz nodded. "I am an unqualified Aztec historian. An intermediary. A pacifier. A librarian."

Alicia evaluated him. "Not a lover or a fighter then?"

"Maybe one. Not the other."

"Damn. Right now I need a man that's both."

After swopping their vehicle for a larger, more robust four-wheel-drive they headed out of Kanab. It was late afternoon and the team had been on the go since their last fitful catnap on the plane, but nobody requested a break. The fact that Coker and his gun-toting entourage could turn up at any minute was not lost on them.

The single road wound out of the flat town and started to climb up into the hills. At first, Alicia was as fascinated as the rest of them by the Wild West country and the once in a lifetime spectacular sights, but she soon decided that once you'd seen one stunning canyon you'd pretty much seen them all. She tilted her headrest back and closed her eyes.

They woke her when Grandview Peak and Little Black Mountain emerged, comparing their map to the curves of the scenery. It was hard to imagine the Aztec warriors in their hide-covered caravans, struggling gamely along the mountain passes until they found a place to hide their gold. Even harder when sat in a burbling vehicle on a straight, asphalted road with an MP3 player and a cellphone strapped to your waist.

Further along they found the Tower of Babel and then Fiery Furnace. Crouch was convinced that they were the landmarks they sought. It was after the final one, the Fiery Furnace, when his nose dipped toward the map again.

"Over the spikes of the furnace," he said. "There appears to be some kind of plateau and a great many trees. Is that correct?"

Their guide, a weathered American with a deep accent and a dislike for communication, nodded. His name was Boots, because he never removed them.

"From up there," Crouch pointed to the plateau, "the calendar notations begin. The good news is that it's in footsteps rather than days. We're very close."

"Won't be going that way," their guide piped up.

Crouch did a double-take. "Sorry?"

"Militia country. Everything past that plateau. Damn fools guard their territory like a bunch of apes around a banana factory."

"You're telling me that the place we want to be—the treasure site—is *inside* the perimeter set up by the High Desert Militia?"

Boots sucked his bottom lip hard. "That I am."

Crouch took a deep breath to settle himself, then said, "Show me."

Darkness had fallen by the time the small group located a parking area and hiked to the top of Fiery Furnace. Alicia took time to scan their surroundings and noted the profuse amount of twinkling campfires down below. Boots told them the Furnace was a regular tourist haunt as well as a place for serious hikers. Alicia began to wonder how the hell the Aztecs had hidden their gold from all these wandering people.

Before she could address the question, Boots was pointing across the top of the plateau. Alicia drew her jacket together against the night chill and peered into the distance. A smattering of stars and a crescent moon added a generous amount of light.

"Trees. Trees. Trees." Boots pointed out each one. "Look between them. Look hard."

Alicia peered. At the edge of her vision she thought she saw a high metal fence. Crouch consulted his map. "From this point." He indicated a significant hollowed out shape in the edge of the cliff that led down to the Fiery Furnace. "From this exact point, the Aztecs turned to marking out the path in footsteps. One hundred paces and turn right, that kind of thing. We're close. But . . . follow me."

Crouch set off at pace, the team jumping to catch up and dragging a protesting Boots along with them. Their leader didn't refer to the map just yet, but walked right up to the fence a hundred yards distant and stared through. Alicia stood at his shoulder.

Flat scrubland spread out to all sides, stretching away to a small collection of metal huts and buildings. Alicia could make out a central square marked by blazing trash cans, beaten-up cars, canvas-covered transport trucks, and a small central dais where a tattered, indistinct flag hung as if in defeat. Old, battered signs—handwritten—clung half-heartedly to the fence: *It's your ass if you ignore this fence.*

She made a face. "Classy."

Crouch evaluated the camp. "How far does it stretch?"

"Few miles. Maybe more." Boots sucked at his lips nervously.

"How many of them?"

"How the hell should I know? But I seen at least thirty or forty at one time. So, probably more than that."

Alicia squinted at their vague guide. "They show any signs of being dangerous?"

"Bad dudes." Boots nodded. "Very bad dudes. I seen them chase down one of their own once, strap him to the back of one of those big trucks and drag him through the desert. Weren't much left of the guy after that. I never seen 'em back down to anyone. Not once. I guess they got the firepower to back 'em up."

"And the law?" Cruz asked. "Do they not become involved?"

"Cops leave 'em alone. Never shown any major inclination to get involved here. Leastways, not without the Army as back up. But the militia do keep themselves to themselves mostly. Don't cause no trouble."

Alicia kept her eyes on the scene. She counted over twenty men lounging around, taking it easy, chatting in circles near the burning cans. Others walked between huts, carrying beer and cigarettes, laughing loudly. Somewhere a husky motorcycle started up, roaring at the night. No surveillance cameras were in evidence and the fence wasn't electrified. The lack of a perimeter guard was all too clear.

"Easy to get in," she said. "But still risky. And dangerous. And that sign about my ass really puts the jitters up me."

Healey snickered.

"We'll need to test them but not tonight," Crouch said. "First we need a plan that centers round getting in and finding that treasure without being spotted."

"Steal it from under their noses?" Healey's eyes shone with excitement.

Russo stole his thunder. "Steady on, kid. We can't lug an entire treasure trove out on our backs."

Crouch grinned. "Maybe we can. We got into this for the

action and the adventure, right? Well, let's have a little of both."

"I'm up for it," Healey declared.

"We sure have the edge on technology," Caitlyn said with a touch of irony as she stared through the holes in the fence.

"This boundary." Alicia generally indicated the fence that stretched as far as they could see. "Is it self-proclaimed?"

Boots stared uncomprehending.

"I mean, do they own the land?"

"I guess so. But who really knows? The government build these fences all over our state, and Arizona and Nevada. Pop up like newborns they do, hush hush secret. A private military base, a so-called research center. A black site. You know how many of them are out there? One day you can walk along a path, the next you're told to turn back or get shot. They can do that. Should they be able to do that? I don't think so."

"Then what you're saying is the High Desert Militia popped up out of nowhere a few years ago and nobody knows if they're here legitimately?"

"That means," Crouch pointed out. "That we wouldn't be trespassing on private property if and when we cross that fence."

"P'raps," Boots agreed. "But ain't nobody that's bothered about it been tough enough to ask 'em."

Alicia turned to her team with a smile. "Well, my friend, that's about to change."

SEVENTEEN

The team wrestled with the problem all the way back to Kanab. How to distract a badly organized but well-armed militia? Crouch came up with the sensible suggestions—distractions or a raid; Healey came up with the thrilling ones—bombarding them with mortars. Russo jiggled his massive head from side to side, suggesting they send Alicia in to drive them crazy. Caitlyn offered a few high-tech alternatives but it turned out they had none of the equipment she required and local supplies weren't as plentiful as they'd hoped.

In the end, it was Lex that fired Alicia's imagination.

"We employ the bikers approach," he said into a lull. "Works every time."

"What?" Crouch half turned in his seat. "How?"

"Militia groups have more than their fair share of bikers in their ranks. For whatever reason." He shrugged. "Some are in hiding. Others just wanted by the law." He grinned at his own joke. "Of all new recruits or visitors, bikers are one of the most likely groups to be allowed inside."

"So you're suggesting *you* head on in there alone?" Russo grunted. "I don't think so."

"I have my jacket. My tats. I'm genuine. All we need to find is a good bike. Or two." Lex eyed Alicia, raising both eyebrows.

Alicia's grin held weight. "Now you're talking. Trouble is, two of just ain't a gang."

"We could be a splinter group."

Alicia bit her lip. "We'd need to sell it. A gang would sell it and escape without a scratch. Just the two of us? I'm not so sure."

"If it helps there's a biker bar restaurant in town." Caitlyn held up her cellphone showing a search result. "It couldn't hurt to try there."

"Let me get this straight," Crouch said. "You two are going to what? *Rent* a few bikes and a gang for the night? Shit, can you get any crazier?"

"Oh, Michael." Alicia smiled quickly. "I'm just getting started."

It took the rest of the night and part of the day after, but by late the next afternoon Lex's plan was shaping up. The biker bar had turned out to be a diluted version of the real thing but Lex did find two bona fide articles, both wearing vests embroidered with various patches. The bikers called them their colors, and attached to them a mass of meanings.

"They good?" Alicia asked him.

"They sure ain't waxers," Lex said. "Let me double-check."

"What's a waxer, dare I ask?" Caitlyn wondered aloud as he walked away from their table.

Alicia watched him go. "Real bikers call weekend riders 'waxers'. Riding isn't their lifestyle. The furthest their bikes go is to the end of the driveway every weekend where it gets washed and waxed until it shines like the sun."

The group watched Lex work for a while, coming clean with the bikers as much because they were his kin as to preserve their safety. After a while he beckoned Alicia over.

"This here's Wrench. And this is Red Head."

Alicia evaluated them. Wrench sported old scars and sunken eyes. A beard covered his lower jaw. The stare he gave her searched for expertise and she saw a hard, experienced brother hiding behind the gaze.

"Army?" she asked.

Wrench grunted. It was enough. Red Head was younger but no less tough or sharp. It was he that spoke first.

"Lex calls you Taz. How'd that come about?"

Alicia flinched. She'd almost forgotten the biker nickname. "Not something I really talk about," she said. "Our boys didn't make it . . . ."

She paused. Wrench put up a hand. "We heard. Don't worry. Lex here says you two are all that's left."

"All that's left running," Alicia admitted.

"So who you running with?" Wrench indicated the team seated at a far table.

"Military group," Alicia told them without hesitating. "Has Lex explained?"

Wrench nodded. "I'm always up for a blast at the militia. Red Head here though, he ain't so on board."

Alicia scrutinized the man. With short-cropped blond hair, a white complexion, and a fuzzy day-old growth it was hard to see the reason behind his nickname. *Always a story,* she thought. And most bikers liked to tell it.

"So, Red Head," she said. "What's the problem? And the name? You want to tell me how you came by that?"

"No real story," he said. "It's the flavor I prefer," he smirked, "in women."

Wrench chortled. "No story? 'Course there's a story. Red Head ain't never been with any other kinda flavor. Blond, brunette, black hair—never. Gets himself very upset when a redhead turns out to be a fake—if you get my drift."

"Wrench," Red Head said warningly.

"Checks early on." Wrench laughed. "Then sometimes storms off leaving the little lady a tad confused."

Alicia turned to the annoyed biker. "I guess I'm safe then. Blond all the way, head to my toes."

"Shit." Wrench stared at her. "Now you're in my head."

"Wait till you see my leathers."

Lex leaned into the discussion. "Did I say you'll be well rewarded? That guy over there, the serious looking one, he'll set you up for a month."

"Sounds dangerous." Red Head was staring at Alicia.

"Is there any other way?" she asked.

"Got a plan?"

"Never do. Always see what comes up first."

Red Head shook his head. "All right, stop the flirting. Lex here had me at reward."

"Flirting?" Alicia snickered. "I hadn't even started."

Wrench looked a little mortified, but quickly asserted his attendance. Alicia walked back to Crouch.

"Four bikers in total," she said. "It will have to do."

Crouch nodded at the others. "Let's get ready."

Alicia pulled on her tight leather pants, enjoying the feel of the soft leather easing up her bare legs. Since it wasn't the most dignified of operations, especially when you got nearer the ass area, she elected to perform this one alone, in her hotel room. Once complete, she took a moment to walk over to the window, taking in the dying ball of the sun as it spread across the horizon.

Where next? she thought. From place to place, country to country; crisis to crisis and adventure beyond adventure. The road stretched ever on and its beauty was that it immersed you in all the various pit-stops along the way, engaging you in a constantly moving picture of diverse life.

The next horizon was always only a day away.

Alicia quelled her wanderlust for the time being and exited the hotel room. The team met with Wrench and Red Head, and looked over the other two bikes they'd managed to rent from occupants of the diner. One was a passable Harley, the other a Honda, nicely outfitted but hardly a biker's bike. Lex stared at it with disdain.

"Shit."

"Roll with it," Alicia said. "We'll think of something."

She straddled the Harley, blipping the throttle to get a feel for the bike. When Crouch and the rest of the team were ready she peeled out after them, making sure Wrench, Red Head and Lex were ahead of her. The mountains came quick and soon they were roaring along the narrow roads, leaning into the corners and letting the engine roar down the straights. High cliff faces echoed with the monsters' roar, replicating and throwing it back at them in a respectful, spirited way. For a few miles there was nothing but the road and the darkening skies, the black ribbon ahead and the feel of the other bikes and their riders, all accomplished, chasing the end of the day until the next dawn.

Then Crouch sent out a warning call through their comms. Alicia, feeling a little self-conscious, slowed immediately and helped rein the rest in. By the time the bikers were under control Crouch had called a halt for a final interchange.

"Good luck in there," he said in closing. "As soon as you have their attention we'll breach as near the map's coordinates as we can."

"Coordinates?" Alicia laughed. "Really?"

"Well, they're as good as coordinates," Crouch said a little huffily and turned away. Despite her words Alicia had complete faith in their boss and trusted him to find whatever was out there.

If anything.

As the treasure team melted away, the biker team took a last moment to remember their stories.

"Hang on tight, boys. This is gonna be a tester." Alicia wasted no time in roaring toward the militia's only gate. Lex followed immediately with Wrench and Red Head bringing up the rear. Red Head muttered something about this not being such a clever idea after all through the comms. Alicia promised to keep him safe. That galvanized the man's masculine pride a little, prompting a spurt of speed.

Alicia stopped outside the gate, Red Head at her side. Lex squeezed past them both, the supposed leader of their little gang. With his Honda mostly hidden by Alicia's Harley he leaned forward in the saddle and stared up into the CCTV camera, making a speech sign with his right hand.

"Now we wait."

Not for long. The militia, on sensing any kind of potential

threat, were always quick to mobilize. A high-sided, canvas-backed vehicle squealed dangerously around the square, loaded with men, and bounced down the rough trail toward the gate. Faces peered at them from every vantage point. Behind the truck came a small jeep. Both vehicles squealed to a stop near the gate, dust swirling from their tires.

A man bellowed at them from the bed of the jeep. "You're on private property! Turn around and keep going!"

Lex kept his voice calm. "We're just like you, brother. Looking for a night's sleep, a few drinks, maybe a party." He grinned.

"This ain't a fucking rave. Turn the hell around."

The man's words were contradicted by at least three-quarters of the men leaning out of the truck, most with a gun in one hand and a beer in the other.

Alicia shifted, drawing their attention. "We'd be grateful."

The shouter jumped down from the bed of the jeep. As he drew closer Alicia got her first good look at him. Unshaven, with hair down to his shoulders and wearing an open jacket that even *looked* like it reeked, he leveled a rifle at them.

"What you want with us?"

"Like I said," Lex waved it away, "a place to sleep for the night. The chance to swop a few stories. We been on the road a while."

"Not much of a gang," the man sneered.

"We're all that's left," Lex said truthfully. "Used to be over twenty Slayers. Got hit in Germany."

This made a few of the men jump down and walk forward, interested. Their leader lowered his weapon. "Got hit you say. You take any of them fuckers with you?"

Lex nodded quickly. Alicia saw from the way he held himself that he was still mourning his true brothers. This gang may be a façade in itself but its back story was a very real, very dreadful truth.

"We got no quarrel with bikers," one man said. "C'mon, Pitts. Let 'em ride in."

Pitts stared at them a while longer. He searched the darkness behind them. Eventually, mostly giving in to his own men's wishes, he ordered the gates to be unlocked. "But watch 'em," he said. "And search 'em. No weapons, cellphones, or any of that new-fangled crap. This is our land. Our rules. You got me?"

Lex held up his hands. "We're just here to drink."

The bikers rode through, following the truck and the jeep back toward the square and the blazing trash cans. Once there the gang dismounted and allowed the militia men to inspect their bikes. Following Pitts' instructions they attempted to search the bikers. A few knives were found on Red Head, a baton on Wrench. Alicia subjected herself to a general pat down but when one of the guys ventured a little too close for comfort she spoke out.

"That hand gets any closer to that right cheek I'm gonna rip it off."

They backed away. One of the men, a scarred, wild-eyed youngster with a swagger and a bellyful of bravado stepped up. "Your fuckin' jackets don't match."

Lex showed them his own, embroidered with his colors and the Slayers' logo. "Alicia here lost hers in the fight. Red Head and Wrench were new to the crew, just joined from the . . ." he looked around at them, eyes asking a very important and overlooked question.

"Iron Horsemen," Wrench said without batting an eye.

Alicia stepped forward. "You gonna show us around then boys, or what? Hey, that's a nice big gun. Can I touch it?"

A shout stopped her. Pitts was approaching. "Just keep 'em in the goddamn square and keep your guns to yourselves. I don't mind helping out a like-minded fellow but I'll be damned if they're touching my guns."

Alicia held out her hand for a beer. "I'll take some of that then."

The militia men grinned and beckoned for her to follow then into the square, toward a blazing trashcan that seemed to symbolize their epicenter. Lex and the hired bikers followed. Alicia downed the beer in one huge gulp, gaining even more attention and caught another in midair.

Lex joined her. "Down in one?"

"Is there any other way?"

Crouch led the remainder of the team to the east, following the outer perimeter of the fence until he found the best entry point. Wearing dark clothes, flak jackets and infrared goggles they were well equipped for stalking the night, but the difference between being able to see through the darkness and search for treasure in it was vast. The team were expecting the search to test all of their abilities.

Crouch knew the maps and notes by heart. He had read them a thousand times. Still, he treble-checked their starting point, traveling around the plateau above the Fiery Furnace to locate the exact landmark from which to start. He took his time. Healey and Russo snipped the fence, letting everyone through, then secured it afterward with metal ties. They left as little to chance as possible. Crouch waited, kneeling in the dirt.

"Eighty five paces," he whispered through the comms. "Northeasterly. We're looking for a totem-pole shaped hoodoo."

The moon and stars glittered down upon them, affording enough light to help their search but also raising their chances of being spotted. Crouch fancied that the militia didn't post outer perimeter guards, but didn't want to test the theory too closely. Crouch took point, Caitlyn a step behind. Russo and Healey brought up the rear with Cruz between them. The Mexican guide had been unusually quiet since landing in the US, blaming his reticence on being outside his comfort zone.

Crouch didn't babysit the man. Soldiers had to deal with that kind of shit their whole lives.

Counting softly in his head, he walked until eighty five paces had passed. At that point a vista opened to their right, its impact tarnished by the darkness, but still with enough effect to take their breaths away.

Crouch pointed ahead. "Totem-pole shaped hoodoo on the edge of the cliff."

The thin spire of rock protruded above the rim, its length shaped into rounded columns as it climbed to its apex. Crouch knelt down and consulted the map. "Okay, so I know it's one hundred paces west," he said. "But that's toward the militia compound so be careful."

Small rocks eased their way, providing areas of cover. Crouch pointed out an ancient rock formation, a huddle of bare stones, and a sprouting of trees that formed the second landmark, then cut north again.

"The good news," he said, "is that the landmarks are actually here. I can understand that one or two may have been lost to time and the elements, but finding none at all would have pointed toward this being a hoax."

Cruz looked at him. "The elders wouldn't do that. They gave their word."

Crouch nodded, saying nothing.

"A wilderness as vast as this," Caitlyn said. "Those Aztec warriors and whoever came after could have been lost out here for days. I wonder how they ever made it back."

"Followed their own map probably," Russo said a little drily but then shrugged in apology. "It is a wild place, doubly so in older times."

Another formation passed them by and still Crouch followed his map, venturing once more closer to the perimeter fence and then stopping near the banks of a briskly running stream. The sound of rushing water broke the silent monotony, a balm to Caitlyn's ears.

"Best sound I've heard in a long while."

Crouch took a drink from a bottle of water. "Saddle up yer pony," he said in a shocking cowboy accent. "The final landmark is at the mouth of this stream."

EIGHTEEN

Alicia carefully tossed another can into the fire, laughing as she scored a direct hit, slowly shaking her hips to a rock beat. To all but the most observant she appeared inebriated, caught in the moment, happy to be among the bikers and militia men, but inside she was as alert as a fighter pilot in a war zone. Her every move was designed to throw the enemy off guard, to take their attention away from the real events that were taking place tonight. Lex played his part at her side, reveling in the role of leader.

The stories he'd promised to tell, whilst turning out to be the center of militia attention, betrayed the pain he still felt for the loss of his brothers. There was the story of Whipper and how she came by her name; Dirty Sarah and the way she could fight. Then came older stories of men now dead—Tiny, Donkster and Lomas.

Alicia moved in closer as Lex spoke of Lomas, the leader of the Slayers and Alicia's last beau. He had died in her arms. The pain she'd experienced at his death surpassed all the hurt she'd ever felt in her life. There was no recovery; no going back.

Only the road ahead.

Lex spoke warmly of the gang leader, telling a bevy of stories. The night grew long and the music vibrated into lighter tunes. The beer flowed endlessly and the laughter rarely stopped. But Alicia never let her guard down and neither did the militia men. Pitts was always present, cradling his rifle, and several of his cohorts watched from afar, perched atop jeeps or standing among shadows as if waiting for something to happen. When Alicia put on an impromptu dancing display, wriggling and cavorting, she turned at the end to find Pitts' eyes on her, evaluating and watchful and totally unmoved.

Lex pulled her back to the trashcans. "Time to hit the sack."

Wrench and Red Head backed him up, enquiring as to a place

to sleep. The latter had been talking to one of the militia women present. With tied back flaming red hair she was a prime candidate for Red Head's affections, but to his credit he quickly backed the team.

"Sleep by your bikes," Pitts told them. "Won't rain around here tonight."

Lex balked for a moment, unsure how to respond to the potential insult. Alicia laid a furtive hand on his arm.

"Sure, sure," he blustered. "Don't matter to me."

The men began to drift away. Pretty soon there was only a hard core left; hard-eyed individuals that rarely let their weapons leave their hands even when drinking. Alicia wondered about the dangers of such an individual having to take a leak. Feeling buoyant now that they'd gained Crouch and the rest of the team so much valuable time to search, she was about to ask the question when Pitts sidled up close to her.

"Something ain't right about you, missy," he said softly. "Those guys they're blinded and guided by what's between their legs. And yours. But me and the senior ranks over there" —he nodded toward the jeep and the men courting the darker shadows— "we see past all that."

"Past *that?*" Alicia affected a high-pitched tone. "To my ass? It's great isn't it?"

Pitts shrugged, slightly tongue-tangled. "All night," he said. "We'll be watching."

Hefting his rifle he purposely swung the barrel so that it crossed paths with all four bikers before ambling away, then glanced back over his shoulder, eyes never straying far. The men of the senior ranks drifted a little closer now, saying nothing.

"So," Alicia said brightly. "Who's sleeping tonight?"

Excitement coursed through the team as they climbed the sharp incline alongside the burbling stream. Full darkness had long since fallen, turning the landscape to a light green discernible only through night vision goggles. The hard ground had been worn smooth, making it difficult to find any purchase, so much so that Crouch found himself crawling before too long, breathing loud in his own ears. The stream cut back and forth across the rock, meandering down its own path and vanishing into nowhere.

At last they crested the rise. A flat piece of rock extended in all directions, leading to even higher ground several hundred feet away.

"The mouth of the river," Crouch said expectantly, "is the pictogram that signifies the final landmark. We're here."

"It's not much of a river and that's definitely not a mouth," Russo pointed out. "More like a leaky plughole."

"Man's got a point." Caitlyn crouched down and peered hard into the small square of darkness from which the water spouted. "Pass me that flashlight."

Healey was already beside her, handing the powerful flashlight over. Caitlyn angled it into the hole, remembering to remove her night vision goggles first. "Just a hollow clogged with pebbles and dust and dirt. If there is anything under there it's well buried beneath tons of rock that we sure can't dig through."

Crouch joined her. "I can't understand it. They surely had to hide a part of the treasure here. Otherwise why all the clues and markers? We were purposely led to this point—for what?"

Cruz was also on his knees. "I doubt a dog could fit through that hole let alone a man."

Crouch tapped the rock with his own flashlight. "What are we missing?"

"If you guys are done looking, turn those bloody flashlights off," Russo murmured. "We're lit up like a Jean Michel Jarre concert."

Caitlyn frowned in confusion but switched her light off. Crouch did the same. "The mouth of the river," he said, shining a penlight over his notes. "If it's not here then . . ."

Caitlyn sat back on a rocky outcrop, scanning the area. The

only noticeable cavern was the astonishing black expanse above them, speckled with stars, a great dusky frame for the moon. The isolation of the area struck her as much as anything. A life could be lost out here and only the vast remoteness would ever know who'd passed.

Cruz moved over to Crouch, studying the notes. Russo and Healey moved a little higher and replaced their goggles, giving the area a once over. After a minute Russo clicked his comms and reported that all was clear.

Caitlyn sighed. "I guess most of the time these treasure hunts will end in failure. And even if there once was something here— five hundred years is a long time."

Crouch shook his head. "Look around you. This land does not change. Five hundred years is but the blink of an eye to the monuments of Utah."

"What surprises me is that there's a stream out here at all," Cruz said. "I wonder where it comes from."

Crouch turned to stare at him. "What?"

"I said, what surprises me is—"

"No. Not that. You said 'I wonder where it comes from'. Is it possible that—" he tailed off, again revisiting his notes.

Caitlyn felt her excitement rise. "What is it?"

Crouch traced the words with his finger. "Mouth of the river," he repeated. "Could it be a mis-translation? Could it really be— *source* of the river?"

Russo and Healey returned, picking up on the sudden buzz.

Cruz nodded. "I believe it's a common problem. But the actual source could be anywhere, right?" He gestured up at the mouth. "Underground rivers, lakes. Some hidden tributary of the Colorado. It passes by less than ten kilometers from here."

Russo snorted. "But at a lower level, genius."

Cruz made a slight smile. "It is not uncommon to find springs at the top of a mountain where rivers run below. The pressure of the weight of the earth on subterranean water deposits can force water up through fissures and cracks to produce elevated springs."

Caitlyn looked up. Her eyes caught the crowd of rocks situated a few hundred feet above them, the highest ground in the area. "I see only one possible source to this stream," she said, pointing. "And it's there."

Crouch jumped up. The team raced up the sharp slope, struggling for a good foothold on the smooth rock but determined to beat the terrain. Crouch hauled Cruz along and Healey dropped back to give Caitlyn a hand, but the black-haired girl waved him away. So far Healey's training had consisted of hand-to-hand combat and incapacitating strikes, but this wasn't a trained killer she was facing—it was an exertion of effort against the mountain and she was damn well going to prevail on her own.

Healey smiled and left her to it. Caitlyn thought about the girl she'd been before she joined Crouch's unit not so long ago— would she have denied an offer of help from a trained military solider?

Not a chance.

With more than one last huge surge of effort Caitlyn made it up to the strange array of rocks. The guys were waiting for her. "Thanks," she panted. "No hiker in their right mind would ever try that. Now what have we got?"

Before her, several rough, surfboard-shaped boulders appeared to be growing up from the ground, pointing at the skies. Almost fan shaped, the arrangement struck Caitlyn as odd but at the same time familiar. It was Crouch's statement that made her remember.

"A natural occurrence," Crouch said. "In the shape of a feathered headdress?"

Cruz pursed his lips. "You're reaching."

"Maybe. But a wandering Aztec warrior might take this as a sign. C'mon."

They squeezed among the boulders, searching the surface of the rocks and around the sides. The rock was thick and solid, but the formation was also quite dense, offering a chance to slip and squeeze among the standing stones and venture into their inner core.

"I can hear water," Cruz said, for the first time looking eager. "Hurry!"

Caitlyn followed Cruz and Crouch, sliding between the smooth rocks, using their tapered bases to keep her balance, resting on the arch where more than one came together. Everyone became stuck more than once and, though she helped push Crouch to force him through every narrowing gap, it was still undignified to have Healey shoving her from behind. Within minutes the team were sweating and panting. Crouch called for a rest.

"Never," he said. "Never did I expect to find myself temporarily defeated by a bunch of bloody rocks."

Cruz, who had been checking every surface as they toiled through, spoke up. "Not a single marking," he said a little dejectedly. "I hope this is worth the effort."

"More importantly," Caitlyn said, looking around. "I hope we can get out."

Crouch waved him on. The team restarted. Caitlyn tried something new, finding it easier to slither around each rock, keeping her entire body in contact with the surface rather than stepping and climbing and pretty soon everyone except Russo was copying her. The big man was having the most trouble, getting wedged where they slipped through and having nobody to give him a boost. Still, he battled on.

Caitlyn, lost now among the tall stones, kept her eyes peeled ahead, the stars and moon an intermittent lightshow above. Her gaze was fixed on Cruz's back when the man suddenly vanished. A high-pitched squeal followed him down. Crouch leaped forward, bracing himself between the pillars and staring past his own feet.

Crouch shouted, "You okay?"

A half-strangled voice floated out of nowhere. "I have no idea."

Crouch turned around. "Cruz fell about ten feet. There's a spring down there, guys. At the very heart of this little gaggle of rocks." Their boss slipped and slid out of sight.

Caitlyn moved into position, seeing for the first time what Cruz had clearly overlooked. A small natural break in the rock formation lay ahead and below, its bottom mostly consisting of a burbling spring. What Caitlyn saw immediately was the run-off to where the spring naturally fell away.

The dark hole was easily the size of a man.

Cruz was already at the entrance, peering within. Crouch was trying not to elbow him out of the way. Caitlyn grabbed a handhold and let herself down the side of a rock, scrambling blindly for a foothold. After a moment of effort Healey's voice, closer than she would have thought, said, "Just jump. The fall is five feet."

Without acknowledging him, Caitlyn let go, landing on her feet and then her knees. A jolt of pain flashed through her limbs but nothing nearly enough to prevent her from rushing over to the bubbling spring.

"A bit of a *Eureka!* moment." She fought away a fleeting image of the horrible events that had recently microwaved her mind and jumped into the action. "Let me see!"

Cruz waved his flashlight at the hole. "Down there," he said. "The spring travels to the right but I swear I can see another tunnel branching to the left. Now, with this rock being situated so high there's got to be room for a cave down there, possibly eroded thousands or millions of years ago before the stream diverted its course." He grinned self-consciously. "That's the hope I'm clinging to anyway."

Once Healey and Russo had joined them the team set about wriggling down the narrow tunnel. The going was wet and slippery, the rock unforgiving. When Russo became stuck it took all of Healey's strength to pull him free.

"Christ, you're going to have to cut down on the burgers, mate."

"Every ounce pure muscle," Russo returned. "It's what separates the men from the boys."

"Muscle? I thought it was brains and chivalry."

"Yeah, and that's why you're a twenty-three-year-old virgin."

Healey choked. Caitlyn managed a smile even as she crawled, soaked, into the all-enveloping darkness. They followed the tunnel Cruz had spotted, lights shining ahead. The rocky ceiling sloped down and down, away from the direction of the stream. The external surfaces were slick, making the going easier. Cruz crawled ahead for some time before slowing considerably.

"Okay, I have total darkness."

Crouch peered past him. "Oh yeah, that's darkness all right. I believe it means we have a large void ahead."

Caitlyn had no idea what it meant. She said as much.

Healey laughed. "Just ask yourself—what would Lara do?"

"Lara?"

"Lara Croft. Tomb Raider."

"I don't play video games, Zack. Maybe you could ask yourself that same question and go from there."

They crept forward. Crouch pointed out that this all-consuming darkness could be part of a vast cave, a deep recess or even a sudden drop-off. Their powerful flashlights picked out the ground a few feet ahead and no more. Presently the whole team could stand five abreast and join their beams to help penetrate the darkness. Crouch broke out the glowsticks and threw a few into the air.

The way ahead gradually became clear.

They were standing at the entrance to a cave. The entire place was a vault of rock, and completely empty. The floor stretched away two dozen feet toward another tunnel on the far side.

"Bit of a let-down," Caitlyn voiced the feelings of the group.

Then Cruz squealed again. Caitlyn flicked her gaze at him, worried he might have fallen, but changed her mind when she saw him loping off to the right. His flashlight illuminated a large part of the cave wall.

"Aztec art," he said, his tone charged with exhilaration. "These are drawings of warriors, maybe the very warriors that guarded the caravan!"

Caitlyn peered at the crude depictions. Many showed men clad in a kind of uniform, reminiscent of an animal. They all carried shields and clubs and what appeared to be a kind of machete-like weapon.

Cruz continued. "See their helmets? That signifies the warrior group to which they belonged. Eagle. Lion. And so forth. The one with the Jaguar head and skin is a Jaguar Knight. All carry a weapon called a Maquahuitl, basically an Aztec sword. It's short and made of oak, and has volcanic stone embedded into the edges."

"Looks a little basic for what we know about the Aztecs," Caitlyn said.

"Don't underestimate them. The Spanish said one of these could chop off the head of a horse in a single blow."

"Why wear a uniform?"

"The more elaborate the uniform the higher the rank," Cruz said. "But this is proof that they were here. My god, this is *proof*."

"These aren't the only Aztec drawings to be found in North America," Caitlyn reminded him.

"And where's the treasure?" Russo asked. "Can't have just upped and strolled out."

Crouch headed for the far tunnel. "Let's see. Hey, that's not a tunnel, it's a room. Oh—"

His flashlight beam suddenly seemed to irradiate, light being reflected back from a solid surface. The further he walked the more the illumination increased. It was a phenomenon that creased Caitlyn's brow in confusion.

Until Crouch fell to his knees and three staggering words fell from his lips.

"This is . . . fantastic!"

NINETEEN

Alicia heard the commotion begin sometime after midnight. The four bikers had gathered their motorcycles in a front-facing half circle and lay with their backs to a solid brick wall. Feigning sleep for over an hour now, and lying with her head positioned so she could see under the bikes, Alicia was relieved when the militia began to show their true colors. It put an end to all the dicking around.

She nudged the others with her foot but they were already preparing. As Pitts approached she eased a concealed blade from the small of her back to the side.

"Did you know about this? Is this you?"

Alicia rose into a melee. Pitts strode into their makeshift refuge, face and neck an unsightly shade of fire-truck red. The rifle he carried swayed carefully between them.

A swarm of angry militia men backed him up. Alicia quickly counted over thirty eager guns, at least half of them being brandished under the heavy influence of alcohol.

"What the hell are you talking about?"

"You!" Pitts ignored her and spat his words straight at Lex. "Is this you?"

Lex shrugged. "Is *what* me?"

Alicia moved to within striking distance. Pitts didn't notice. He fired a shot between Lex's feet that kicked up a swirl of dirt. Alicia would have pounced then, but knew to do so now was suicide. They had to find a way to thin the herd.

"Lights were seen out by the old stream. We have trespassers."

Lex spread his arms. "It's just us, man."

Pitts waved his rifle. "Cover them."

His men spread out to all sides, weapons raised and well apart.

Alicia had just seen her problem grow existentially.

"You're coming with us," Pitts growled.

"With you?" Alicia repeated. "Where the hell are you going?"

"Gonna smoke us some intruders," Pitts said. "Bastards are about to wish they'd never been born."

Crouch was speechless, rocking from side to side on his knees, flashlight wavering ahead. Caitlyn dropped to his side, her own vision stunned into stillness. By the time Cruz, Healey and Russo joined them Crouch was finally able to speak.

"In all my years I have never seen anything like this. Never."

The small cave revealed by the light of the flashlight was full of gold cladding. It was attached to the walls, stacked high on the floor, leaning against all four sides. Where it had fallen from its original perch it appeared tarnished, spoiled by layers of dust, but even then nothing could prepare the treasure hunters for the true measure of what they'd found.

"So this is all the gold they stripped off the walls?" Russo asked in his quietest tone ever. "Must have been quite a city."

"Greatest of its time," Crouch said. "Destroyed by greedy men that coveted what they did not have."

Caitlyn sighed. "And so it goes."

Healey walked forward, approaching the entrance to the gold room. "It's solid gold, not too thick, but still—entire planks of the stuff. One thing's for sure, we can't hump it out of here."

Crouch squeezed past him, basking in the glory of the find. With the gold all around him it appeared that he was standing in the deepest underground cave, immersed in sunlight. He closed his eyes for a second but the light didn't dim, it lit up his dreams and substantiated every decision he'd made so far.

All his life he'd been heading toward this moment.

As a boy he'd read the books, dreamed of the sparkling buried troves, watched the movies; and then life had intruded, offering him a fresh journey of discipline, camaraderie and leadership. As a man he'd fully embraced the challenges, leaving little time spare to pursue his dreams, even when work was done. Through the years he'd pushed the old urges aside, drowned them in new responsibility. The dreams had faded and almost been forgotten like a boyhood pet—an old love that forever owned his heart but had no significance in the present. When unfortunate opportunity landed him with a second chance he'd jumped straight in, determined to give it his all.

Now . . .

Caitlyn laid a hand across his shoulder. "Well done, sir. This is . . . incredible. The Gold Team earn their stripes."

"What happens next?" Cruz wondered. "The Nahua will want to know that we have found their birthright."

"Next?" Crouch repeated, still dazed. "Well, next we find the second trove."

"All this," Cruz said. "Needs to be safeguarded."

"Of course. We'll slip out of here and I'll make the calls. What do you take me for? An idiot? We always knew we'd find a treasure sooner or later. We have protocols in place to secure and preserve the find."

Cruz smiled. "I knew you were the right choice."

"Oh God," Healey groaned. "Does that mean we have to tackle those bloody rocks again?"

"Afraid so." Caitlyn swatted his behind. "C'mon bucko, giddy up."

Healey sprang forward as if he'd been stabbed. Caitlyn watched him go, then made a face at Russo when the young man didn't look back.

"Whoops, hope I didn't offend him."

"Nah. After that slap he's probably hiding an erection."

Russo strode off, leaving Caitlyn blushing. After a minute Crouch retreated out of the gold room, camera in hand. He proceeded to document the find, covering both caves with infinite care. Cruz wandered over to the drawings again as their boss worked.

"My heart breaks for these warriors," he said. "Sent on a perilous journey away from their home they were gone many months, but finished their task, lost men along the way and still some returned. To find what? A city destroyed. Homes razed. Families murdered. The burden that fell to them was insurmountable."

"And this is how they would want to be remembered," Crouch said. "Knowing that they safely preserved their city's wealth and cultural treasures to be returned to its descendants another day."

Caitlyn saw that Crouch was finished and headed out of the cave. Darkness enfolded her once again, but Healey and Russo waited just ahead, ready with their flashlights. The way back was much easier and quicker. Soon they were scrabbling up the slick slope where the watercourse branched off and then back among the standing stones.

"Shit," Russo said. "Look at that."

Caitlyn stared in the direction he was pointing. A faint red glow buffed up the far horizon, making the skies appear lighter.

"Dawn?" Caitlyn was amazed. "We've been down there all night?"

"Well, technically we've been beyond the fence all night," Healey said. "Took a while to find the cave."

"Sure, but—"

"Time flies when you're treasure seeking."

Russo squeezed out from the final stone, turning around to help steady the others. At last they were free, standing on hard ground and searching for the most direct route back.

"All we have to do," Crouch said. "Is head back down to the stream, then go northwest, stay away from the camp, and retrieve our vehicle. After that I'll start making the calls and we can plan our next move."

"I wouldn't make too many plans," a rough voice said from behind them. "They're hard to fulfil when you're dead."

The sound of dozens of rifles being cocked sent Caitlyn's heart into overdrive.

TWENTY

Alicia placed herself in prime position to incapacitate as many militia men as she could with one devastating move. The time was fast approaching; it was all a matter of experience and anticipation. Guys like this, they had to work themselves up to a kill; make it feel justified and reasonable in their own minds. If it felt wrong they'd just shout and threaten until it felt right.

Pitts had led thirty of his men and the bikers to the small stream, then tracked Crouch's team to the standing stones. After that, it had been a simple matter to lie in wait until voices were heard then lie in concealment. Weapons had been trained on the bikers the whole time. Now though, Alicia watched as Lex positioned himself between three men, and even Wrench and Red Head realized it was in their own interests to take as many enemies down at once when the time came.

Pitts walked closer to Crouch and the boss helped close the gap. Healey and Russo ranged out to the side, drifting in. They appeared to be unarmed. Alicia was betting her life that they weren't.

"You're trespassing," Pitts spat angrily. "What you doing in there?"

"Sightseeing," Crouch replied. "I don't believe it's against the law."

Pitts brandished his weapon. "You crossed our fence!"

"We've been here all night. I didn't see any fence in the dark. Did you guys?" Crouch turned to his men, face set hard and eyes blinking twice to give them the two-minute warning, still drifting closer.

Pitts spat into the dirt. "Don't matter what you saw. All I need to know before I pepper your asses is: Do you know these four pieces of work? You all planned this in cahoots or not?"

Crouch stared at Alicia. Not a flicker of recognition crossed his face. "I don't believe I do."

Pitts frowned. "What kinda accent is that? Australian?"

"English. Like I said we're touring." Crouch would never force a battle. He'd talked himself out of more than one tight space and saved countless lives. Admittedly some of those lives popped back up later toting Uzis but he would still never cause pointless bloodshed.

"Don't look like tourists to me."

Crouch shrugged. "Are you really going to kill us in cold blood?"

Pitts' smile gave Crouch all the answer he needed. "Been done before. Ain't nobody around here to see. Them boys back there they need their target practice."

"Are you telling us to run?"

"I likes me a good hunt."

Crouch swept a glance across the thirty faces. Not a man among them appeared regretful, not a single evil grin was false. They had done this before. They'd never do it again.

"Time," he said.

Pitts blinked. "Wha—"

The whole area burst into frantic action. Healey and Russo whipped .45s from beneath their jackets and fired into the group of men standing furthest away from Alicia and the bikers. Alicia whipped around, disarming her closest opponent with a twist and jerk of his arm whilst side-kicking a second in the throat and a blocking a third with his pinwheeling body. Less than a second later she shot the first man and the two behind him, then ducked to the floor. Crouch jumped into Pitts, wrestled his rifle down to the ground, flipped his body over a raised shoulder, and let it fall hard onto the rocks. Cruz and Caitlyn leaped behind an upstanding boulder.

Militia men screamed and fell, momentarily overwhelmed by

the planned onslaught and the sheer terrible force of it. Healey and Russo continued to pick men off. Alicia saw Lex disarm a man and wound another. She saw Wrench and Red Head wrestling enemies, the first biker with more than a modicum of military skill, the second with brute force. She smashed the butt of her rifle into a nose, spun the weapon around and fired twice. Bodies fell, twitching. Healey and Russo dropped to their knees and kept up a withering salvo.

The militia shrank back but they didn't waste away. For all the bad that they were, they remained hard, determined men. Crouch had already anticipated this, so when the private army started getting it together he shouted a quick retreat.

Instantly, his team spilled away, a deadly torrent parting. Alicia called to the bikers, indicating a nearby rock cluster, and covered their dash. Healey and Russo fell to their stomachs, the jagged rise of the slope affording them just enough cover. Crouch fell back to where Caitlyn and Cruz were concealed.

"My men!" Pitts was screaming. "You killed half my men!"

"Let that be a lesson to you," Crouch called back, holding Pitts' own rifle in the air. "Besides, most of them are just wounded. They'll heal."

Pitts gasped and sputtered so much he couldn't form words. As Crouch peered carefully around the boulder he saw the man wrench a gun out of the hands of a confederate and take aim.

"Shit." He ducked back in.

"Charge 'em!" Pitts screamed. "Kill 'em all!"

Bullets pounded against the boulder, some glancing off its edges and depositing a reddish powder in the air. Crouch made sure his colleagues' heads were firmly down near the floor before angling his own rifle over the top of the boulder and returning fire. Still in his line of sight were Healey and Russo, taking advantage of their clever perspective to pick off charging enemies. For a minute all was battering noise and bloodcurdling yells; until Crouch heard the scrambling of feet close to his shelter.

Anticipating the attack he stepped out at the right moment, met Pitts head on, and smashed the man's rifle aside with his own. Pitts brought it straight back down but Crouch caught it along the length of his own, using it like a sword. When Pitts furiously snatched the rifle away to gain space, Crouch used the predictable moment to end the fight. He smashed Pitts' larynx, putting an end to the insane bellowing once and for all, and brought a knee up hard as the man fell. Crouch made sure he felt the nose break before allowing the inert body to slip to the floor.

Another man burst around the rock. Crouch peppered him full of holes. He used the falling body for shelter as he grabbed another quick glance. Men were collapsing before Healey and Russo like sacrificial robots, the mindless and foolish led to the slaughter. Alicia and her three cohorts were firing intermittently around the sides of their sanctuary, working as a team.

Crouch tried something. "Pitts is dead!" he shouted. "Go home!"

In truth, the state of Pitts' health was undetermined but his soldiers couldn't know that. As a man they slowed and then paused, each staring to the other. Then, in unison, they began to back away. With guns raised, and some still discharging, they retreated until they were no longer a threat, then turned to hightail it back to their compound.

Russo jumped to his feet. "Sir! We have to pass right by that compound to get out of here and they probably know that. We should hurry!"

Crouch knew it. Already helping Caitlyn to her feet, he waved frantically toward Alicia. "Come on!"

Alicia waved back, grinning before remembering their predicament. Within seconds the entire team was running, crossing the tumbling stream and slipping across the glassy surface. An open plain soon unfolded ahead and the team ran as if being chased by dust devils.

"Did you find what we were looking for?" Alicia jogged at Crouch's side.

Despite their dilemma Crouch let his face expand into a wide smile. "Sure did, Myles. Biggest bloody treasure trove since Tutankhamen."

"Damn. Can't believe I missed the big discovery."

"Don't worry. When we get out of here there's going to be another that'll make *this* one look like a quick trip to Tiffany's."

"As if I know what that is."

Alicia checked her crew as they ran. Red Head was puffing a little, but keeping up. Caitlyn was struggling; even carrying no gear the girl was slow. Alicia, finding new depths of character, fell behind to encourage her.

"Not too far," she said. "Then you and Healey can get laid out in the back seat."

"Don't bank on that." Caitlyn panted. "I slapped his arse and I don't think he appreciated it."

Alicia failed to choke down her mirth. "You what?"

"It was a spur of the moment thing. We'd just found treasure. You get it, right?"

"I just wish I'd been there to see it."

Still they ran, taking the most direct route back to their vehicle. The rising sun beat down; not even a breath of air stirred the sparse scrub and stands of trees. Thinking about their quandary Alicia realized the car would be a tight squeeze now since their bikes were lost, and another costly bill for Crouch when they returned to Kanab.

Behind, she saw nothing. Russo noticed her checking and shook his head. "Assholes will be reloading," he said. "And I'm down to my last six shots."

"One more for the niggles list," she said. "Pack more ammo. Truth be told I only have four."

Crouch added a full mag and Healey another five bullets. A minute later their car was in sight and Russo was untying the fence. The engine started with a roar. With three in the front, four in the back and two in the hatchback space the team would have opted to fight it out if the force facing them had been smaller but now wasn't the time to take such a chance. Guns were positioned and heads twisted to the best vantage points as they slithered across the dirt, hitting the asphalt hard. The sudden jouncing of the car elicited a chorus of pained groans.

"Suck it up," Crouch told them. "Long way to go yet."

He powered the car along the winding road. The perimeter fence flashed by to their right. In only a few moments Crouch had confirmed the worst.

"Damn fools have parked a truck broadside, blocking the road. Armed men to every side and in the gateway."

"Can you get past?" Russo readied his gun.

"Not a chance."

"So what the hell are you going to dooo!" Healey's last word was drawn out as Crouch trampled the gas pedal to the floor and swung the vehicle hard right. The front end bounced over the raised asphalt, hitting dirt and fighting for purchase. The car slewed left and right, the tires grinding. Men scattered from in front of the militia compound gates, not having time to fire even a single shot.

"They didn't expect that!" Crouch shouted.

The car sped through the open gates, straight in to the militia compound. Crouch let it pick up speed for a minute and then spun it around the square, throwing up a wall of dust. He waited before the central dais, underneath the drooping flag, waiting to see what their enemies would do. Alicia quickly pointed out their bikes.

"If we get chance . . ."

"Too exposed," Crouch said.

"I didn't mean ride *past* them."

Crouch caught her meaning and ran through the likely upcoming scenarios in his head. The obvious one had the militia blasting straight toward him in that big truck.

"All right. Do it."

The four bikers slipped out of the car, sprinting hard across the square and through the smoking trashcans. Alicia reached her bike first, flicking the foot rest and fiddling with the starter. Lex, Wrench and Red Head jumped aboard their own bikes. Lex kept his eyes on Crouch.

"Ready?"

They waited close to the brick wall where they'd sheltered the night before, out of sight of the militia. Wrench took the moment's respite to tap Alicia on the shoulder.

"Hell of a side trip you provide."

"And on the house." she replied. "Never let it be said that Alicia Myles doesn't offer a good ride."

Wrench chuckled. "I don't doubt it."

The roar of a powerful truck's engine snapped Alicia's attention back to their perilous situation. Crouch raised his hand, just visible behind the wheel. Alicia arranged her bike so that it would go first and the others pulled up alongside her. Another heavy bellow and the truck roared along even faster, out of sight to Alicia but clearly powering toward Crouch's vehicle. The sound of gears being forced bit at the air. In the moment that Crouch's hand fell, Alicia opened her throttle, making the bike spurt forward at full speed. She held on tight, yelling as the adrenalin surged.

This would be close.

Three bikes sped along at her side, gaining momentum; silver chrome, aluminum and darkest black flashing in the corner of her eyes. With no helmet her blond hair streamed out behind—a warrior Valkyrie riding like a bat out of hell. The four-bike race was fluid, molten, the blur of dirt, metal, leather and flesh flowing together as their speeds increased.

A moment more and Alicia launched herself out of the seat, tumbling clear. Her motorcycle sped on, a missile that struck the front of the truck. The next three bikes in line hit the front wheel, the side and the rear wheel as one, causing the driver to lose control and the men in the back to go head over heels across the flatbed or tumble over the low sides.

Crouch floored the gas pedal, shouting for his men to throw open the doors seconds after they'd already done so, then screaming to a halt alongside the battered bikers.

"Move!"

Alicia dived across the back seat. Wrench and Lex landed on top of her. Red Head struggled to climb over the rear seats. Before anyone could even think Crouch burned rubber again, upsetting their balance beyond control. Healey leaned out of the front window, loosing rounds out of Crouch's rifle. If a head rose, Healey took it off.

The car screamed through the militia compound and out of the gates. Bullets, fired more in frustration than in any hope of finding a target, clanged off the bodywork and thumped into the dirt around them.

Crouch heaved a sigh of relief. "Make yourselves comfortable, people. We have a long ride and a hundred phone calls to make."

Healey powered shut his window. "And an even greater treasure to find."

TWENTY ONE

Kanab saw the departure of Wrench and Red Head, both carrying thick green wads and riotous new memories. Crouch barely took a breath between phone calls, contacting friends in authority, the World Heritage Committee and other organizations, following the framework of his protocol to the letter.

"The machine is booting up." He broke his procession of calls one time. "Sadler and I established our procedure even before the members of this group were finalized. To be putting it into play so soon is frankly astounding."

Alicia tuned him out as he took another call. The trip to Kanab had been incident free, but somewhat cramped. By the time the team returned to their hotel everyone was ready for a shower. Alicia locked her door and stripped off, letting the clothes pile at her feet. A whiff of her armpits made her frown.

"Major degunk in order," she said to the empty room and padded across the bare floor. She caught a glimpse of herself in the full-length hallway mirror and stopped to look. It was a rare moment. The laws of her life required that she never stopped; in that way the past would always be behind her.

If she was forced to confront her current wants and needs, and then the next step; the results of that inner search, she feared, would lead to some kind of breakdown. She studied the lines of her body. Her muscle tone was clearly defined, her pale skin marked by old wounds and fresh bruises. Nothing sagging yet, but whereas time hadn't yet taken its toll the job certainly had. Old healed scars were beginning to crisscross with new ones. Alicia hurt only when she stopped her forward momentum—in more ways than one.

The shower cooled and purified her, at least for now. Ten

minutes later she was dressed in fresh clothes and entering Crouch's room, not surprised by the look of excitement on his face.

Crouch held up a hand, covering the phone. "I have our benefactor, Rolland Sadler, on the line. He's already said this find in itself will fund our team for years through various celebrity benefits and news exclusives. The Nahua will be prioritized . . ." He went back to his call.

Alicia drifted inside and perched on the arm of the sofa. Crouch finished up with a, "Yes, Rolland. We're about to sit down and study the map." Then he turned to her.

"Whoa," he said. "Our boss is a real slave driver."

"They're all the same." Alicia waggled her eyebrows.

Caitlyn entered the room and walked straight over to the table. "So where's the map and the notes?"

Alicia and Crouch exchanged a glance and smiled. Motivation was high after the recent find. But in addition to the many positives it offered, Crouch knew they now faced a mélange of undesirable consequences, not the least of which was the return of Coker, his boss, and others like him. If Coker had lost touch with them in Utah the underground rumor network would certainly have put them back on the map by now.

With Healey and Russo fetching coffee and croissants, the map and notes were laid out for Caitlyn to study. Crouch knew them by heart, but he sat down alongside her.

Caitlyn re-familiarized herself with the poem:

"Through the great, endless river you must travel,

"Past canyons and rocks of waves,

"The Shield Arch shows the way,

"But heed our warnings to the mushroom rock,

"Then beyond the known territory of the braves,

"Look between Hummingbird and the ritual for your final guidance,

"And betray the sacrifices of your loyal warriors not."

"The river has to be the Colorado," Crouch told her. "I think if you were an Aztec warrior wandering the desert five hundred years ago, the Colorado would seem great and endless. Plus, it fits perfectly with the directions."

"How close can the directions get us?"

Crouch sighed. "The smallest measurement this time I'm afraid, is in days. We can get to the general area, but we can't pinpoint the particular stretch where they traveled it and crossed it."

Healey interrupted as he handed out paper cups full of steaming coffee. "Wow," Alicia said. "Even the smell of coffee makes me more alert."

"Everything's approximate," Crouch went on. "From our guestimate of how many miles per day they traveled to how far they wandered off their straight line. We have to assume that the bulk of the finest treasure is there. The Wheel of Gold that Cortés valued at 3800 gold pesos and later Castillo valued at more than 10,000 pesos. 'As big as a cartwheel,' he said, and later known as the pieces of eight. And more—statues, coins, idols. Possibly even manuscripts, every one of incalculable worth. I've lost track of the number of people who've sought this treasure down the years but I'll say this—the mountains keep their secrets well."

Caitlyn traced the map with a nail as she searched Google Maps on the computer. "At the very least," she said, "we need to relocate. Kanab's compromised as a base now."

Alicia looked over, following the line of her finger and noting where it ended up. "You're kidding?"

Caitlyn turned a happy grin on them. "Nope. Haven't you ever wanted to go there?"

"I've been to Vegas several times. Trust me, it never ends well."

"Won't it make us more . . . conspicuous?" Russo wondered.

"If anything," Crouch acceded. "A big, busy city might be the better place to stay. Not only does it provide a certain anonymity, but we're less likely to become open targets there. So long as we stick close to the main drag."

"The Strip," Caitlyn said happily. "They call it the Strip."

Alicia tapped the girl on the shoulder. "Reality check. We ain't heading out there to party, love. We're on a mission."

"I understand that," Caitlyn said. "It's the victory celebration that I'm looking forward to."

TWENTY TWO

Sunset Station sat southeast of Las Vegas Boulevard, about ten miles from the staggering casinos that formed its heart. Busy, colorful, extensive and bristling with security they agreed it was the best place to stay. Nobody could predict what a South African crime lord might order his men to do, but ordering an attack on such a high risk target seemed unlikely.

Crouch enthusiastically set about determining their best starting point, using the old Aztec distance and directional system. Caitlyn called Healey over to work on the rest of the poem.

Alicia gazed out of the eighth floor window. "It's all so flat."

Russo drifted over. "Guess that's why they call it a desert."

"Funny guy. How'd ya like to—" Alicia started to retort and then saw a slight smile curling the big man's lips. She understood. They'd fought together now, spilled blood together, saved lives and ended them. The bond they shared was no longer built on reputation, it was built on respect.

Alicia nodded in silent response. Caitlyn argued softly with Healey over the unknown meanings behind the poem's mysterious descriptions. Wave rocks, shield arches and mushroom rocks might be anything, but at least two of those word pictures pointed to an Aztec narrative.

Alicia's phone rang. Looking down she was startled to see the call was from a not-so-old friend.

"Drakey!" she cried into the handset.

Matt Drake started to laugh. "Same old Alicia. Ay up, we're missing you over here. Team's just not the same without your . . . panache."

"Shit, that's a big word for a Yorkshire dimwit."

"I have more. How about élan? Flamboyance? You still there?"

Alicia saw Crouch glance over. "The boss is giving me the evils for being on the phone at work. You know how it is in gainful employment."

"Can't say that I do. And Hayden says she's fine by the way. Almost back to normal."

"I was going to ask." Alicia pouted.

"Listen, before you left we were starting to hear rumors, stories filtering through about a nasty new group. Some kind of secret organization called the Pythians."

"I remember," Alicia said. "We believed they were recruiting hundreds of mercenaries from all over the world and trying to put some very high-profile objectives in place."

"Yeah, well, they appear to be the kind of secret organization that just doesn't want to stay secret. Reports are popping up from Tokyo to Los Angeles—"

"Something about Pandora wasn't it?" Alicia interrupted.

"We haven't nailed it down yet. The whole thing's just . . . very fluid. And that's the problem, and why I chose to call you. Something this fluid, this fast, means it's about to happen. The fuse is about to be lit, Alicia, and it's gonna blow big. Every major government has raised their threat level *without* an ounce of direct information. War cabinets are being called. The airwave chatter is so high they've drafted in twice as many men to cope. I wanted to warn you."

Alicia covered the handset and repeated the information to the room, more directly at Crouch. Their boss nodded.

"Ask him if Argento is involved."

Alicia mentioned the Interpol agent's name.

Drake affirmed. "Yes. The SPEAR team is heading this one up, but every country has their own way of doing things, of course. And every country has a team. And Interpol," he sighed. "They have bloody dozens."

"Stick with Argento," Alicia said. "He's good and if he recommends any team it's safe to say they'll be one of the best."

"How about you guys?" Drake asked. "You ready to fly anywhere at a moment's notice? This thing is global."

"Sure. As soon as we find the treasure."

"Good. Stay safe, Alicia."

"You too."

Alicia ended the call and spoke into the abrupt silence. "Seems there's more going on in the world than our little treasure hunt. Who woulda known?"

"Drake," Russo said wonderingly. "Isn't that your old . . ."

Alicia turned a fiery gaze upon the man. "What?"

"Boss?"

"A loose term but partially true. We worked together in the same unit and then with SPEAR. Drake and I have more than a history together. We shared life and death for almost ten years."

"I've heard of SPEAR," Healey put in. "Good team."

"Best in the world," Crouch said. "And we'll stay on standby for them. Drake wouldn't call unless it was terribly urgent. All that tells me one thing—we're on a brief timetable here, guys. We need to move fast before the real-life shit really hits the fan." He took a deep breath and returned to his notes, a worried frown stretched across his features. His sense of responsibility would not allow him to seek out a five-hundred-year-old treasure whilst friends and soldiers struggled to protect the rest of the world.

"We need to find the rest of our Aztec gold. Now."

TWENTY THREE

Highway 89 snaked through a rolling wilderness, broken in parts by rocky, often vertical buttes, flanked by mountains, lorded over by the sprawling blue skies. Their vehicle, a black 4x4, powered its way toward the Colorado Plateau, jammed full of bodies, equipment and gear as high-tech as underground satphones, trackers and laser field glasses to items as innocuous as suntan lotion and small inflatable rubber dinghies.

Predictably, Alicia was the first to point out the obvious. "Mr. Crouch sir," she said in a small voice. "I'm putting in my protest right now. Either we trim the team or get bigger vehicles. I for one am not overly happy about three- or foursomes on the back seat every time we take a journey."

Russo half turned from the front seat. "Isn't that kind of your forte?"

Alicia gave a mock laugh. "Oh har-de-har. Look who's lightened up since we found a few pieces of gold."

"Point taken," Crouch broke in. "I'm surprised you left it so long before complaining."

Alicia shrugged. "Kinda enjoyed it at first."

Healey unconsciously shifted his leg away from hers. "Ah, not much further now."

Alicia grinned. "You prefer it if Caitlyn and I swopped places, Zack?"

With no answer forthcoming, Alicia turned her attention to the outside landscape. Mile marker twenty-five flashed by and Crouch quickly applied the brakes. At first Alicia thought their boss had lost his mind; no road was visible, but then the 4x4 jounced onto a dirt track, slewing slightly across the gravel.

"A dirt road now?" Alicia grumbled. "Really?"

"Only gonna get worse from here," Crouch warned.

Jose Cruz, ensconced in the cramped but functional rear compartment, cleared his throat. "Excuse me, I hate to be a bother. But I'm quite sure we're being followed."

Crouch glanced at him through the rear-view. "Assuredly. Bastards have been on our tail ever since we left Vegas."

"That long?" Russo whistled. "I only clocked them after Mesquite."

Alicia stared straight ahead. "What are we dealing with?"

"Three, possibly four SUVs and a helicopter. Civilian, unless it's been retrofitted. I'm guessing Coker."

"Just a matter of time." Alicia nodded. "So he picked us up in Vegas? Anyone with the right connections could do the same. You thinking his crime lord boss still wants us dead?"

"Not before we find the gold." Crouch smiled grimly.

"Wait a minute." Cruz's face creased with confusion. "If we know Coker is following us why are we leading him straight to the gold?"

"You should pay attention," Alicia said. "We're following a five-hundred-year-old map, interpreting directions noted down by warriors, not cartographers. And," she smiled, "we're leading them out into a wilderness that we can control."

Cruz shook his head with weary acceptance. "Soldiers," he intoned.

Crouch bounced the 4x4 between bumps in the road, staying clear of the sand and scrub that marked the sides of the track. With the air conditioning cranked up high the car's temperature still rose.

"Damn, if only it coulda been raining." Alicia tapped a side window with a touch of British humor.

"This road could have been impassable if it had been raining," Crouch said. "Don't wish yourself into even more trouble."

Alicia shrugged wistfully, about to comment further when Crouch pulled the vehicle into a makeshift parking lot, empty except for two cars—a white pickup and a sky-blue van. The only structure was a vault toilet; beyond that the flat scrubland stretched immeasurably.

Crouch turned off the car, stretching his back. "We ready?" Alicia exited and walked around the back, slipping dark sunglasses over her eyes. The packs had all been assigned back in Vegas, filled with each person's essentials dependent on their job. Her own mostly contained weapons and ammo; firepower she believed every girl should pack. Well, every girl with her kind of past, present and inevitable future. The days when life surprised her were long gone.

The group hefted their gear and moved out, deliberately paying no further attention to their followers, only the helicopter that could currently be seen in the far distance—a mere speck in the sky. Crouch quietly estimated they had at least a half-hour head start.

"Let's make it count."

A sandy track led west out of the parking lot. Crouch drifted slowly, cross-referencing their position with several incomprehensible scribblings he'd made on his own map.

"It's as good a point as any to make a start," he said. "The Colorado is at our back. I estimated a line between the place where the Aztec warriors' dateline and calendar put their passage across the Colorado to where the subsequent entries ended. According to their notes, the Aztecs followed a strict line in the dirt. Even if we take into account impassable features they'll still have returned to that line, more or less. Yes, the search grid is wide but it's what we have. All we need is to find a single reference point."

"Canyons and rocks of waves." Caitlyn secured her pack with a grunt. "That's our next clue."

"Looks like the right kinda country." Russo eyed the distant mountains.

The track led downhill for a while, turning east as it entered a little wash. The stony slopes made the going heavy and increased the chance of mishap. When Alicia glanced back she no longer saw any sign of pursuit. With the way ahead becoming more demanding she bent her head to the task, reveling in the tough grind to help clear her mind. The future always lay before her.

Walk on.

Steep hiking came next, all the way to the top of a ridge. Healey broke out a large bottle of water and offered it around. A tiresome sun burned down. The ground was pure rock, mountain country, offering the questers no clues.

"Technically," Caitlyn said, looking back the way they had come. "You could call that a canyon."

"More a crack," Cruz said. "A stitch. But I admire the wishful thinking."

"Trail splits ahead." Crouch pointed. "We'll cut left, I think. The right-hand trail veers away drastically from the route I've mapped."

Taking his words as their cue to continue, the team moved out. As they walked, Alicia turned to Caitlyn. Though reassurance was not normally a weapon in Alicia's arsenal their newest recruit had been through enough severe adversity of late, enough to warrant an exception.

"I heard it mentioned before that many other treasure hunters have sought out Montezuma's treasure. Now, I understand where we're different, having the old warriors' notes at our disposal but surely at least *one* of the prospectors should have come close to finding it."

Caitlyn bobbed her head, black hair ruffled. "One man in 1914 brought photographs of petroglyphs from Mexico, convinced that they stated the treasure had been brought here, an instruction from the old Aztec priests. Skeletons were soon found, even staircases cut into the rocks—later attributed to the Anasazi, but no treasure. Another location was Three Lakes, where men ended up scuba diving, attesting that they found a man-made entrance at the bottom of a lake. The men never returned and the find was later denied by locals." Caitlyn shrugged. "Truth? Conspiracy theory? Locals with Aztec ancestry protecting their heritage? Nobody knows. Montezuma's treasure is as much a grand old fable as the Holy Grail and the actual Pacific Treasure Island. Before Michael came along the most accepted story was the one where a struggling and well-liked prospector and his wife were shown a cave of riches by local Indians, allowed to leave with a cache of the treasure, but blindfolded so they would never be able to find the cave again. Apparently, the prospector had saved the life of one of the Indians' wives. The man settled close by but never did find the cave again. Now, that area is at the junction of two rivers—the Colorado and the Virgin, and since that time the Hoover Dam has been built . . ."

Caitlyn paused for effect.

Alicia finished. "Leaving the cave underwater?"

"Actually under Lake Meade." Caitlyn shrugged. "Perhaps it was a whole different treasure. Who knows?"

Alicia nodded at their leader. "He does."

"You're that confident?"

"I've worked with Crouch a long time, mostly indirectly. If he said the Holy Grail was hidden in the Ghost Train ride at Blackpool Pleasure Beach, I'd follow him inside."

Caitlyn laughed as the team went east, spying several rock domes on the flats way below. Staying on an eastern heading the trail again dropped sharply. Another wash claimed them from view for a while, the dry creek displaying not even a trickle of water today. Alicia knew that in times of rain it could fill treacherously fast but saw no danger in the blazing sunshine that was starting to creep down the sky vault above.

"See that ridge?" Crouch said as they again ascended. "It's slickrock. We head that way. Keep it in your sights."

Using the ridge as a marker, Alicia trusted to their boss's instincts and research sense. If he was winging it he was doing a good job of hiding his speculations. All the while he and every other member of the team kept their eyes glued to the landscape, searching for rocks of waves, canyons, mushrooms and arches, but the lines of the poem were as ambiguous as a politician's election promise. After a few more moments Russo spoke up.

"Damn, I just spotted Coker's team. They're on top of the first creek bed, heading our way." He pocketed his small pair of Steiner binoculars, infrared lens still flashing. "Bloody bloodhounds."

Crouch pursed his lips. "All right," he said. "Then we go to plan B." He sent a private smile in Alicia's direction, knowing exactly who the phrase reminded her of. "A few more miles and then we stop for the night. We'll grab a few hours' kip and then head out when it's still dark and whilst they're still snoring."

"Break camp?" Healey asked. "They'll surely have a scout on us by that time."

"Leave the camp in situ," Crouch said. "And risk that we'll find what we're looking for before we need it again."

"Couldn't we just—" Alicia made a sniper's shot with her fingers. "You know."

"I want no further loss of life on this trip," Crouch declared. "We're hunting treasure, not lives."

"And if they don't feel the same way?"

"Then I guess that's a whole different story. But we will not fire first. Understood?"

"Sure."

As they approached the slickrock ridge, Crouch pointed out the best place to make camp; one with a narrow ravine at its back that offered a covert escape route under cover of darkness. Risky, he confirmed, safety-wise, but the forecast was for no rain throughout the next several days. The team made a show of setting up several makeshift tents and lighting a small campfire as the sun began to wane in the west. Russo and Healey were assigned to keep a close but surreptitious eye on their followers,

151

in case Coker's crew suddenly decided to come in for a closer inspection, but the ex-Ninth Division soldiers soon reported the formation of a similar camp a few miles away.

Alicia made her way to the top of the ridge as the western horizon became a broad, fiery expanse of vibrant color but it was the bleak land below that drew her attention. The land was uninhabited, wild, free. With freedom came a particular loneliness; it had been the darker side of the pendulum her entire life. Cut loose and leave those who cared about you far behind or stay with them and feel limited. Would she ever learn?

The train of thought brought more recent complications to the surface. There had been a time a few months ago when she thought an old flame might be rekindled, the one man that had held and impressed her year upon year, a man that offered limits she would like to be a part of, but then *his* old flame stepped into the breach.

Alicia sighed. Who knew what the future held? Treasure? Pandora? And after that?

She turned her back on the freedom in front of her as she saw into its true heart, noted the wrenching seclusion, and made her way back to the companionship offered by her team.

As the campfire flickered, waxing and waning across the assembled faces, Cruz suggested they tell old ghost stories. Caitlyn blinked and Crouch fixed him with a stare before realizing the Mexican guide was joking. If they'd had time Alicia would have liked to quiz Caitlyn further, to dig into the real reason behind her leaving MI6 at such a young and promising age; she might even have liked to get to know both Healey and Russo a little better, but now wasn't the time. Their little sham was working; nobody from Coker's team had ventured closer than a mile since they set camp, most likely thinking they wouldn't be crazy enough to set out through this wilderness at night.

It was Crouch's only thought. The maps he'd brought were explicit in their detail of the land's topography—they wouldn't fall down any unexpected canyons and despite dangers like quicksand, deep stitches in the ground and a hundred other pitfalls—and he remained incredibly determined to continue. The discovery of the Aztec gold was now within his grasp—just one of many boyhood dreams that had chased him down the years, unending, magnificent in its scope and, until quite recently, just another vision out of reach. A fantasy.

Some people dreamed of fast cars. Island paradises. Movie celebrities and music stars; youthful aspirations and goals that faded as the weight of the world grew heavier with every passing year. Michael Crouch's somewhat sentimental dream had never waned within him—he was a treasure hunter through and through.

Allowing Coker to simply tag along and lead him straight to the Aztec gold was not a possibility.

As soon as he deemed it murky enough, Crouch signaled to the team. Nobody had slept; the tension was simply too high, the risks too great. Sleep could wait until tomorrow. With adrenalin pumping, the five men and two women crept through the narrow ravine and over the slickrock ridge and into even deeper darkness, using the silvery moon and starlight to guide them. Crouch took several moments to regain his bearings before continuing.

"Slowly now," he whispered. "One slip and we're done for."

"You really think those bastards won't have seen us?" Lex wondered.

Alicia glanced speculatively toward Russo and Healey. "Not if these two fine soldiers did their jobs properly."

The camp had been veiled, disguised to match what the enemy would expect even down to lumps in the sleeping bags. The gamble had been played. They were all in now. The backside of the slickrock ridge was unexpectedly steep, falling at a far sharper angle than the front. After a quick consultation Crouch stuck closely to the line he'd already drawn, bearing south.

"Stay as high as you can," he passed along the line as they traversed the ridge. "The further we descend the steeper the fall." Alicia stuck to the narrow path, taking great care where she placed her feet. The going was made harder by the vistas that opened up to every side, temptations offered with each passing step. After ten minutes of cautious walking, Crouch stopped and pointed ahead.

"See the large mountain? That's where we're headed."

"You sure?" Cruz sniffed, gazing back and forth with more than a little skepticism. "One place looks pretty much like any other out here, especially in this light."

"Of course I'm not sure," Crouch snapped, the tension of the situation getting to him. "But we have to trust the old warriors. You of all people should know that. And for the rest of us— mostly soldiers—the notion of following their lead is nothing more than natural."

Cruz bent his head. "We're just following in the footsteps of thousands."

"That we are," Crouch said. "But even now no official trail of this region is provided to hikers. They are left to navigate and fend for themselves. The entire area is a challenge where travelers must find their own route. It's very common for people to get lost and never find the landmark they're searching for."

Alicia checked on Lex. The biker, along with Caitlyn, was struggling more than a little, but the terrain ahead was starting to ease somewhat. With more time to scan her surroundings, Alicia looked to the mountain ahead, noticing for the first time the long, vertical crack in its side.

"Well, that's a great landmark," she said, nodding. "Surprised the Aztecs didn't use something like that."

Crouch shrugged, still staying high on the ridge but walking easily now. "Perhaps it's too obvious?"

Russo, who had been trailing behind, now caught them up.

"No pursuit," he said. "I figure we've gained at least an hour on them. If all continues like this we should pull out two or three."

Crouch nodded, not stopping. Using flashlights at the more awkward places, the team continued south, alert for anything. At this point, Crouch wasn't particularly worried about missing a clue or even the treasure itself—the line he had drawn through the map pointed toward many more hours of travel yet. They squeezed past the sandstone slabs, bearing toward the marker, and passing two large buttes not surprisingly known as the Twin Buttes. Crouch checked the land's layout, directing them to the right and through yet another wash. Caitlyn swigged from a bottle of water and again recited the poem out loud.

"As if we could forget," Russo grumbled.

"One thing I've learned is you can't be too prepared," the young woman said. "Because whatever you do—life will surprise you."

Alicia again wished they had more time. Caitlyn clearly had something she was struggling with. The one good thing about their new situation was that Healey was staying close—maybe the two younger members of the crew could help each other.

Across to the opposite side of the wash they circumvented two multi-colored domes, the whole team in awe of the area's beauty, its natural wonder. Alicia imagined the Aztecs wandering this way for the first time and being party to so much idyllic scenery—perhaps they'd imagined they'd been blessed by their gods after so much toil and travel. Maybe that was why they secreted their heritage out here.

The sandy path now continued in an upwards direction, passing by the domes and entering a new section of the land. Crouch forged on ahead.

And suddenly stopped, switching his full beam on for clarity.

"Oh my." His back was stiff, frozen. "This . . . is more than unnerving."

Alicia slipped around him to investigate, then stopped in

stunned disbelief as many flashlights lit the scene. Before them lay a phenomenon unlike anything she had ever seen. Depressions and hills in the rock were formed of thin ridges of undulating, wave-like patterns, eroded by time and runoff and wind ripple. The rolling forms appeared to blend into each other, one vivid, colorful sandstone swelling rolling into the next.

"Fantastic." Caitlyn said. "Carved by the elements."

"It sure is stunning," Healey said. "See how the whole landscape rolls."

"Not only that," Crouch breathed. "It is our 'rocks of waves'."

Caitlyn smiled. "The first landmark. Though I guess it's not exactly definitive."

Alicia studied the many-hued chutes, marveling at their permanent yet eternally fragile appearance. This was the wild earth revealed in all its splendor, a dramatic piece of isolated beauty.

"Once you've experienced something like this," she said. "How will Oxford Street ever look good again?"

Russo eyed her. "Somehow you don't strike me as a girl that shops on Oxford Street."

Alicia narrowed her eyes. "Nah, but I might actually strike you."

"Next, the Shield Arch," Caitlyn said. "Which is more of an Aztec reference don't you think?"

Crouch picked his way carefully through the small canyon. "I agree, since their shields were quite distinctive. Let's keep moving. We couldn't do better now than to get this landmark at our backs to help throw Coker off our scent."

Continuing past the phenomenon and down the far canyon the group resumed their march. Time passed, measured only by the sound of their own breathing. The night began to wane, giving way to the early beginnings of a superb sunrise. By now the canyons and washes were beginning to blend in to one another, but Crouch kept them on as straight a course as possible. Arches did indeed grace the surrounding landscape, but none that resembled a shield, and none even close to Crouch's planned route. Down a scenic canyon they walked, stopping to drink from a trickling spring situated to their right. After that Crouch pointed out a fault-line crack in the canyon and matched it to the plotted course on his modern map.

So far, their route matched the one originally taken by the old Aztecs.

More fault lines passed. If this were rainy season they'd be walking downstream, or worse. Other canyons branched into their own and at each one Crouch took a good look around, searching for the next landmark.

Eventually, he paused.

"So this is Paria Canyon," he said. "Which makes that—" he indicated an open seam to their right "—Wrather Canyon." He stared toward its extremes. "Do you see that?"

Alicia peered hard as the sunrise made a heady blush of the horizon. Not far, possibly no more than a slight kink away from Crouch's hand-drawn line, stood a high arch. Alicia squinted.

"The Shield Arch?"

"It's the closest yet to the shape of an old Aztec shield and the only one on the right path." Crouch nodded. "The Wrather Arch I believe it's called."

"Is it on our route?"

"Within a hair's breadth, I'd say. Either way it's the only arch on their route so far that's shaped like a shield."

"Wait." Caitlyn had advanced further into the canyon and was peering hard around its natural curve. "There's another. And another. In fact, they all pretty much look the same."

Crouch moved to her position. "All right," he said in a rather lackluster voice. "Let's take a look."

Arches were common to this part of the world, Alicia soon realized. Caitlyn soon pointed out several more as they gained a higher position.

"The Wrather Arch is still my favorite," Crouch said now that they stood beside it, gazing up at its truly amazing formation. He motioned back toward the trail. "And only a moment's walk from our trail."

"How can you be so sure the trail stays so perfectly straight?" Healey asked.

"In truth, I can't," Crouch admitted. "Except for the expertise of the Aztecs themselves. If they wandered through this desolation, we're lost. But then *so would they have been*. Making their route arrow straight worked in more ways than one, including as a form of backward navigation. I repeat – the Wrather Arch is the closest to our trail—I say we count it as a clue."

Despite the doubt, Alicia felt the excitement creep into her gut. "What's next?"

"But heed our warnings to the mushroom rock."

Alicia peered ahead. "So what the hell are we waiting for? Treasure this valuable doesn't just find itself."

TWENTY FOUR

The canyon soon began to widen, Crouch marveling at the emerging layers of sandstone that continued to make a miracle of the surrounding rock. The miles lay behind and before them, but despite their lack of rest none of them complained of weariness. Yes, the treasure had been waiting five hundred years, and no it could not wait a moment longer. Crouch kept in touch with their benefactor via satphone, carefully arranging their protection and cover for, if and when the find was made—another secure measure in place to negate the effects of Greg Coker and his trailing band of mercenaries.

They negotiated some large boulders that had all but blocked the canyon at some time in the past; an obstruction that might put off all but the most ardent of explorers. Beyond the boulders the slight trail grew into the closest thing yet that resembled a path, twisting away from the broken walls of the Paria and on into the distance. The path turned and bowed but always came back upon itself, following Crouch's line closely enough that he didn't feel the need to call a detour. Canyon walls rose and fell to each side; buttes and washes dotted the way, natural springs burbled along time-bled stitches in the rock.

Alicia saw the mushroom-shaped rock first. She stopped and pointed to the right and at the same time Crouch gestured to the left.

"Is that—" Alicia began.

Crouch stared. "A mushroom shaped hoodoo!"

The formation stood hundreds of yards off their track, spiraling up through the wilderness. Nevertheless, a side canyon slid through the rock towards it. Both Healey and Russo started down the narrow ravine, but a few words from Crouch stopped them.

"It's not right."

Caitlyn frowned. "Because it doesn't follow your path?"

"Exactly."

Now even Alicia felt a touch of frustration. "Michael, it may not be arrow straight. The hoodoo is exactly what we're looking for. Let's check it out."

Crouch wrestled with the problem, a dozen emotions crossing his face. "Damn. All right. Let's take a look."

The team threaded their way through the high rock walls, Russo taking the time to watch their backs. "Coker's men could trap us down here, guys, if they wanted to. It's a great place for an ambush."

Alicia grinned. "Sure, John Wayne. Just lead on."

It took almost a half hour to reach the hoodoo, the shape lengthening and rearing up higher with every step they took toward it. The narrow canyon gradually widened, its walls spreading out as its floor lost much if its steepness.

"Bloody hell," Crouch moaned. "We're nearing the valley floor."

"If that's the hoodoo," Caitlyn pointed out. "Then where's the 'warning'?"

Alicia recalled the poem. *Heed our warning that leads to the mushroom rock.*

The team stared into the extensive wilderness, so great that all four directions blended into one gigantic expanse. Alicia circumvented the bulky spire, studying its rocky surface and the floor to all sides. If there had been other boulders or twisted formation close by, she would have examined them also, but the hoodoo stood in its own splendid isolation.

"There's nothing," Healey murmured, following her around. "Just . . . nothing."

Crouch turned to gaze back up the canyon they'd traversed. "And nothing the way we came," he said. "No wall writings. No caves. Is this where it ends then?"

Alicia squinted at him. "That doesn't sound like the Crouch I know and love."

"To put it bluntly – we're winging it here. One wrong step and the entire mission is thrown out of whack. What if this is that step?"

"We go back to the last place we're sure of." Caitlyn said. "The rock waves."

"If we're thrown off the path this easily—" Crouch paused.

"Just remember the arches," Lex said with a shrug. "We didn't find just one. I'm damn sure there are a hundred of these friggin' hoodoo things out here."

Crouch stared at him. "I guess you're right."

Alicia noted the downcast faces, the questioning frowns and saw for the first time, a pall of uncertainty and doubt falling across her team. "It's ultra-important now that we stay strong," she said. "Keep to our faith. God knows how many times I've said that to myself over the years, but belief is everything. Right now. Right here. If we trust in ourselves that we can do this, we *will* do it."

The team chalked it up to a misstep and scrambled back up the canyon, this time going against the slope and finding progress hard. Russo and Healey ranged ahead, alert for any sign of Coker's men. By the time they reached the spot where they'd strayed from Crouch's 'perfect' line, they were sweating and irritable.

"The next person who says we don't follow the line," Crouch growled. "Stays in the desert. We follow the age-old philosophy: 'Your best guess is always your first'."

Alicia didn't respond, and was glad to see Caitlyn holding her tongue. The team took a short break for water and a quick scout of the terrain toward their rear and then started forward once more, following the twisting path. The ridge line dipped and rose, wound left and right, led them past breakneck plunges and across narrow rims. The canyon wall widened and narrowed with every turn, constantly undulating, until even Crouch himself began to wonder if this were the correct path. Twice more he took out his improvised map, doubting himself, wondering where they could possibly have gone wrong.

Perhaps the rock waves weren't in fact part of the land formation they'd already found. What else?

Then, an abnormality in the rolling formation of the canyon walls caught his eye.

"Look here," he murmured.

The team gathered around. Crouch indicated the canyon wall to his left. A series of orange figures had been carved into the dark brown wall; men, women and animals with curved horns drawn all in a row. The people had arms outstretched and bent at the elbows, the bodies elongated and the legs strangely short. Other creatures may have existed there at one time—faint depictions of turtles, dogs and snakes that had all but eroded by now. The row of figures led directly toward an altar where a figure lay prostrate, a priestly man with a dagger upraised above him, blood running from its blade.

"A warning?" Healey wondered.

"That leads to the mushroom rock." Alicia drew their attention to the formation ahead. "This, more than anything yet proves we're back on the right track."

Crouch eyed her speculatively. "We hope." The man's confidence had taken a severe beating after their wrong turn.

The rock arrangement was called a hoodoo—a thin upstanding spire, narrower through the middle, carrying a wider, almost block-like structure at its apex. A mushroom pillar. It rose out of the lands below, impossibly balanced, both a testament and a defiance of the elements that formed it.

Crouch and Caitlyn barely gave it a glance. "Then beyond the known territory of the braves," they said in unison. Crouch gave the surrounding lands a shrewd frown.

"All this rock," he said. "Is known as Navajo limestone. The

Colorado Plateau, this part of Arizona, is made up of it. All the lands around here once belonged to the Navajo Indians—whose warriors were often known as braves. The Aztec warriors themselves would have respected the title."

"Going back to the petroglyphs." Caitlyn nodded at the rock drawings. "The Aztecs are notorious for their belief in human sacrifice. To them it was a religious practice, simply the cultural tradition of the peoples of Mesoamerica at the time. It might not mean anything."

"Priests." Russo shook his head. "Always blood-letting at the heart of religion."

Caitlyn blinked. "Not true. If you're referring to today you're referencing gruesome fanatics twisting religion to accommodate their vile needs. In ancient days the priests believed the gods sacrificed themselves so that man may live. The Aztecs, under pain of death, said 'Life is because of the Gods; with their sacrifice they gave us life . . . they produce our sustenance . . . which nourishes life'. What they're saying is that ongoing sacrifice sustains the universe."

"Sacrifice in all its forms." Alicia surprised herself by joining in the debate. "Not just physical."

Crouch pointed past the mushroom hoodoo. "Navajo. Hopi. Beyond those lands and past the terraces the old map changes its measurements from the Aztec representation of passing days to one of footprints." He smiled even wider. "We're almost there, my friends."

"But how far do the Indian lands stretch?" Lex asked, the ever-present worried expression turning his young face into a middle-aged man's.

"Not far." Crouch checked his maps. "I have current and past versions right here. Beyond the flatlands there, where the ground starts to rise." He pointed at the middle distance. "That's where they end."

"Doesn't look very hospitable," the biker grumbled.

"All uninhabited," Crouch affirmed. "No roads. Barely a trail. We're already past any known site previously claimed for Montezuma's treasure. Seems the old prospectors didn't look far enough."

"Or deep enough." Caitlyn thought about Lake Mead and then shrugged. "But not to worry about that, eh?"

The team trudged on, dropping further into the lowlands with every step, now being pounded by the rising sun and lack of shade.

"Just great," Lex complained. "Perfect. We get the high cold mountains at night and the low hot desert during the day."

"Stop whining," Alicia sizzled back at him. "Unless you want me to spank you in front of all these folks."

Lex blinked quickly and shut up, savvy enough to take Alicia at her word. Crouch grinned at them both.

"Smart man," he said. "I wouldn't put anything past our Alicia."

"Sun's not fully risen yet," Russo pointed out. "If we hoof it we can probably get among those small mountain rises ahead before it does."

Crouch led the way, picking up the pace as they entered the expanse of flatland. Green and brown shrubs dotted a hundred twisting sandy paths. In one place a tiny river turned into a mini-waterfall as it suddenly fell into a round man-sized hole cut into the rocky ground—just another remarkable natural spectacle.

As they approached the rising mountains, Crouch slowed and stared at his map. "So we're nearing the end of the lands of the braves. Up next we have 'among the terraces'. Out here . . ." he scanned their surroundings. "I'm lost."

"Great observation." Alicia bobbed her head, blond hair flying. "Out here—everyone's lost."

Russo passed among them. "We have company."

"What?" Lex almost turned to scan their rear but Russo, thinking him the one most likely to turn and give the game away, placed a huge arm across his shoulders.

"Don't be a dick."

Alicia also hugged into Lex. "Big unit?"

"One man." Russo shrugged, almost lifting Lex off the ground with the simple action. "Must be a scout."

"But he'll be in radio contact." Alicia said, thinking about what had to be done. Ahead, Crouch stared up at the layered mountain as it rose up out of the desert, each fifteen-foot-high level a large step of pure jagged rock jutting toward them in wedges.

Alicia knew they had to draw the scout in. If he was any good he'd be in constant contact with Coker, have eyes on all their party in case someone suddenly vanished, be fully armed, and might even have a secondary spotter further back.

"No choice." Crouch also seemed to be computing the scenario as he stared up at the multi-ridged mountain. "We have to capture him. It's the only set-up that buys us time."

"How long would the cavalry take to get here?" Caitlyn wondered. "If you pushed the button now?"

Crouch smiled at her. "Out here, Caitlyn, that's a beautiful analogy. They used to film all the old westerns here and over near Kanab." He seemed lost for a moment, the sentimentalist in him taking over. Alicia imagined what it must have been like watching the legendary Audie Murphy, John Wayne and Alias Smith and Jones gracing the silver screen.

"Michael?" she prompted gently.

"Oh yes. Well, it would take them an hour to mobilize and reach us. But I can't push the button until we find something definitive. The resources involved in steaming to our rescue in sufficient force are tremendous and it's not just about money. Entire units and groups of men and women have to literally put their lives on hold to make this happen properly."

"I get it," Caitlyn said. Alicia knew Crouch wasn't just talking about cops or soldiers, he was referencing Aztec specialists around the world, important security professionals that couldn't afford to order an operation on bad information, key members of the World Heritage Committee, even Interpol would have an interest in Coker and his boss and were ready to lead an operation of their own in conjunction with the United States.

"Oh my God," Crouch suddenly breathed, still staring up at the ridges rising out of the desert, and then repeated more slowly. "Oh . . . my . . . God."

Alicia raised an eyebrow. Crouch wasn't exactly known for his proliferate cursing. Now what?

"It's the mountain," he whispered. "It's formed of fucking terraces. Look!"

Alicia looked up. Something that had been staring them in the face all the way across the flat desert now became apparently obvious. The line of the poem ran through her mind—*among the terraces*—making her heart soar as yet another clue presented before them.

Lex grunted. Alicia realized it had actually been an exuberant shout but thanks to Russo's arm—as thick as an anaconda—the cry had escaped as little more than a mumble.

Crouch almost fell to his knees, the only thing stopping him the knowledge that Coker's scout was undoubtedly watching them. He knew they'd already lingered too long. "Drink break," he said. "I need some time. Just grab a perch and take a break."

He refrained from breaking out the map, its contents already committed to memory. Still, he wanted to. He was a man of paper and files, and pen and ink; pre-Android. Yes, he could navigate his way around a mainframe universe with the best of them—but he didn't really enjoy it. Comfort was holding the evidence physically in his hand, not something encased in plastic, metal or rubber.

Among the terraces,
Look between Hummingbird and the Ritual for your final guidance.

The guiding line he'd drawn, now firmly in his mind, dissected the cliffs in half. They should stay on track. He would leave the problem of Coker's scout for Alicia and her crew to take care of. He took a swig from a water bottle and motioned Caitlyn across. "Any ideas?"

"Only that the Ritual clearly points toward the Aztec belief in sacrifice. Ritual bloodletting was an accepted norm at the time, as customary as vacation time and Sunday trading hours are to us."

Cruz took over, remembering his lessons. "The Ritual stems chiefly from their primary god, Huitzilopochtli, god of war and symbol of the sun, built around a belief that every day the young Aztec warrior must banish from the sky the creature of darkness using the weapon of sunlight. But every evening he fails and the creatures are reborn. He needs sustenance for his fight and his diet is human blood."

"And the people accepted this?" Caitlyn wondered. "Their fathers. Sons? Daughters?"

"The priests were a powerful ruling body," Cruz said. "As were the kings. As the Aztec empire grew it ensnared more captives for human sacrifice. The increase in captives led to the need for more war. And retellings of gruesome, bloody ceremonies strikes terror into the hearts of their enemies."

"A long-used method in the art of war," Crouch said.

"Indeed. I have read that when the great pyramid in Tenochtitlan was enlarged in the fifteenth century the resulting ceremony and celebration comprised of so much killing that the lines of victims stretched out of the city and the massacre lasted four days. You think the Spartans were hardened and bloodthirsty? They had nothing on the Aztecs."

"Non-stop sacrifice," Crouch said. "And all to their gods."

"But how does the Ritual help us now?" Caitlyn wondered

Cruz shook his head. "I don't know. Perhaps we'll find an altar up there. But an annual reaping of twenty to fifty thousand victims clearly means something to these people. And with most of them being sacrificed to Huitzilopochtli, the sun god, it is he who is of most importance."

Crouch eyed the rising sun. "I have a feeling we should hurry. What more do you know of this sun god, Jose?" The boss rose, packing his water bottle away.

"My Aztec knowledge is unfortunately limited," Cruz admitted. "Gleaned through only a few months of lessons under Carlos, browsing and speed reading. The Nahua tribe and their old ancestors are not my only job function, you know. And they had so many gods—" He shook his head. "Only a professor that devotes his life to their history would know more than a smattering about all of them."

Crouch gave Caitlyn the eye. "Perhaps you could help?"

The young woman produced a tablet computer. "Equipped with the best signal boosters money can buy, though no doubt we'll get a better signal out here than in Marble bloody Arch."

Crouch shrugged into his pack. "Ready?" he called out, enquiring with that one word as to how they were planning to deal with the scout.

Alicia gazed on ahead. "He's about thirty feet behind us. Used our snack time to creep up. He's good, but not as good as us. Start climbing those . . . terraces, sir. We'll bag him."

Crouch set off, eager to stay well ahead of Coker. The rocky terraces didn't pose a problem to the climbers, despite jutting out one above the other and rising for hundreds of feet; their sides were crumbled and eroded, and angled to provide enough purchase for scrambling—a technique not without its hazards but not terribly dangerous.

Crouch went first, pointing out the safe purchase points. Caitlyn paused in his wake, allowing tumbling rocks to pass her by before starting up. Lex came next, employing a similar tactic, and then Cruz; leaving the three soldiers to bring up the rear. Laughing aloud, Alicia shoved Russo ahead with an ass-jab that made the big man squeal. Healey declined her gracious extended offer and motioned for her to precede him. The scout behind would have no idea they knew of his presence.

On the first terrace, Alicia confirmed their suspicions were real. As they moved from its front to its back where the mountain rose, they effectively passed from the scout's sight. Three terraces and they had carefully monitored his progress, learning his habit. On the fourth Alicia spoke quickly.

"Who wants to do it?"

Excitement lit Healey's eyes and even Russo's. Good soldiers. Alicia felt a similar eagerness to enter the fray. The battle called to her as much as it had to the ancient Aztecs. Maybe soldiers never changed.

"Rock, paper, scissors?" Healey suggested.

Alicia groaned. Out here, among the stone terraces, on the trail of Aztec gold and with armed enemies at their back, the youngster wanted to play a game. So be it. Quickly she thrust her hand out three times and then held it palm down, the accepted sign for paper. Both Healey and Russo held out clenched fists.

"Whoa," Alicia said. "I think we found our first battle contest. And I won."

"Not next time," Healey said a little hotly. Even Russo looked like he wanted to complain.

"Tell you what," Alicia said sweetly, patting Healey's cheek. "Complain to your relevant politician. But don't mention his expenses."

With that, counting in her head, she pulled on the rope attached to the piton they'd fastened into the rock wall to double-check its safety, and then ran hard toward the edge of the terrace. Without a sound she leaped into thin air, sixty feet above the desert floor, and used the rope to swing out then back in toward the lower rock wall. A brief memory flashed through her mind— about the last time she'd fought using ropes during the Bones of Odin quest against Matt Drake—and then her body was jockeying to change the position of her flight as her feet kicked out, slamming into the chest of the stunned scout. The man folded instantly and stumbled back into the mountain, not even a grunt escaping his broken chest. Alicia let go of the rope, landing lightly and at a run, reaching him before he had a chance to draw a weapon.

"Surprise!"

She hefted him over her shoulder and threw him back toward the cliff edge. The man landed in a tumbling heap, reflexes finally catching up to his predicament and arresting his roll. By then Alicia was on him once more, lifting him by the straps of his utility jacket until she could stare into his eyes.

"Radio?"

The scout struggled in her grip, surprisingly strong. Twisting sideways he moved until the rising sun flashed and blinded her, pushed away and drew a knife.

"Won't matter," he said in a thick South African accent. "Boys are coming."

Alicia heard the scramble as Healey and Russo made their way down the slope from the terrace above. She debated waiting until the sheer force of numbers intimidated the scout into submission then decided it just wasn't in her nature.

"Let them come," she said, striking at the knife-hand with one arm and the neck with a flying foot. "They'll last about as long as you."

The knife hit the gouged, rocky floor with a clatter; the neck jerked sideways. The scout fell to his knees, grasping for the deadly blade. Alicia drew one of her own.

"Come nicely," she said. "Or I'll feed your carved bones to the coyotes."

Healey and Russo arrived, the latter bouncing off the rock wall, the former staggering as his foot caught in several deep channels cut into the ground. Exposed up on the terrace, Alicia had no time to dither. Her peripherals also noted the arrival of Crouch, Caitlyn and the others but her concentration focused solely on the scout and his whirling blade. The first thrust went under her arm, the second across her chest, missing by less than an inch. Alicia stepped in and broke the arm, now hitting hard with her own knife, jamming it into the soldier's ribs to the side of his vest. Eyes opened wide, still uttering no sound, still coming at her, she drove the knife in again for good measure.

This time he staggered.

Alicia let go, allowing the body to fall heavily away. Healey and Russo raced up.

"Took your damn time."

"It was that or fall off the bloody rock," Russo returned, indicating the edge.

Crouch arrived with a worried frown plastered across his face. "I'm seeing bodies."

Alicia stared out across the open plain, toward the distant hills where they had traversed Paria Canyon. There, antlike, were Coker's crew, heading this way, purposeful and plentiful.

"I guess an hour, maybe more," Crouch said. "Depends on how much this guy managed to tell them. *We're nowhere!* We're here, but we're nowhere. Might as well be trolling around Vegas."

"Hey," Caitlyn called, staring down at them from the ledge fifteen feet above. "According to the Aztec scholars Huitzilopochtli was the god of war and the sun. Remember the greatest Aztec treasure—the Wheel of Gold shaped like the legendary Pieces of Eight. Well, that was a representation of him, that obviously upped its value. Huitzilopochtli required a blood sacrifice, not always in the form of human martyrdom. Sometimes a ritual bloodletting was used."

Crouch stared up at her, the rising sun at his back. "What does that tell us?"

"The Aztec's also called him the Hummingbird."

Crouch swallowed drily. The poem's last line stormed through his head—*look between the Hummingbird and the Ritual for your final guidance.*

The sun god and sacrifice.

Slowly, he turned around, saw how the rising sun developed, extending its rays in piercing beams, spectacular in the dawn. He saw how the fiery blush of the sun played against the walls of the mountain as it rose, marking a straight line as perfect as the one he'd drawn on his map.

Oh my God.

The straight and accurate line, their headstrong route of travel, had been a clue.

Then his mind switched to the Ritual and immediately sent his gaze downward to where the scout's body lay at their feet, bleeding.

Blood trickled along rivulets that had been carved into the rock floor, seeping toward the mountain's rock wall.

"Between the Ritual and the Hummingbird," he said. "I know where the treasure is."

TWENTY FIVE

Crouch scrambled at double speed up toward Caitlyn and let out a shout of exultation, quickly tempered.

"Rivulets, tracks in the floor, have been cut on every ridge," he said, inwardly berating himself for his outburst. Though stupid, even as he rebuked himself he knew exactly why he hadn't been able to hold the enthusiasm in.

Here was the culmination of a lifelong dream, a ridiculed fable he'd proven to be true, a treasure found that a murdered and imprisoned culture had once owned and lost, a vanished heritage that attested to their true greatness.

Spurred on by urgency and desire he raced for the next slope. "We have to find the one that leads to something more than the face of the mountain."

"Between Hummingbird and the Ritual." Caitlyn fixed the line of the rising sun in her mind as she pounded after him. "Between that line and these channels . . ."

Alicia and the rest ran in their wake, the force at their back immaterial now. What would happen was inevitable. Crouch needed his proof to initiate the call for help. When Alicia chanced one more glance at their backs she saw Coker's force traversing the far slickrock ridge and two small specks above them, birds in the sky.

"Bollocks," she intoned. "Coker has at least two helicopters with him."

Russo kept his head down. "As soon as he realizes the scout's been neutralized he'll send 'em in. Shit."

Above them, Crouch reached the fourth, fifth then sixth tier of rock. The older man was starting to pant. Caitlyn disregarded etiquette and pushed at the small of his back, helping him over the more awkward parts. The seventh ridge passed and they were nearing the top, over a hundred feet high. Still, the rock face was solid, offering no sign of a niche, cave or even a tunnel in the floor.

Alicia, Healey and Russo caught up to them. "Still nothing?"

Crouch scaled the final slope, breaking free of the ascending mountain and emerging onto a wide rocky plateau. Before them a spacious escarpment ran back toward the ridged beginning of some expansive upland terrain, stretching as far as the eye could see.

Crouch wilted. "No. There's . . . nothing here."

Caitlyn felt her own passion wane. "But these grooves were made by somebody." She kicked at the dead-straight furrows. "Oh dear, the sun isn't as direct up here."

As she said it, the line of the rising sun, clear against the mountain wall, had expanded and dissipated across the open landscape, making the Aztec's guidance almost impossible to follow. It was only because she'd fixed the spot so firmly in her mind that she was able to point in all seriousness to the soft ridge that led to the plateau ahead.

"The troughs end right there."

Crouch moved forward, every step a battle as he fought against elation and failure. When he closed in on the small ridge his steps grew smaller, less frequent. Any moment now he'd have to admit that their quest had been unsuccessful.

But we found the initial treasure . . . the words were already formed on his lips.

Maybe there was another cave, another room back there. Maybe it had been found previously and the sheets of gold left abandoned—its secrets lost between warring treasure hunters. Maybe . . .

The minor ridge was solid, a knowledge that fell heavily on his heart, but then he realized that it ran at a slight angle away from him and was formed of a series of bulges. They'd have to walk its entire length to check around every one.

Luckily, the grooves pointed them straight at the right one.

Caitlyn skipped past Crouch, unable to contain her high spirits. Alicia was merely surprised that Healey didn't follow in her wake. When the girl bent down and then looked up, her face shiny and bright, she made Crouch's heart skip a beat.

"What is it?"

"A narrow entrance, made against the rock wall and against the natural angle. Without the clues we followed this hole would be almost impossible to take seriously."

Alicia reached the girl, staring down. The narrow hole was barely wide enough to admit a man, clogged now with debris and practically unnoticeable. There was something very cunning about how it had been formed *behind* the natural angle of the ridge; a person's eyes would automatically follow the regular line.

"No time to waste." Crouch fell to the floor and started to use his hands to dig out debris. "Spread this out in as regular a manner as you can. Coker won't find this hole without help if he tried for a thousand years."

In minutes the hole had been cleared and Crouch was chest-deep inside. Alicia evaluated the scene at their back, seeing nothing but the two distant specks in the sky, perhaps moving closer now. Crouch soon disappeared and then Caitlyn, Cruz and Lex. Alicia eyed the two remaining soldiers, none of them overly pleased about wriggling into a hole in the ground.

"Rock, paper, scissors again?"

"Fuck it," Russo grumbled. "I'll go."

"Ah, shouldn't you go last?" Alicia asked innocently. "Since you're more likely to plug up the hole. I mean that in a good way."

Russo ignored her and struggled through. Healey jumped up next and then Alicia grasped the edges and slowly lowered herself down. The curve of the hole fitted against her body like a small chute. She slid along carefully, using arms, elbows and knees to grip the sides. When she glanced up the last thing she saw was a small circle of daylight, blue wilderness sky unbroken by cloud or vapor trail.

Then, the darkness.

Crouch shone a flashlight over her as she located her own. In addition to the handheld version, she carried a weapon-fixed and head-mounted variation, the latter of which she also employed now.

In the glare of many flashlights, the age-old blackness reluctantly brightened. Dust and untouched debris coated the floor. Already the cave was larger, both ceiling and walls beyond reach. Crouch illuminated their surroundings.

"Nothing to see," he pointed out. "Probably intentional in case anyone happened to stumble into this place by accident."

Alicia read his mind. "Which means we've a long way to go and no hope of getting out of here before Coker arrives. How far down does that phone signal of yours reach?"

"I guess we're about to find out."

Time played tricks with their minds as they descended. Minutes felt like hours as each twist and turn, and even each footfall, needed careful attention. The initial shaft brought them into a sub-chamber that could be exited only through a similar tunnel. With no more clues to guide him, Crouch was thankful the chambers hadn't been littered with a warren of tunnels. The tunnel fell at a comfortable angle until he estimated they'd dropped a hundred feet and were heading back toward the desert floor. It also occurred to him that each ridge's set of troughs actually pointed toward this hidden place—a guide or a frustrating obstruction devised by the ancient warriors?

Still lower, and now the angle evened out, leading them into the heart of the great primordial mountain. The moment their going became easier, Crouch pointed to a carving on the wall.

"The first sign," he said, "that our crazy quest is almost at an end."

Alicia gave the picture a passing glance, taking in the now familiar stick figures and accompanying snakes, spears and swords. No doubt that these people were warriors and made of the hardest metal. Flashlight beams flew across the rock all around her, the sounds of their footfalls echoing through the surrounding perpetual dark. She might have imagined a deep feeling of isolation when trekking hundreds of feet below the earth, but the team she'd become a part of were close and the bonds they'd already formed were already easing her burden.

A dozen feet more and an archway materialized out of the gloom, its uprights covered in symbols.

Crouch heaved a great pent-up sigh. "This is it."

TWENTY SIX

Beyond the archway there were no more secrets, no more pretense. Gold and gems, wealth and riches glittered in the lights of the flashlights as if a thousand campfires had suddenly been lit. Piled high around the chamber, stashed against the walls, a nation's fortune beyond imagining lay in opulent abundance, catching and reflecting the new light with an eagerness that matched that of its discoverers.

Crouch fell among the strewn treasures. "This is so much more than I imagined."

Alicia moved to his back, mouth open, still trying to wrap her brain around the sight before her eyes.

Caitlyn said, "It's . . . wonderful." Tears deepened her voice.

Alicia stopped trying to take it all in and focused instead on one area at a time. Here were Aztec gold coins, heaped, stacked and amassed in endless dunes. Over there was a huge lifelike solid gold alligator head, snarling in the shadows. Bird and snake sculptures occupied one entire corner of the vast chamber, only now revealing its scope as Lex and Cruz ventured further inside. Cruz was practically crawling, stunned, eyes shiny with pride, amazement and undiluted awe.

To her right sat objects studded with gems; emeralds, rubies and garnets of deep hue. To her left dozens of double-headed snakes. Masks of silver and deep turquoise lined the way before her, guides that formed a path through endless wonder. Ceremonial figures stood around the walls, clutching staffs, spears and swords formed of beaten gold.

Crouch found his feet. "I guess that now the cavalry can be called."

"Wait," Caitlyn said, reveling in the moment. "Just wait."

Crouch didn't need telling twice. Like an old pirate, gold

digger or a treasure hunter from ancient days he dug his hands into the stack of gold coins and threw them into the air. Alicia couldn't keep the smile off her face.

Then Cruz cried out and the whole team looked up.

It wasn't through fear, it wasn't pain or doubt; it was through that which he finally beheld—the wonder of all wonders.

There, fixed to the black rock at the rear of the chamber, hung the greatest treasure imaginable—the Wheel of Gold—and it was indeed a wonder, shaped like and as bright as the sun. The god for which it had been formed sat at its center, the circle around him made up of glyphs with square, triangular and circular shapes creating the outside, eight of them, which was how the cartwheel had earned the nickname—pieces of eight.

Intricately carved, gloriously finished, the Wheel of Gold was a wonder itself, but as a part of this vast treasure—mindboggling.

Caitlyn made her way to the back of the chamber, staring up as if in worship. All around her the Aztec treasures sat in state as they had for half a century; lost, lying spellbound in the darkness, a richness of wasted energy and effort, taken by chance, time and vicious circumstance.

"I don't mind saying I doubted you, Michael," Alicia said. "But after this . . ." she shook her head.

"First time out." Crouch couldn't tear his eyes away from the Wheel. "We all had a few doubts. But now . . ."

Healey and Caitlyn stood together, as close as possible without touching. Alicia blinked in wonder as the treasures that surrounded them seemed to catch fire, gold reflecting light.

"They should reproduce this cave for the eventual display," she said. "It would make a great spectacle."

Crouch shrugged himself into life. "Yes, yes, and we should get moving. Coker can't be far behind us. He dug around for the satphone.

"How's the signal?" Cruz asked him.

"Non-existent. God knows how far under the rock we are."

Their boss looked like he might never want to leave this place.

"Well, if we ever want to see sunlight again," Russo rumbled, "the way is up."

Lex, the only one of the team who had remained quiet during the staggering discovery, backed toward the cave entrance. "Yeah, and I guess even I can lead us out since there's only one path."

Alicia, engrossed in the surrounding riches until now, suddenly fixed the biker with a calculating stare. A small revelation hit her—that ever since they'd arrived in London she hadn't had much time for Laid Back Lex. Small wonder, since she'd been put in charge of a new team and had been trying to prove she was worthy. Earning the respect of soldiers was one of the hardest things in the world. Alicia had moved everything else in her life to the backburner in order to lead. Not to fit in, she could never do that, but to become accepted as a team leader. Factor Lex and his moods into that and you eventually fashioned a ticking time bomb. On a good day Lex was self-destructive, stand-offish and aggressive. Alicia originally took the man under her wing after dozens of his friends were killed in action, determined at some level to save him from the terrible downswing she knew his exploits would begin to take. At least by her side, she could control his behavior.

Time to re-evaluate.

Instantly forgetting the treasure she moved to his side. "Let's go."

Lex eyed her. "What's your deal?"

"No deal. I said let's go."

The biker had to be handled just right. Too much compassion would make him hostile. Too small an insult would make him suspicious. Alicia wondered briefly what the hell she was doing. Caring really wasn't in her nature.

Something drove her. An instinct that said now was the time to learn how to become a better person; now was the time to shine.

Their entire future would soon change. And not because of Aztec gold.

Thinking of Crouch and his new venture, of Matt Drake and his woman, Mai Kitano, of the world as it was and how it might become, she ushered Lex out of the chamber and made sure the others were following. Russo came last, not through awe but because Caitlyn and Cruz lingered until the last possible second and had to be coerced. Alicia watched Caitlyn stumble into the rock wall as she stared transfixed at the receding horde of riches.

"Don't worry," she said. "It'll still be there when we return."

TWENTY SEVEN

Daylight hit them like a direct blow to the brain, stomping in on their awareness and making Lex bite into his lips, knowing he couldn't make a sound. Alicia had already appraised him of the various punishments for giving their position away, none of which were pleasant and only two sounded of interest.

Alicia poked her head out of the hole, eyes squinting. The rock plateau was empty to the west, running all the way to the flatlands with little cover. By inching her body forward she managed to survey the open land that led back toward the stepped escarpment.

"All clear," she said with more confidence than she felt. As bodies started to crowd around her she snapped. "Wait!"

Scanning the skies for the metal birds of prey was not enough. She had to inspect the area, cast a trained eye over the hard ground and the eroded ridges; test for a dozen other disturbances and study the lands. Despite the relative openness of this place Coker could still have placed a sniper or two out there and man-sized delves and nooks were everywhere, courtesy of the timeless elements.

Even Crouch peered around her. "See anything?"

Alicia sighed. "To do this properly I'd need another fifteen minutes if you're prepared to wait."

"Well, not really."

"Can't you . . . call the cavalry?"

"Of course." Crouch disappeared from view.

"Wouldn't it be easier to just stay in the caves?" Cruz wondered.

Russo fixed him with a stare harder than a Death Valley rodent. "We're soldiers not fucking rabbits."

Alicia stepped out, then crouched down, alert to every movement. Russo covered her back, Healey stepped out to the flank. Two minutes of careful reconnoiter inspection yielded nothing.

Crouch returned. "All good. Once they got over their shock and excitement they agreed to send help."

"I really don't like this." Alicia never took her eyes off their surrounds. "Coker *should* be somewhere around. Unless he's a total incompetent he surely saw us reach the top of the cliff."

"Maybe he's still climbing," Caitlyn said.

At that moment Alicia's eyes were temporarily blinded by a sudden silvery flash that came from the distant hills near Paria Canyon. "Damn, he's got a scout out there."

Almost instantly, the roar of powerful engines signified the close proximity of the two choppers, though Alicia could still not see them. Her judgment needed to be fast. Return to the caves and become potential rats in a trap, also leading Coker straight to the gold in the process, or make for the rock terraces and flit among them like deadly ghosts.

"Come on!"

She raced out of hiding, Russo waiting for the others to break cover before following. The team ran hard, realizing their lives probably depended on pace right now, and made the edge of the plateau in less than a minute. Alicia pulled up, Lex at her side, as a panther-black helicopter rose up right in front of her, so close that the features of the pilot could clearly be seen through the tinted cockpit glass.

Alicia didn't miss a beat, veering to the side as the chopper hovered. Like a suddenly unblocked stream the rest of her team followed, Russo and Healey raising weapons in warning to their enemies.

The second chopper reared up, shooting over the top of the cliff and roaring above their heads. To a person the team ducked, but the metal bird passed in an instant, already hovering and lowering slowly toward the plateau they had just vacated.

Alicia reached the slope to the side of the first jutting wedge of rock and scrambled down its length. Her eyes registered no surprise as a dozen men came into sight, clearly positioned and waiting for her. As one they raised their weapons, but Alicia had no intentions of being captured.

Ever.

Sliding down the last few feet, she plucked her handgun from its holster and picked off the first three men. She crashed into the next two, toppling them like skittles. Behind her Healey also opened fire, his bullets finding men that were firing themselves. His shots struck first, spinning their bodies and sending their bullets against the mountain or into the skies. Then he was also among them, making himself their priority as the rest of his team still came down the slope.

Alicia disarmed a man with a handlebar moustache before hurling him off the cliff edge. As her eyes flicked momentarily down she saw more men gathered on the ledge below. A quick count put the number at six but she couldn't be sure. That left the rest of Coker's crew and the man himself probably up top on board the choppers. Her team was well and truly boxed in.

Crouch was among them and struggling with a big merc whose face bore the tattoo of a dragon. Russo was torn between covering their rear and wanting to join the fray. So far nobody was following them down from the plateau above but it might only be a matter of time. On the other hand Coker could already be inside the treasure cave . . .

Russo grabbed Lex, jammed a pistol into his hand, and yelled, "Watch our backs!" Then raised his gun and took aim. A bullet slammed into the rocky outcrop at his side, another skipped along the channeled floor. Alicia threw a second man toward the valley below. Healey fought hand to hand with a stocky man with a bright red face. Crouch stumbled and went under his opponent, taking a heavy blow to the side of the head. Russo relieved him of his burden with one bullet and saved Healey from being knifed in the back with another. Then shock jolted him as a bullet struck his side, smashing like a hammer into the flak jacket he wore. He staggered, almost dropping his gun, but fought through the pain and surprise to regain his feet a moment later.

Looking up, the world had turned red.

Surprise hit him, followed by bewilderment and uncertainty. All this passed in less than a second and then it was the barely remembered feeling, the bursting, raging need to cause chaos, bringing it all into focus. This was a feeling he'd only experienced once before, years ago. It was the craze of a berserker falling over him; the turmoil of violent battle had suddenly become his best friend. Back then it had taken over, consumed his soul, winning the battlefield and saving most of his comrades but making a blight of the place he used to call his heart.

Not now. Not again. Whatever the circumstance he wouldn't let it destroy him.

Bellowing with rage, an outlet, a red-hot steam vent, he pounded the ground like a man trying to bring down the mountain. Gradually, the red receded. Pure battle hatred ebbed away, leaving his gut and chest full of bile. At last his eyes cleared.

Lex was beside him, covering whilst he recuperated.

"Thanks, man."

Lex grunted. Russo breathed hard. Alicia dropped a third man over the edge, this time making sure he fell among his climbing colleagues. The trick gained them precious minutes.

"Other side!" Crouch suddenly yelled.

Alicia saw it immediately. As they plowed their way through the mercs on this ledge and more scrambled up from below, the descent on the other side of the rock ledge, though steeper and more dangerous, was clear. Coker had positioned the majority of his men up top.

She engaged another merc, forcing his gun arm down and between his legs before head-butting under his chin, the force of her blow lifting him off his feet. Stepping in she hurled him over her shoulder, toppling a second man and the last that blocked her way to the other edge of the ledge. With cold indifference she placed bullets in the two men that otherwise would have had no compunctions in killing her.

Crouch materialized at her side. "Risky," he said, looking down.

"My fucking middle name. And our only chance. Even then they'll be right behind us."

Alicia turned, beckoning the team over. Healey dealt with the last merc even as a bullet whizzed close to his skull, fired by the climbing enemy force.

"Quick!"

Alicia whirled and jumped through the air, landing hard amidst a pile of shale and rock dust, slipping and sliding down the steep slope. There was a good reason they hadn't chosen this side of the mountain to ascend. Steeper, with a sheer drop to the left and strewn with sharp-edged bits of rock and potholes, debris and partly eroded edges, the way down was unjustifiably perilous. Alicia's intent in sliding down first was to at least clear some of the dangerous rubble out of the way. She would trust in her own catlike instincts to stay on the path.

Down they slithered and slipped, not even Caitlyn or Cruz slowing them up; a team connected by more than a little esteem and a vast burning desire. Alicia gained the second ledge down and hit the rough slope again, kicking timeless elemental wreckage from her path. From above came more shouts and then a familiar voice blared down the mountain.

"Crouch! For God's sake!"

Alicia paused, slowing. Peering over the top ledge was Greg Coker, his eyes squinting into the blinding sun.

"What the hell's your deal, man?"

"Stop. We can talk."

Crouch turned slowly, staring upward. "From what I hear, Greg, the best thing for you to do right now is step off that cliff."

Coker looked momentarily shocked, then tried to wipe the expression off his face. He failed. "I could really use your help, Michael." After a moment he seemed to realize how that sounded and added, "To find the treasure."

Crouch seemed to think about Coker's double meaning. "Then find a way to talk to me. But it sure as hell isn't going to be through a bevy of dumb mercenaries."

Coker's expression softened as he appeared to absorb that. "Stop or die," he said without missing a beat. "That's what the man in charge wants me to tell you."

The team continued downhill. Crouch answered for them. "Without us you'll never find that treasure."

"He's willing to take the chance."

Alicia snorted. "Yeah, that figures. Senseless, irresponsible silly crime lords. They're all the fucking same."

"It's the power," Cruz said at her back. "Being from Mexico I know a little about them. More than I'd like to."

Crouch urged them on. To Coker he said, "It's your choice, Greg, but at the moment you're definitely playing for the wrong team."

Coker's face disappeared quickly, replaced by others and then the cliff edge above was bristling with guns. Alicia darted underneath the next outcropping, followed by the rest of her team, only Russo at the back having to dodge between bullets.

"For a big man you're even slower than I'd imagined," Alicia told him as he rolled at her feet.

Russo jumped up and dusted himself off. "Stop flirting, Myles. You ain't my type."

Alicia sputtered, momentarily dumbstruck. It wasn't often a gibe caught her off-guard but Russo's had done the trick. Before she could retort Russo and Healey were returning fire.

Crouch nodded. "Good. We need to remind them that it's not worth their while to fire down this mountain side."

A screaming body tumbled past their little refuge, arms and legs flailing. Alicia listened as a lull interrupted the clamor from above. "All right. Time to move."

Again they ran, Healey and Russo covering their flight. It took all of Alicia's concentration and skill to clear a path, stay safe and ignore the peril at her back as she descended the mountain.

Outcroppings—what the Aztec had called terraces—slipped by at a rapid rate and the valley floor grew closer with every passing minute. Twice more the mercs above attempted pot shots and twice more Healey and Russo dissuaded them. After a while their enemies must have decided that pursuit was the better option; the trained soldiers could move faster than Crouch's team.

Russo called along the line. "At least nine to a dozen still chasing us."

Alicia surveyed the floor of the valley, now huge and startlingly close. Sunlight bounced off the rocks and filled her forward vision. For all the tech Crouch and Caitlyn had brought to the team, the one thing they had forgotten was bloody sunglasses.

Still, it had been a wild ride since leaving Mexico.

Just how she liked it.

Gaining the flat ground, she immediately unslung her weapon and covered her team's race to safety. Once they passed her she turned to run as Healey in turn dropped to one knee. Running this way, shielding each other, they traversed the exposed ground, moving more slowly but in a far safer formation. Crouch made them zigzag their run and drop behind random boulders, further confusing the pursuit. Alicia reminded them that Coker had left at least one man positioned back at Paria Canyon.

"Then it's the Colorado." Crouch pointed off to the left. He knew that America's great river snaked within a few miles of this position and, although inaccessible for much of its length, offered two manageable staging areas not far from where they were.

"Satnav it, Caitlyn," he said. "We haven't a moment to waste." As she worked and ran he put in another call to the authorities.

Alicia took her turn once more, protecting their escape with a few well-placed shots. Ahead now another ridge line became visible, a mini-cliff that formed the higher banks of the Colorado at this point. Caitlyn guided them toward a break in the ridge, where satellite photos had earlier revealed a viable route down to the river. More of a plan D, Alicia had never expected to be white water rafting during a treasure hunt, but those that adapted quickest survived. Or so she believed.

Reaching the top of the incline, and with Coker's men about a quarter of a mile in their wake, Alicia swung her pack around and unfastened one of the zips. Dragging out a soft object in a bag she readied herself for the upcoming maneuver. The dinghy would inflate automatically and she'd have to be inside it by the time it hit the river. There were three dinghies between the team, the others held by Crouch and Healey.

Alicia slid between the upstanding rocks, each spire craggy and pockmarked, worn with age. The moment they dropped out of sight of their pursuers the team didn't waste a moment, spurring on and wrenching out their durable dinghies, first reloading and then stowing away guns and electrical equipment. Below them, the dashing waters cut their way through the canyon, running narrow and fast and not without risk here.

The team inflated their dinghies and Caitlyn and Cruz, Lex and Russo jumped headlong into the crafts as Alicia, Crouch and Healey held them as steady as they were able. Water smashed against the side of the canyon and splashed back into their faces; the low, narrow boats bounced from trough to trough, unguided at first. Alicia gauged their distance from their pursuers as they paused beside the river.

"If they have dinghies they'll be right at our backs."

Crouch's phone rang. With a laugh and a finger aimed toward all the gods of inappropriate timing, he unzipped his pack, unwrapped the phone and put it to his ear.

"Yes! This better be bloody good!"

Alicia tried to guide their dinghy whilst watching the enemy. After a few fruitless minutes she gave the primary task to her boat's other occupant, Laid Back Lex.

"Keep us away from the friggin' rocks."

"Oh thanks, never would have thought of that!"

"Belligerent bastard."

Alicia felt her heart sink as Coker's mercenaries broke out rubber dinghies of their own, flinging them easily into the water and jumping aboard. Within a few moments there was a hot pursuit down the Colorado, bullets pinging and whickering through thin air and bouncing off the sides of the canyon.

Crouch's shout drowned out even the automatic gunfire. "No way! You've got to be fucking kidding!"

Alicia again found herself shocked by the man's outburst. The stresses of this expedition and the weight on his shoulders might be bigger than running the Ninth Division, but still Crouch was not a man partial to nonsensical flare-ups.

The news had to be bleak.

Crouch shouted into the phone, his words lost as a hail of gunfire pounded into the approaching rock wall and Alicia screamed at Lex to adjust their course. Raging waters sprayed and splashed to every side of them. A moment later, Crouch, in the lead boat, turned to shout.

"Our recovery team's been grounded," he cried, his words bitter with disbelief. "Sounds like someone in charge was paid off. They're effectively buried for now with no idea when they'll be cleared."

As if in answer, Alicia ducked under another onslaught. Coker's goons drew closer. Now their flight wasn't just about staying safe for an hour, it was about returning to save the treasure too.

And they were going the wrong way. *Fuck!*

"Someone stopping the recovery team isn't simply about grounding a chopper," she told Lex quietly. "The authorities were en route too. Military maybe. Who can call off that kind of rescue operation at a moment's notice?"

"The President?" Lex struggled to keep them away from a midstream rock cluster.

Alicia pouted, taking a face full of water. "You've clearly never met him. And shit, I didn't mean anyone of such importance. I'm thinking more local. I've come across my share of corrupt politicians in my time."

"Shocker."

"Point taken. Police then. Army. Do they have a mayor of Arizona?"

"How the hell would I know?"

Alicia gave up, knowing Lex wasn't exactly in the mood to talk and, for now, was probably right not to. She concentrated on shouting directions as Coker's men heaved closer and the stream quickened, dropping through a series of narrows with white water cascading over the sides at every twist and turn.

The front of their dinghy smashed hard into the left rock wall, rebounding and losing momentum. Alicia staggered. Lex paddled hard to align their course. A bullet skimmed off the surrounding waters, skipping over the waves. Alicia decided enough was enough and returned fire, though the ever moving craft blew even her careful aim to bits. She began to think the best way to score a hit was to bounce a bullet off the damn canyon wall.

Ahead, Crouch let out a warning cry. Alicia gave up the potshots to take a tight grip of the side straps as their dinghy plunged through a set of rapids. With the bows dropping at an alarming angle the team simply held on as their crafts fell and crashed through churning water, their back ends skimming to left and right. Alicia felt them being bounced from rock to rock, fizzing across rapids, controlled by the torrent. With a huge jolt they hit the bottom of the sudden drop and found themselves in calmer waters.

Crouch used the reprieve to bark an order. "A little further up to the right," he shouted, "is our second potential entry point. We need to use that now as an *egress* point and get back to that mountain!"

Alicia fired once more as their pursuers hit the rapids, claiming a lucky shot as a bullet ripped apart a plummeting dinghy and spilled out all three of its men. Before she could utter a word their enemy's first dinghy was upon them and Crouch was shouting about another, worse set of upcoming rapids.

"Time to fight or die," she told Lex. "And earn my respect, biker boy."

TWENTY EIGHT

A crazy melee broke out on the waters of the Colorado River. A man leaped from his dinghy to Alicia's and found her hands at his throat. Struggling to bring any skill to bear in the constantly shifting craft she bore down on the man, tripping him and holding his head under the water that swilled at the bottom of the boat. Sputtering, he punched out, catching her with a blow to the ribs. Lex smashed at his head with a paddle. The dinghy nosedived down another furious cascade and a second man scrambled up the side of their dinghy, scrabbling for purchase. Lex crabbed over to him just as the dinghy veered to the right through the fast-moving water, sending him onto his back. Their enemy's dinghy was keeping up through the rapids, bumper to bumper, a third man inside now somehow standing upright and aiming his pistol.

He vanished in a spray of blood, taken down by Russo in the next dinghy. Alicia held her assailant until he stopped moving, then looked up . . .

Straight into the eyes of the second man, now climbing up over the side of the dinghy with a knife clasped between his teeth.

Alicia glared. Then Lex barreled across her vision, striking the man and taking him over the side. At the last moment Alicia managed to grasp Lex's trailing leg, then held on as his body was pummeled by the mini-waterfalls. The dinghy fell directionless, spinning around. Alicia felt its momentum finally arrested and looked up.

Russo had a good hold and was pulling it after his own, toward the bank. Crouch and Caitlyn were already there, the former resting on one knee and using the solid ground to improve his aim.

Alicia heard the screams as Crouch put an end to their pursuit.

"Now," he said. "Let's go grab our treasure."

*

The journey back was swift, a straight run across the already darkening flatlands. Crouch figured that the Paria Canyon lookout would have relocated by now, and if he hadn't then the game was well and truly up. But it was all they had left—seven brothers in arms racing through the twilight to save one of the grandest treasures ever found.

From shrub to shrub and boulder to boulder, from rocky terrace to rocky terrace; straight up treacherous slopes and across ridges that bordered on sheer drops, they gained the top of the mountain, tooled up and prepared for battle.

It wasn't difficult to find Coker's operation. It wasn't tough to spot his guards. The man had clearly gone 'all in', seeing the treasure as a way to some kind of freedom. Both choppers were on the ground, gently whirring, surrounded by a rough ring of armed men. These men smoked and talked and looked bored, as if they'd been there all day. Beyond them lay the hole in the ground, and out of this emerged more men, carrying a selection of gold and jewels. They were not laden down, nobody struggled; it was as if Coker had instructed them to take a cross-section of the loot.

Crouch indicated they lie low. "In a way it's good that Coker didn't come well prepared. He can't take all the treasure."

Cruz looked aghast in the shadows. "Whatever he takes it's a shameless theft. The only people it belongs to are the Nahua."

Alicia placed a hand on his shoulder. "The world is full of arrogant, privileged men that believe they may take whatever they want. That's why there's people like Crouch and Russo and I to help permanently modify their thinking."

The team waited and watched as a slow trickle of mercenaries emerged from the hole in the ground, carrying various items toward one of the choppers. Alicia saw bags of gold coins, garnets and rubies; a small statue; carvings and tablets; a wealth of riches seeing freedom for the first and possibly last time in five hundred years. Darkness fell across the desert in all its heavy shrouds. Crouch checked his satphone for messages, saw none and made sure it was switched to silent. Plans swirled around his head, most of them pretty damn desperate.

At last, Coker appeared, panting a little. Behind him, three men carried a heavy object between them, taking great care as if their lives depended on it, shuffling forward only half a step at a time. Even then Coker continually winced at them.

"Careful. Bloody careful there."

Cruz drew an agonized breath. Alicia had to clamp a hand across his mouth to stem the outburst. Caitlyn spoke for them all.

"Oh no. No. He has the Wheel of Gold."

The greatest treasure of treasures was being stolen beneath their very noses.

Alicia made an instant decision. She turned toward Caitlyn. "Go. Now. All of you. Caitlyn, turn on your tracking system. If I can join you later, I will."

Healey's eyes were wide. "What are you going to do?"

"Whatever it takes." Alicia said, checking her weapons by touch alone. "But I won't let this thievery stand."

Crouch knew better than to question Alicia in her very element. He quickly turned and started to head down the mountain, every member of the team turning to stare at her one last time. Russo was the last to go.

"Fight and stay free," he said, touching her with his eyes alone.

"Fight and stay free," Alicia returned with a genuine smile. "Keep 'em safe for me, Rob."

In the next moment she was running, eyes peeled ahead, scanning for targets. In her right hand she cradled her semi-automatic; in her left a small pistol. When the first man saw her she took him out then drifted wide of his position. The sudden tumult in the camp helped her cause. She fired at and felled another three. Coker was shouting, his men starting to panic.

Those carrying the Wheel of Gold went absolutely still, acting like rabbits caught in the headlights. Alicia hit the ring of men hard, shouldering past one and elbow-striking another. Like a dark desert puma she raced, shooting to left and right, darting through one shadow-struck space to the next, until the guards almost shot each other in their confusion.

It was shock and terror, it was a burst of awe-inspiring violence that she couldn't hope to maintain but trusted she could keep up just long enough. Bullets flew everywhere, but not at the treasure helicopter and not near Coker and his carriers. Alicia sprinted in that direction, terrifying the men that couldn't reach for weapons, making Coker's face blanch under the stark lights offered by the chopper.

"You're weak, Coker. So fucking weak!"

Surprisingly his face twisted into a snarl. "You have no idea. You don't have a wife and child!"

Alicia knocked him off his feet, confident now that she wouldn't be shot in the back, and then broke toward the treasure chopper. A man had caught up to her and sought to clamp her throat, but Alicia broke his arm and left him groaning. Another crossed in front of her. Alicia merely helped him on his way, adding enough momentum to send him sprawling. Without slowing for an instant she dropped and slid underneath the chopper, passing below its rounded black belly and clamping the tracker on as she glided past. Up and out the other side she again sprayed a hail of bullets at the guards, scattering their ranks.

Rolling, scrambling, she vanished into the dark.

Coker was screaming. "Load the gold! Load it, you arseholes. I have to get the fuck outta here! And find that bitch."

Alicia crouched down low, a restless spirit at nightfall, enfolded in shadow. Guns lay before her, a knife at her side. To chase her was to die and these men's deaths would be anything but pretty. Breathing shallowly, she waited, listening to their very thoughts reflected in the lights of the chopper through their wary eyes. All emotion, all distraction, was beyond her now, a distant part of the galaxy. Only the battle existed and the opportunity to support her team.

The men backed off, not able to see her in the dark but somehow sensing that their lives hung in the balance. They may be dumb, these men, but they were soldier enough to know a superior predator when they were up against one.

"On! On!" Coker was supervising the Wheel's loading, not paying an ounce of attention to anything else. When the gold was packed he clambered aboard. All the remaining men immediately jumped into the second chopper and loaded the wounded, some hanging off the skids, ready to chance a mid-air fall rather than Alicia Myles.

Within moments the choppers lifted off, the monster from the dark now at their backs, her reputation enhanced to the nth degree.

Alicia moved out, determined to catch up to her team. The chase wasn't over yet.

TWENTY NINE

Crouch spurred the team through the darkness, their way lit only by the barren moon. Caitlyn tracked the choppers even as they thundered overhead. Crouch burrowed through his pack for his satphone, then contacted his best hope.

"Armand? We've been fucked, my friend."

"Ah. If I had a silver dollar for every time I hear that . . ."

"Who do you have in Vegas?"

A pause and then, "It is all good. I have one or two assets as does almost everyone. It all depends on what you want them to do, eh? Tour guide? Traffic cop? Dancer? What do you want with them?"

"I don't want a party planner. I want . . ." he paused. What did he want? Even at this stage he wouldn't risk an innocent's life.

"I need a spotter," he said. "We can track a chopper from this end but when it lands I need somebody to follow it and whatever emerges."

"I have a girl who is not Interpol. Is that good? I have her available at a moment's notice but where do you want her to go? Last time I checked, amico mio, Las Vegas was a big place."

"Truly, I have no idea, Armand. This is a last gasp scenario, but everything depends on this girl and you."

"Ah, another time honored phrase that I love. And 'off book', that is another of my favorites. The Americans won't be pleased if they ever hear of my involvement, Michael."

"They won't hear it from me. And besides, it is somebody in America that is trying to destroy everything we have worked for."

"Well then, in that case . . . leave it with me. Do you have battery enough to keep this line open?"

Crouch checked. "I'll ring you back in five. Oh, and try to find me a man in authority to help secure the rest of our treasure."

"Hmm. Make it ten."

Crouch urged them on, Paria Canyon showing them its multitude of colors even in the gloom, at length becoming the marvel known by the Aztecs as wave rocks. Beyond the canyon and time felt like it was speeding by, propelled by a desert storm. Alicia caught up with them but didn't feel like talking. Her own urgency spurred them to even greater speed.

Crouch shouted up as they ran for the cars. "We have Armand's asset ready to go in Vegas. She's stationed herself behind the Strip, pretty central I imagine. As soon as you get a fix, Caitlyn, let her know." He passed her the phone.

Caitlyn's face was scrunched with the heavy responsibility of it all, her gaze never once lifting from the tablet screen she held rigidly in front of her. Crouch gunned his vehicle out of the parking lot and headed up the track toward a highway; this time nobody complained about the cramped conditions. As they sped, the landscape flashed past, the vault of the night now just another hindrance to their quest.

Caitlyn kept them apprised. "Still on the same heading. Straight for Vegas."

"How far out are we?" Healey asked.

"Too bloody far," Crouch complained, coaxing the vehicle to even greater speeds.

As the miles passed and the tension grew, Caitlyn watched the chopper inch ever nearer Las Vegas. Their asset—a woman called Kate Stanton—promised she was ready to go, her M V Augusta warmed up and her body encased in black leathers.

Lex immediately perked up. "Damn. She's hot."

Alicia opened her mouth to rebuke him, then thought about what had been said. "Actually yeah, she's hot. When do we meet?"

The critical time soon approached. Coker's chopper winged its way over the mountains that surrounded the desert city, dropping fast. Caitlyn took a chance and told Kate Stanton to head immediately east. She reported that she was leaving South Valley View Boulevard and heading up West Flamingo to East Flamingo. Her progress was fast, too fast, as both she and the chopper passed like speeding wraiths in the night, one hurtling through the air and one racing across the ground, prompting Caitlyn's screech of warning.

"Go back!"

Kate's voice was muffled. "Back where?"

"The way you came. The chopper's starting to slow. It's really close to the Strip."

"I can't use the Strip. Too much traffic and too many idiots. Find me a clearer route."

"All right." Caitlyn surveyed the helicopter's wind speed and position even as Crouch found a long stretch of open road and stamped on the gas pedal.

"Use Koval to Sands Avenue. Is that okay?"

"It'll do." Kate grunted. The sound of her revving the bike's powerful engine could be heard by everybody in the car. Lex's face was split into a permanent grin.

Speed dominated the moment. Three vehicles vied for the right to win, to take home the spoils of victory. Caitlyn reported on the helicopter's flight, almost squealing as it slowed and began to lose altitude. Kate's dulcet tones filled the car.

"Give it to me, honey. I can't follow those squeals to a destination."

Healey, leaning over Caitlyn's shoulder shouted directions. "It's the Venetian. D'you see? Treasure Island opposite, LAVO's nightclub there." He jabbed at the screen. "My best guess is they're landing at a helipad, one reserved for guests."

Crouch swore. "Blood money wins again."

"They haven't won yet," Alicia growled, seeing the road dip ahead and a great bowl filled with glittering golden light appear. The city of Las Vegas, a flaming bastion against the dark.

"Somebody will notice all those soldiers climbing out, surely," Lex put in.

"My guess is, they changed clothes," Crouch said without even a hint of sarcasm. "Healey, tell her where the helipad is. Fast. Even narrowing it down to the Venetian means it's still a bloody huge search area."

"Around the back," he said. "The altimeter says they're landing at ground level, so it's not a roof. Is there a road that leads off Koval?"

"On it." Kate revved the Augusta, the result a melody of pure power and exquisite engineering.

"Look to your right. The chopper's down but only just."

"I'm seeing nothing. Shit! Nearly took out a goddamn tourist couple wandering across the road. Wait! I have them."

Silence filled the interior. Crouch jammed his foot hard to the floor. The car twitched in protest. "We're twenty minutes out," he said hopefully. "If I can find a way to navigate the worst of the traffic. Make that forty."

"I can help," Kate whispered back, no longer astride her bike. "I'm standing on the seat, watching over a wall. They don't seem in a hurry. Nobody has surfaced yet. Oh wait, a Venetian security team is approaching them. Now, stay on 95 until you reach Tropicana. Head down there but don't go all the way. Turn at South Maryland, don't let McLeod tempt you—there's a mess of roadworks up there."

As Crouch followed Kate's directions, the rest of the team prepared. Ammo was low, they had a back-up stash in the car and reached for that now. Alicia took a moment to speak.

"Coker and his men are the targets, guys, but be careful. The very people we're sworn to protect will quite probably get in our way out there. Don't hurt them. The damage to your soul and theirs, as well as their families just ain't worth it."

Kate's voice interrupted. "All right. Men dressed in jeans and t-shirts are climbing out. They're all carrying backpacks, except for one man who's pulling one of those suitcases on wheels. A big one. Sucker looks heavy too. He's a big guy . . . and he's puffing like a steam train. Identical. Strapping on and seem to be waiting for someone. Oh, hang on, here's a dude now, kind of stressed looking, waving his arms and barking orders. Yup, they're heading out."

"Where to?" Crouch swung into South Maryland. "We need to know where they're going."

"Damn, this is gonna cost you extra," Kate murmured with a slight grunt.

"What are you doing?"

"Climbing over the friggin' wall. What do you expect?"

Alicia nodded in appreciation. Argento sure knew how to pick his assets.

"Don't get caught," Lex said encouragingly.

"Thanks dude. I really needed that."

Minutes passed. Crouch, following Kate's earlier directions, cut down East Twain to Sands. As the rear of the enormous Venetian hotel and casino started to dominate the windshield he found a parking space and stopped.

"We ready?"

Sporting all the accepted tourist paraphernalia; light back packs concealed in huge shopping bags they'd bought days ago, shoulder bags to conceal small weapons, thin jackets to hide bulletproof vests, and with earbud communications planted, hidden trackers activated, and even disposable cameras with CCTV fitted.

Kate talked them in. As they hurried through the enormous, lavish lobby she reported her observations of the last twenty minutes.

"I caught up with them just as the last was heading into an elevator. Managed to confirm they're on one of the top floors. Beyond that I honestly can't say. I've been scoping out the same set of elevators ever since but nobody has come down."

Alicia approved and said so. Coker's men were unlikely to use a different set of elevators on their downward trip. "You'll have to direct us in. This place is huge."

Kate guided them through the windowless maze. Even now, the team found it hard not to be taken in by their surroundings. The spectacle was mesmerizing. Crouch walked as fast as he dared whilst not drawing attention. He was quite aware of the security stats of this place—at least two thousand cameras, sixty surveillance screens watched over by dozens of guards in a small fifteen feet by thirty feet room; about five hundred VCRs recording even the tiniest action. Eyes were in the ceiling, the walls, the lights. Crouch even fancied they might be in the floor.

Kate was hard to miss. She sat in a relaxed pose, scooping ice cream from a small Haagen-Dazs tub, a floor plan of the casino laid out beside her and a half-eaten burger on a plate from I Love Burgers by her side. Alicia saw the bank of elevators immediately, just visible if Kate leaned to her left.

Crouch sat without introduction. "Great job."

Lex squeezed in beside her and grabbed the burger, taking a bite. "Hey, you don't mind do you?" The biker was already smitten.

"Not at all, dude. Wasn't mine. I was using it as cover."

Lex choked. Alicia frowned at him. "Don't you dare bring that back up, Lex. We're trying to stay under the radar."

Kate leaned back in her comfy chair. Alicia saw a raven-haired woman with locks tied back, slight creases in her face where the helmet fitted snugly and a fit body encased in leather. Her demeanor told the world that she was at her ease but her eyes betrayed a little worry at the sight of all the new arrivals.

"Biggest crew I ever saw," Kate commented. "Except for the one I followed to those elevators."

Alicia shrugged. "They were even larger before we went water rafting and mountain climbing with 'em."

"Either way I'd rather not get in the middle of your playdates."

"Fair enough," Crouch said. "We can take it from here." He eyed the elevators as they swooshed open. "Thanks for the great help, Kate."

"Well, next time I put in a cameo appearance I'd like cash up front." A slight twinkle lit her eyes as she stared transfixed at Alicia.

The Englishwoman returned a sparkle of her own. "Well, we could always offer Lex here as a down payment."

"Ugh. Bikers just don't do it for me. But still, call on me whenever you're in town."

"Be sure to." Alicia showed her teeth.

As Kate moved away, Lex raised his hands in anger. "What the hell were you doing, Alicia? She was just my type!"

Alicia pouted. "But you weren't *hers*. Me however . . ."

Lex stared. "Jesus, that doesn't make her less appealing, you know."

"I know."

Crouch hissed to draw their attention. "We only just made it, guys. Our thieves are exiting the elevator right now, and they have our treasure on their bloody backs."

THIRTY

Crouch rose immediately, more plans than Venetian slot machines chirping inside his head. Coker's men had returned to the Venetian for a reason, a major one. The operation had been full of risk to start with, but to succeed and then bring at least part of your loot and military force into a Las Vegas casino for forty minutes seemed . . . inexplicable.

"The big player is here." Crouch suddenly saw it. "Coker was forced to bring the plunder for that bastard to see, otherwise why not take it straight to an airfield? The South African has to be staying here."

"Two birds—" Alicia began.

"Too bloody right," Crouch said. "I've been messed about one time too many during this trip."

Russo counted men as they slipped out of the elevator. "At least a dozen plus Coker, sir. We're gonna need everyone."

Crouch tightened his lips into a stubborn line. "I won't let this bastard go. Healey, we're leaving you here. Orders are to scope the South African out; survey but don't engage. When we return we'll want enough information from you to formulate a take down. Got it?"

Healey was wide-eyed with surprise and sudden self-doubt. Crouch moved away briskly, leaving him to it, but Russo and Alicia pulled the young man aside.

"Walk the halls. Purchase a room up there. Try to talk to his men. Follow them. Learn their habits. If you can do all of that tonight we might even treat you to a Denny's ice cream." Alicia winked.

"Do what you can, mate." Russo said. "If we had time we'd juice up one of the security team to help, but . . . ." He shrugged.

Coker's team headed out. Crouch lingered beside a bank of slot machines, Caitlyn and Cruz already playing. Alicia gave Healey one last punch for good luck and walked away. Quickly, they tracked Coker's men to the casino entrance for Las Vegas Boulevard, the opposite side of the complex to where the chopper had landed.

Crouch looked mystified. "What on earth are they playing at?"

Caitlyn pointed out the time. "It's almost midnight. I would hazard a guess that they have an alternative method of moving stolen treasure out of the country. Perhaps on the back of an eighteen wheeler to an unguarded coast."

"Good guess," Crouch commended her. "Off the top of your head?"

"I've worked stolen art a few times for MI6."

"But first they have to get it to the eighteen wheeler." Russo parted from the group, keeping their movements as innocuous as possible.

Alicia drifted in the other direction, alone now. She emerged from the casino into a path of glittering lights, the famous Campanile Bell Tower and Rialto Bridge off to her left, a perfect expanse of polished flagstones leading in that direction. Down a set of steps she went, staring at the sights but not really seeing them as the peripheries of her vision were all that she cared about.

Coker and his men dawdled deliberately down the steps, mingling with the crowds, the man with the suitcase struggling. At first Alicia thought they were aiming for one of several parked cars or the taxi rank but then they pointed themselves directly toward Las Vegas Boulevard and put their heads down.

Crouch came in over the Bluetooth connection. "Full reconnaissance mode. Split up. Let's go front and rear. I want to know exactly what they're doing, but stay wary. They may have their own set of spotters in the crowd too."

Alicia put on a surge of speed, meaning to spy on their quarry from in front. Russo dropped back and Crouch stayed at a safe distance, surveying all. Caitlyn linked arms with Cruz and moved to the very back of the men, close enough to touch their backpacks if she'd wanted. Even that close the couple could barely be distinguished from dozens of others. Alicia watched as the man with the suitcase called a temporary halt, moving his hand to get a better grip of the handle, muscles bulging as he started to pull again. As Kate had said that 'sucker' had to be heavy. Or maybe the merc was a lightweight, all testosterone and steroids? Alicia shrugged it off. They would find out soon enough.

Toward Treasure Island and across Las Vegas Boulevard they walked, almost running in their haste, dodging between moving cars and freewheeling cyclists. Coker's men picked up the pace, suspicious to a point but making speed their priority. Alicia leaped over the hood of a car as it braked, then ducked behind another as one of Coker's men turned to stare in the direction of the sudden squeal of rubber. She snaked around the car's rear, emerging as a wandering tourist. Russo and Crouch came together on the sidewalk, the big man noting a McDonalds sign and shouting, "Grab us a burger!" in his loudest voice. The din and tumult of the crowds served to anesthetize Coker's attentiveness, some partygoers even pushing into his men's backpacks as they squeezed by. A boy-racer revved his engine on the Strip, bright lights flashing underneath his car. Crouch used the distraction to drift even closer. If Coker had turned at that point the men would have been face to face.

Alicia wondered if Crouch was hoping for it. They certainly couldn't afford to let Coker escape today.

More tire squealing and happy shrieking split the night; the sounds of the nearby Mirage volcano eruptions resounding above it all. Alicia watched Lex eyeing up a green superbike and hoped fervently that he wouldn't try to steal it. In another moment both Coker's team and her own were entirely swallowed by a huge hen party; girls with names strapped to their backs and faces gaudy with makeup, cackling like a brood of chickens. Most of them carried long-necked bottles sporting straws and small black handbags sporting the name Fendi or Louis Vuitton or Calvin Klein in subtle lettering. Alicia fought her way through as the group were threading between the big pirate-themed Treasure Island hotel and The Mirage along a palm-tree-lined road called Siren's Cove Boulevard. Even with calmer side entrances to Treasure Island the foot traffic along here was less intense, forcing Crouch and his team to fall back. Alicia ranged ahead, using parked cars and the huge amount of foliage to conceal her surveillance, moving like the sleekest panther in the night. As the road widened and led them even further away from the Strip, Crouch's team were forced to hop from concealment to concealment, fleet of foot, staying as low and unobtrusive as possible. Even Alicia ran out of foliage and was forced to crabwalk along a line of parked limos to stay active. Coker's men hustled along, military training giving them a single-mindedness that pointed them only toward their ultimate goal. The road became Buccaneer Boulevard and now the buildings looked more industrialized; even though many of them were signed Mirage and Treasure Island, the sheer quantity of warehouses told Alicia that this was a bit of a woolly area—vague as to its uses.

Pickup trucks were parked most of the way down the road and in parking lots. Small cranes and white trailers stood all around. Alicia saw and heard Coker shouting into a handset as the group approached South Industrial Road, a six-lane road running parallel to the Strip but far easier to navigate.

A tall white van waited at the side of the road.

"Forget the eighteen wheeler," Alicia hissed. "All these goons need is a quiet road and a van."

Crouch groaned. "Damn it. We can't let them get away now."

With a shake of his head and a quick rub to relieve stressed eyes he shrugged off the potential consequences and issued an order.

"Take them down."

Alicia acted instantly, pouncing out of hiding and drawing her weapon. "Stop right there!" she cried, feeling a little foolish and wondering if her surroundings were making her sound more American than usual.

Coker spun around, as did most of his men, only half a dozen steps from the van. In the light cast by the overhead traffic lights and street lamps his face went bleach-white, his frame suddenly flaccid.

"What are you doing?" he managed before his men dropped and opened fire. Alicia ducked behind a palm tree as he shouted, "I won't let you kill them!"

Crouch and Russo came in from the other direction, firing as they walked. Mercenaries screamed and twisted, backpacks crashing down first as they fell backwards. In a moment both Crouch and Russo were among them and a full-fledged melee broke out in the middle of the Las Vegas street.

With the skies as black as a criminal's heart above and vehicles moving slowly past, with the scene lit starkly by streetlamps and the ever-changing traffic lights, Crouch, Russo and Alicia met with Coker's remaining force of men to fight for the stolen Aztec gold. Alicia threw a right and a left, connected with a square jaw, and saw the man drop like a stone. Russo threw an opponent into the side of the van, heard bones shatter and saw the entire vehicle shift. One of the side doors slid aside to reveal even more men crouched inside. With weapons already drawn they hesitated on seeing the open brawl outside.

Alicia didn't give them time to reassess. Firing from the hip, she approached the van, taking out the first two and sending the others scrambling into the shadows. She jumped up onto the passenger side and grabbed hold of the door handle.

The driver stared across at her, alarmed.

Alicia broke the window, but then a man grabbed hold of her ankle, forcing her back to the sidewalk. She quickly put him to her heel and the van roared as it sped off.

"No!" Coker practically shrieked. "Oh no."

Crouch rounded on the man, giving him no chance to start a dialog. He struck again and again, refraining from using the pistol in his left hand but showing no mercy with his fists. Coker staggered back and then sat down heavily, blood coating his cheeks. He didn't even try to stand up to Crouch, but stared with those haunted eyes.

"What have you done?"

Russo launched men left and right like a missile silo. Alicia used her quick, devastating strikes to take even more out, for the most part ensuring that one blow was enough. Some of these mercs were more highly trained than others, but none were her match. The men at their core, four of them, formed a last stand with knives and pistols at the ready.

Alicia was three feet away. She couldn't move faster than a bullet. Crouch and Russo were even further away. With the suitcase inside their circle the last four men still gave a grim outlook to the proceedings even with half a dozen of their comrades sprawled about them.

Coker struggled to rise. "Still a chance," he muttered. "Damn you, Crouch. You were always an overachiever."

"Give it up, Coker."

"Never. It's a stand-off. Walk away."

Alicia flicked her gaze toward South Industrial Road, saw what was coming hard across its flat, gray surface, and winced.

"Shit guys. I'd fucking duck if I were you."

Before anyone could react, the roar of a Kawasaki Ninja blasted out a few seconds ahead of the bright green superbike, ridden hard by Lex, and pointed directly at the heart of the mercenary's four-man circle. It was without doubt the same one he'd been admiring back at Las Vegas Boulevard. At the last moment Lex leaned back, raising the front wheel so that the bike clipped the curb at speed and rose into the air, tires spinning, traveling several feet off the ground and splitting the mercs' formation apart. When it landed the bike spun to the side, sending Lex into an uncontrollable spin. Caitlyn and Cruz ran to him.

Alicia winced but didn't fail to take advantage of the new situation. The flying bike had broken one merc's arm and knocked a second into unconsciousness. The last two were picking themselves up as Russo and she plowed among them. A knee to the face and an ungainly pounce from Russo put an end to their battle.

Crouch rounded instantly on Coker. "You're going to prison, my friend! What the hell are you doing with these maniacs?"

Alicia rounded up all the backpacks and the particularly heavy suitcase. A quick peek inside revealed the Wheel of Gold, a treasure that had been the cause of so much death and mayhem down the years it ought to be drenched in blood.

"My family." Coker's eyes suddenly filled with tears. "He has teams watching them twenty four hours a day. He sends me fucking video updates of my wife taking a shower or my daughter making dinner with her husband. Every day." Coker folded into a fetal position, body wracked with sobs. "I can't fucking . . . stand it . . . anymore."

And he lunged for the nearest gun, snatched it up, and aimed the barrel at his own head.

THIRTY ONE

Zack Healey felt more alone than at any time since being the youngest member of a family consisting of two brothers, a sister, a father and a mother. He'd quit on the family at age seventeen, sixteen years after they'd quit on him. Their father had never been interested, their mother absorbed by her own friends and tea parties; his brothers only ever beat and humiliated him, and his sister found it better to keep a low profile. Only on Christmas Day did they come together, and even then it was a spartan, forced, loveless affair.

A high-school dropout, a video-game freak, Healey needed not only a team but also a father figure to succeed. The luck of his life had been to cross paths with Crouch in the second year of his stint in the Army.

Now, even trained and battle-hardened as he was, the sense of separation he felt on being left behind heightened his feeling of insecurity. Once the team departed all he could do was stare fixedly from left to right for ten whole minutes, the numbness overcoming him. Never had he been left alone before; even on missions through enemy territory the team had always stuck together.

Was Crouch testing him?

When a security guard gave him the eye, Healey progressed to slotting a few coins into a nearby machine. The sound of the elevator doors gliding open refocused his mind.

Coker's vicious boss was here at the Venetian. Upstairs somewhere on one of the top two floors. Speculation would say the penthouse suite but then Healey had never been one to presume. To him life was black and white, not gray. For instance, he didn't just like Caitlyn and want to dart around her for several

212

weeks, he wanted to take her out to dinner, flirt and see if they might have a solid future together. He was only waiting for the operation to end before he broached the subject.

The slot machine sang out. Healey won four dollars. Alicia's suggestions finally came back to him and he figured she might have given him the most legitimate way to scope out the upper floors. He drifted over to the check-in desk and managed to secure one of the more expensive rooms on a low-thirty floor using the team's AmEx card, that was registered to Redway Enterprises. Taking only his shopping bag, Healey marched toward the elevators and punched a button. Rising fast, he fingered the smooth key card, trying to decide on a plan.

The room was vast and lavish, gleaming and clean. He threw his bag on the bed and plonked down in an armchair. After a moment, feeling more tranquil, he decided that this just wouldn't do. His colleagues were in harm's way, fighting Coker. Besides, he should start walking the halls to determine which door his target was lurking behind.

Outside, the halls were quiet and sumptuous, the carpets patterned and colorful. From door to door he walked, excuses on the tip of his tongue in case he were caught, but this game of chance didn't sit well with him.

Despite his surroundings.

He mulled it over. Even if one of the South African's goons did put in an appearance how the hell would he even know? Surely most of the type of people that rented rooms up here, wealthy men and women, had an array of bodyguards—that, once squeezed into a suit, all pretty much looked the same.

Case in point. A door opened ahead and a bald head jutted out, catching the corridor's lights. On seeing Healey, the man frowned, but Healey smiled and sauntered past. A quick glance inside revealed none of the inner room, but confirmed that the man was a bodyguard and carried a gun.

Still didn't tell him anything.

Twenty minutes after leaving the room, Healey was beginning to feel a little incompetent. Already on his second surveillance loop he was thinking the hotel security might be watching him. It wouldn't do to get to the point where they came into his room and found the shopping bag.

He picked up the pace, thinking of Crouch, Russo and Caitlyn, chasing the treasure through the busy, benighted Vegas streets, and he envied them. The thrill was out there. His eyes glazed over as he felt the excitement rise, taking his focus away. A soldier for long enough to know better, but still young enough to be naïve, Healey smiled to himself as he imagined taking down Coker and regaining the Wheel of Gold.

Lucky bastards.

Outside his room, he paused. The sound of heavy footfalls signified at least three men coming along the corridor behind him. Could be nothing. A sudden thought hit him as he stared at the security cameras dotted at intervals along the ceiling.

What had Russo said? *If we had time we'd juice up one of the security team to help out . . .*

"Oh shit."

It hadn't occurred to him until now that the opposite could also be true.

The door opened inward. A gun was thrust into his face.

"Don't move, asshole." The guttural South African intonation made him flinch. "Or I will blow your fucking head off."

THIRTY TWO

Crouch flung his body straight at Coker, risking a bullet to save the man from himself. Crouch impacted hard, knocking Coker to the ground, but the trigger was squeezed and the gun went off with a resounding explosion.

The bullet flew over Coker's head, slamming into a tree three feet to Caitlyn's left. The shock on her face was clear, the evasion much too late. Crouch wrestled with Coker across the sidewalk, the two men rolling down the high curb and into the road.

"Leave . . . leave me," Coker choked out.

"Tell me." Crouch fought for the gun hand. "Tell me how we can help."

"If I die—" Coker grated. "My family will live."

"No." Crouch brought all his weight to bear on the gun and took a punch to his exposed ribs. "They won't. A man like that will kill them anyway for his own pleasure. For revenge. Either that or he'll enslave them."

Coker's eyes, glazed with pain, suddenly cleared and fixed hard onto Crouch's. "What?"

"You know him, Greg. What do you think?"

Coker relaxed, letting the gun drop to the floor. Alicia kicked it away with her foot and drew the men's attention to the sound of approaching sirens.

"Your call, Crouch," she said. "Run or explain. To the cops. But I'll say this—dead mercs, guns, knives, British operatives and lost treasure ain't gonna explain itself overnight. So unless you have some mega-influential suit we don't know about . . ."

Crouch pulled Coker to his feet. "I do as a matter of fact. One of the biggest suits in the world. But I only have one favor due and this situation doesn't warrant calling it in just yet."

"Wow." Alicia blinked. "Must be some favor."

"Oh, he's some guy."

Lex was groaning as Cruz dragged him to his feet. The sirens grew ever closer. Caitlyn and Cruz ran to the backpacks, both of them struggling to heave one onto their backs, while Russo heaved the suitcase up. Lex steadied himself against the palm tree, staring forlornly at the dented bike.

"We ready?" Crouch scanned the area.

"Where we headed?" Russo asked.

"Back toward the Strip," Crouch said. "We'll lose ourselves in the crowds."

Alicia wiped blood from her face. "Is that wise? Doesn't Vegas have more cameras than Canon?"

"It's not the cameras that'll track us, it's the men behind them. And we're better than them. Also, somebody clearly got to the authorities earlier today. So handing over all this treasure—that worries me most of all."

Alicia accepted their boss's judgment. Lex stared wistfully at the Kawasaki. With the backpacks secure and the team's weapons retrieved, Crouch grabbed Coker and urged him into the foliage. "Everyone, move."

"You have to let me go," Coker groaned. "I couldn't live with myself if anything happened to them. If I'm caught—"

"We'll send men to protect your family. My next call's to the FBI."

"But I could work for you from the inside."

"Greg, you're not thinking this through. By now, your South African crime lord—Solomon was his name I believe—knows you failed. The delivery team had to have had protocols and at least one of those would have covered transfer of the treasures to the white van. If you go back to him he will kill you."

"And so will his men," Alicia added.

Coker forced his eyes closed and put his head back. "Jesus, I just can't stand the idea of them being watched. One time, I received a video tape of my daughter searching for her favorite pair of boots. One day later I found them sat outside my apartment, a thousand miles away, with a note reading: 'do as we say or next time it will be her head'. They have up-to-date pictures, video, recordings. It's the creepiest thing I've ever seen. How the hell do you guard against something like that?"

"Normal people can't. Even normal soldiers can't. Fortunately, we're now in a position to take their surveillance apart. Maybe we'll get something on this Solomon in the process."

"One thing escapes me," Caitlyn put in as they double-timed it back up Buccaneer. By the sound of it the cops were already approaching the battle site. To her right Lex hadn't wasted time in grabbing the green bike and was now wheeling it along rather gently. "Why did they choose you? I mean. One man out of thousands. Why you?"

Coker made a face of resignation. "Solomon is nothing if he's not a bottom feeder. The man thrives off people's weaknesses. Mine—gambling. I ran up a bad debt when I was over working in SA, couldn't get out from under it. Solomon bought the debt and suddenly I was working for him. You name it he's into it. Anything that involves gambling with humans or animals. Dog racing and fighting. Underground drag racing. Mixed martial arts where they battle to the death. Word has it that he even staged his own mini-Olympics once where the top two teams received money and mansions and the bottom three were executed. He sells the recordings through an underground network. I think he fancies himself as a modern style Roman emperor."

Alicia whistled. "Screwball."

"And that's not the half of it."

Crouch's phone rang. A brief glance at the screen showed him it was Healey. "Oh good," he said, answering. "I was just about to call you. We're—"

"Boss," Healey said in a quiet voice.

Crouch stopped in mid-stride. The stress in Healey's voice bled through the connection as clearly as if it throbbed through a vital vein.

"They've got me, sir. The damn bastards got me."

Crouch gripped the handset hard. "Explain yourself. What the hell do you mean—"

Another voice came on the line, its tones throaty and deep, its inflection murderous. "What he *means* is that he's now a guest of mine. And will remain so until my treasures are returned."

Crouch held his breath. "He better not be harmed, Solomon."

By now the rest of the team were crowding around, Russo and Caitlyn drip white and Alicia gritting her teeth.

"Everything's intact, more or less. For now. Your next move will determine if he stays that way."

Crouch held the handset away from his mouth, squeezing his eyes shut until they hurt. As if dozens of cops, dead mercenaries, and stolen treasure wasn't enough. How could an operation that had started out so simple end up consisting of so many complications?

"All, right," he said, seeing a way out of it. "We know you're at the Venetian Hotel. How about the lobby in ten minutes?"

Solomon laughed. "Do you think I am so stupid?"

Caitlyn had recovered from her shock enough to unzip her backpack and take out the team's master tracking device. She switched it on.

Crouch took his time. "So where would you like to make the exchange, Mr. Solomon?"

"South Africaaaaa." Solomon drew out the last letter with a guttural slur. "Two days. You find us. I'm sure you have the means. Oh, and be sure to inform Mr. Coker that his wife and daughter will be dead within the hour."

Crouch cursed as the line died. Coker gripped his arm. "Dammit, Michael! Call the FBI!"

Caitlyn held out the tracking device. "They're already in the air." Tears fell off the ragged edges of every syllable.

Crouch looked back toward the road. Flashing lights could be seen through the trees. "Bollocks," he said. "It looks like I'm going to have to call in that special favor after all."

"And Healey?" Russo demanded. "What happens to Zack?"

"What the hell do you think?" Alicia growled. "We go save the youngster's ass and kill the assholes that dared to take him."

THIRTY THREE

"Now," Crouch said, finishing up his special call. "Everything changes."

The team waited expectantly. Alicia was mindful of the cops a few hundred feet beyond their position. Even now any gung-ho marshal could throw a spanner into their plans.

"What's the plan?"

Crouch took a deep breath. "All right. One thing at a time. First—Lex. Pack him onto that Kawasaki and set him going. He'll be of no further use to us for the rest of this mission."

Alicia winced and opened her mouth to protest. After all, hadn't Lex just saved them a whole lot of hurt back there? Then she remembered who she was talking to—Crouch would have a very good reason.

Russo and Cruz were already helping the tender, complaining biker onto the green machine. Truth be told, by Lex's standard he barely offered any protest. Alicia saw he was more injured than he was letting on. Before she could say a word, the moment Lex's hands touched the handlebars, his eyes lit up, his head went back and he was creeping away, heading toward the Strip.

Alicia grunted. "Put him on a bike and he loses all sense of where he is. All thought—gone."

Crouch nodded. "I thought that might be the case."

"He's probably chasing after Kate."

"Lex can't help us with this next mission. We'll be going dark and into serious, deadly resistance. So the same goes for you, Mr. Cruz. You will be staying here to liaise with the new team Argento is helping to put together. I want you to oversee the removal and cataloguing of the treasure. It will all start today."

Cruz's face shone with pride and relief. "I won't let you down."

"Now, Greg." Crouch stared at the ground. "The FBI should

be with your family by now. And New Orleans is a fair distance by car, so why the hell are you still here?"

Coker stared open-mouthed at Crouch as if he might want to kiss him. "Are you winding me up, Michael? Don't do that."

"To my mind a man protects his family at all costs, puts their welfare above everything else. That's the only crime you're guilty of, Greg. Protecting your family. Only next time, tell me sooner."

Coker turned away, clearly finding it hard to speak. Caitlyn laid a hand on his arm. "Go to your family," she said. "Shelter them. Mine was destroyed, murdered a few months ago. There's no coming back from something like that."

Coker nodded and began to run. Alicia evaluated Caitlyn with a piercing stare. She knew for a fact that Caitlyn's mother had died of a heart attack recently and that her father was very much alive and well. What was the girl up to?

Then Crouch eyed Russo, Caitlyn and Alicia. "That leaves us on a plane to South Africa."

Russo nodded, eager to get going. "What I don't get is why this asshole has to drag us halfway around the world to make the exchange. We're all here now, and so is the treasure."

Caitlyn glanced at Crouch who nodded. "My take is that since he's a South African kingpin he can't operate here as he's accustomed to. In the US he has a huge protection detail, a small army, an extravagant lifestyle. But we can still get to him. Doesn't matter how many men he has or where we meet, we could arrange to take him down anywhere. If he's back home, on his own turf, he can control what happens even as far as paying off the authorities. Those who matter."

"Exactly right," Crouch said. "Now we have to go. If the US government knew we were carrying this gold in their country we'd never see the light of day again."

Alicia narrowed her eyes. "Your 'special' friend isn't an official?"

Crouch snorted. "Are you kidding? Could you name any politician or bureaucrat who wouldn't take advantage of our situation?"

"Dare I ask then?" Alicia ventured.

"Movie star," Crouch said in an offhand manner. "Known as—The Fortress. Big health advocate, gym god and all-round nice guy. He has access to the fastest private jet in the world and a new movie for which he's now setting off on a promotional world tour."

"Shit," Caitlyn breathed. "The Fortress? Do we get to meet him?"

Crouch laughed. "Yeah, and he might even cook for you if he's feeling good. But stay focused. By the time we land in Joburg we need a foolproof plan."

Caitlyn blushed a little as if realizing she'd lost sight of Healey's peril. By now the team were back among the crowds on Las Vegas Boulevard, staring up at the $40 million fountains of Bellagio. Waters swayed and twisted and swirled in their dramatic, bewitching manner, sometimes shooting over four hundred feet into the air. As they watched the show, the team paused for a moment as if relishing the last stunning vision they might ever see.

"Remember the last time you were in South Africa?" Crouch suddenly said to Alicia.

"Yeah. The Ninth Division. It's where I met Matt Drake."

"Try not to blow the damn place up again."

THIRTY FOUR

The plane journey was a study in the extremes of the surreal dream and the hard-hitting nightmare. The Fortress—aka Reece Carrera—proved to be a charming, muscle-bound, witty distraction. Even Alicia, not a woman to dally with the famous or associate herself with the trappings of fame, found herself drawn to the handsome, larger-than-life movie star. There were no airs and graces, no false self-importance, just a man that loved living and took from life the best of what it had granted him. To Alicia, Carrera epitomized the true vision of the sharp-dressed man.

Crouch drew the team around whilst Carrera cooked for them in the luxurious kitchen. "I have Argento on the line. He's already found Solomon's compound, a ranch several miles east of Joburg, toward the coast. Trouble is, Solomon isn't heading for his ranch. He's heading here—" Crouch jabbed at an image he'd brought up on a computer tablet. "The eastern cape. And in particular the Isidenge Forest."

"How can you tell?" Caitlyn peered at the screen.

"Argento has the flight plan. Not only that, but Solomon owns a huge tract of land out there."

"Reasons?" Russo wondered. "More easily defensible. Quieter. No authorities."

"And isolation," Alicia added. "He'll be able to do whatever he wants out there."

Crouch nodded. "I see this as a bit of a break for us."

Alicia grinned. "I know exactly what you mean."

At that point Carrera slipped his bulk around a kitchen unit, into the main cabin. "So you guys like red meat, huh? Black beans? Spices? Tequila?"

"You got me on all four," Alicia said quickly. Caitlyn giggled.

Crouch signaled that they'd be with him in a few minutes.

He turned back to the screen. "Our three-man team, with Caitlyn doing what she does best—the surveillance part using all that high-end software—should be able to get in and out of there very quickly. The approach is through forest, almost jungle. See all the ravines and streams? A massive amount of cover. The escape is obviously the same. We stay clear of the road. Solomon's compound is protected by a chain-link fence," Crouch couldn't keep the smile off his face. "Shit, I've seen ole Carrera back there do this a hundred times."

Alicia saw that Crouch was trying to buoy the troops, so didn't mention that Carrera was more than a little removed from real life in work and play, despite all his efforts to prove otherwise. Solomon's compound would be crawling with guards and surveillance equipment, most of it lethal since nobody was around to complain. A crime lord of his caliber would have every angle covered.

"Not a three-man team," she said.

Crouch frowned. "What?"

"It should be a two-man team. Caitlyn stays out of harm's way, agreed. But so do you. Russo and I are the best field soldiers on this team. We will know Healey's exact position thanks to his tracker. And less bodies on the ground means less chance of being spotted. This is a two-man operation."

Crouch looked ready to argue, but appeared to weigh Alicia's talent and tactical skills against his own. "I guess I would serve the team better by overseeing the op," he consented. "But that means we'll have to be relatively close by. In case of difficulty."

Alicia accepted the compromise. "Fine."

Caitlyn brought up a detailed map of the area and pointed out an e-mail that had just landed direct from Interpol—Argento's brief on the man and monster, Philip Solomon.

"Everything is as we expected. Solomon's your archetypal villain. Coker was right when he told us he built his empire through underground gambling activities. If there's illegal money to be wagered somewhere around the world you can bet Solomon's in the thick of it. Of more interest to us, he's also had his hand in more than a dozen antiquity thefts, though none can be linked to him. Indirectly, he owns an export shop in Berkeley Square, London, that deals in all manner of ancient artefacts."

"On the level?" Russo asked.

"Yes, perfectly legit. Except—" Caitlyn panned down through the statistics. "The shop has never made a profit."

"A front then. Maybe for stolen art. Artefacts."

"It doesn't matter now," Crouch said. "We're inbound to save Healey. The treasure is ours and will soon belong to the world if the US government doesn't dig its bloody heels in. Either way, we have finder's rights and permits. Let's go eat this bastard for breakfast."

Carrera stuck his enormous head around the corner. "Breakfast? Did I hear correctly? I've been cooking dinner for an hour."

Alicia gave him her best smile. "Well, well, Mr. Fortress," she said, rising to her feet. "Let's see if your cooking is as tasty and entertaining as your physique."

THIRTY FIVE

Alicia and Russo made it to the Isidenge Forest area with a day to spare. Realizing they had an abundance of time the team had ditched Carrera and his luxurious aircraft at Adelaide airport and rented a car to take them through Fort Beaufort and on up the A352 toward Keiskammahoek, a small rural town and the location of the Cata Lodge, the only nearby lodging area that offered all the amenities they would need. Crouch rented out chalets and both Caitlyn and he set up whilst Alicia and Russo started on the fourteen mile hike to the Isidenge. Thanks to Caitlyn's cutting edge tracking system she would be able to relate Healey's location in relation to theirs, but was able to offer nothing better. Access to the technology she needed just wasn't possible out here.

Alicia and Russo hiked in silence for many miles, eventually recognizing the forest through satellite pictures taken on the plane, the trusty compasses in their hands and Caitlyn's assurances through their headsets.

Alicia dropped to her stomach. "I guess this is it then."

Caitlyn came through loud and clear. "The Isidenge is a sprawling, sometimes flat sometimes mountainous area. You've still a long way to go. As with most state or national parks in Africa the degree of protection therein is questionable and can vary on a daily basis. Hence Solomon's occupation. Fighting was reported there at least as recently as 2013."

Alicia and Russo rose and hiked some more before dropping out of sight again at Caitlyn's request.

"You're three miles away, due north of your target."

Alicia turned her head toward Russo. "Here's where it gets harder. You ready, big man?"

Russo was already scrambling forward. "Let's go bring Zack home."

Alicia crept along for a while, then stopped in mid-crawl. "This is South Africa, right?"

"Well done for catching up. Yes, it is."

"I'm thinking—spiders. I once saw a sand spider in Babylon. Sacred me half to friggin' death."

"Babylon? Shit, how old are you?"

"Oh, har har. Russo cracks a funny. Dude, you started off being a bit of a wanker but now I'm actually starting to like you."

"Oh, thanks. So long as you don't try to shag me we'll be all right."

Alicia filled her sigh with disappointment. "Okay then."

An hour passed. The two-person team worked their way in slowly, mindful for traps and observers. The Isidenge River put in an appearance to the left, a narrow waterway at this point overhung by low branches and plants, but offering some shade. With sweat stinging their eyes, the sun blazing down almost directly above and insects flitting about their extremities they finally reached the area Caitlyn designated as hyper-sensitive.

"Outskirts," Russo said unnecessarily.

Alicia moved to follow in the man's wake, reasoning that one track was better than two. Through the trees ahead the pair finally saw the glint of steel—Solomon's chain link fence and the boundary of his compound.

"We're here," Alicia whispered.

Crouch's voice answered immediately. "Any sign of surveillance? Guards?"

"Nothing so far."

"I don't get it. All this is entirely too blasé for a criminal overlord. What are we missing?"

"Only this," Alicia said. "A guard tower inside the compound every ten feet. One hundred yards of no-man's land, possibly mined. Rolls of razor wire after that with only . . . one clear path that I can see. Past that, sentries on constant patrol. And more cameras than a Hollywood movie."

"Ah."

Alicia looked at Russo, then clicked the comms. "Ah? Is that all you can say?"

"Wait. Can you get a sense for the size of the compound?"

Alicia scrutinized the fence as far as she could see. "It's bigger than Harrods. Does that help?"

Crouch sniffed. "You can bet your life on one thing. Once you're in it'll be easier to get out of than Harrods. Hold for a while."

The comms went dead. Alicia nodded at Russo. "Screw that. Russo, you scan the perimeter in that direction; I'll go this way. We'll meet on the other side and get a better picture of the place."

Russo nodded, already mobile. Alicia took her time, staying low enough to scrape her chin along the ground. The border scan was arduous but necessary and it took them almost two hours to complete the circuit.

Alicia went first. "I have a front entrance, obviously heavily guarded, to the east. Road in leads past the guard towers to a row of parked jeeps, all unmarked. At the north side I saw a long, round-topped building that I'm guessing is the soldiers' quarters."

Russo pursed his lips. "To the west and northwest lies nothing but a large, block built office building in the corner. Two stories and with a roof lookout post and helipad, I believe. You can see a pair of rotor blades up there with two satellite dishes and other paraphernalia. I visibly counted twelve guards."

Alicia let out a breath. "And I counted eight, not including the towers. Michael, what do you have?"

Crouch answered as if his reconnaissance team hadn't just disobeyed an order. "Your only way in is to scale the office building. Out here, Solomon might not employ the sensors he would in the middle of a big city. Now, Healey is positioned at the northern end of the guard's quarters, quite close to your current position actually. I'm guessing there's some sort of holding cell area inside."

"Any communication from Solomon yet?"

"No. We still have three hours left according to the message he sent with proof of life. That's almost sundown."

"Distractions?"

"These are trained military men. With Healey's presence they'll be on hyperalert and will suspect some kind of distraction. It'll only draw attention."

"So it's stealth all the way." Alicia flicked her eyes over Russo. "And I chose to team up with an African elephant. Fantastic."

Russo gave her a hurt gaze. "Have I concerned you yet?"

"What concerns me is how the hell we're going to scale that two-story building before sundown and without the proper gear. Mr. Crouch, sir, it's time to do what you do best and come up with a plan."

"Already done," Crouch said a little haughtily. "I had plenty of time to think it through whilst you two kids were pissing about on your bellies."

Alicia flicked dirt from the back of her hand. "Do tell."

Buildering, also known as urban climbing, counted on being able to climb walls, often vertical, finding the right handholds to complement the correct body positioning. Whilst achievable on some modern buildings their evenness and uniform surfaces made it a lethal, illegal sport though several daredevils still tried it. Once Alicia had surveyed Solomon's HQ a little more closely and despite its lack of drainpipes, she determined the weathered, dried and crumbled nature of the block construction offered sufficient handholds for Russo and her to climb it. Positioned as it was, close to the northeastern side of the compound, they agreed that it was also the most screened position. Of course, not every angle could be foreseen, but they had already determined that

Solomon employed no forest-mounted CCTV, no motion sensors outside the compound and no traps. To assume the same for the interior would be foolhardy, but Alicia and Russo were at the top of their game—the situation demanded a little risk.

With no more time to waste, less than an hour to Solomon's deadline, and the bright sun beginning to dip toward the west and now no longer visible above the treetops, Alicia and Russo found the best hand- and footholds at the base of the concrete block wall. As her fingers gripped the crumbly rock, Alicia got a feel for the sharp edges and unreliable cavities and voids. She scraped rubble out of a crack before testing it with her weight.

"Ready?"

"Just go, Catwoman. I'll be right behind you."

Alicia took her time. Falling now would have the same effect as being captured—it would scupper their plan. The handholds were regular but most didn't offer enough of a grip or crumbled away to dust. Russo followed her every move, figuring that if she could do it he could do it. A warm breeze turned Alicia's sweat cool. At one point her left foot slipped, unhinging the right and she hung by her fingertips. Russo guided her boots back to safety.

"What I want to know," he said. "Is who saves me?"

"Maybe a fucking baboon will recognize you as part of the family and lend a hand."

Alicia inched up the wall, her vision consisting of nothing but concrete, forty feet high now and still several feet from the top. The forest made noises all around her, hoots and growls and catcalls. Light slipped from the skies. She would let Crouch play for time his own way. This mission was now do or die. At last she reached the top and paused, allowing her forehead and eyes to rise over the apex of the wall.

A rough square flat roof met her eyes, the larger part of which was occupied by a helipad and chopper, with a high, triangular-roofed, guard tower at the far side. Alicia saw movement there. The guard was smoking hard, his gaze lost far out across the tops of the forest trees. With a quick heave she slipped over the top and fell to the tarmacked floor, rolling and scuttling underneath the chopper. When she looked back Russo was in her place, watching the guard.

Two minutes later he lay at her side.

"Phase one complete," Alicia radioed in.

Crouch came back immediately. "Christ, is that all? Get a bloody move on. I've arranged to meet with Solomon in forty five minutes."

So much for playing for time.

"Where?" Russo clicked his mic. "Here?"

"Yes. He knows that we know where he is. There's simply no point pretending."

"I'm just thinking that might make the job of extracting Healey harder."

"Like I said, get a bloody move on."

Alicia rolled out from under the chopper, moved to the guard's blind side and made some noise. When his head popped out into the open she was more than ready, aiming and squeezing her silenced trigger in less than a heartbeat. After that all that remained was his cigarette, floating down through the air.

Russo ran past her. "Cameras?"

"Not up here. Clearly privacy is maintained for the type of person that might visit."

Russo shrugged. "Who cares? It's time to fight."

Alicia vehemently agreed. Together they half-slid, half-climbed down the guard's ladder, all the way to the floor of the compound. Two men saw them and drifted over, unsure. Alicia taught them to be more careful with bullets to the head. Now inside, the pair could afford to plant one or two distractions. Alicia unpacked blocks of C4 and jammed them into various niches before arming a simple transmit and receive device. Russo disabled two Jeeps and readied another before she beckoned him.

Together, they made it to the side of the guards' quarters,

crouching low in the shade but now in full view of the southward facing towers. It was only a matter of time . . .

"There!" The cry went up. "Stop!"

Alicia instantly blew the C4 which was set on a delayed timer, starting the mayhem. Russo ran forward, spraying the tops of the towers with bullets. From out of the HQ emerged a score of men, hardened faces beset with fury. Another blast of C4 went off, sending soil and wreckage among them, blasting most off their feet. Guns flew high into the air. The HQ shuddered as its windows blasted in, the catalyst to even more shrieks of pain.

Closer by, Alicia set off a third blast, this one placed against the wall of the guards' quarters and as far removed from Healey's last known position as was possible. She waited for the debris blast to pass then ran instantly into the hole she'd created, even as more rubble rained down.

The interior was high, hot and disorderly. Cots sat all around the edges of the room, most unmade and with boots and jackets slung atop the covers. Pitted tables ran up the center, covered with unwashed plates and decks of cards, newspapers and magazines. A sink sat in the far corner and a tall refrigerator next to it. Ten years ago they might have been white. At the far end of the building Alicia spied a row of cells, simply bars that had been hammered into the concrete floor to segregate prisoners from the guards. Maybe the guards themselves were sometimes disciplined there.

In any case a face she recognized pressed through one of the bars. "Hey!"

Healey!

Alicia and Russo took off at a sprint, but the view was suddenly obscured as men came in from all sides of the building; those who had been snoozing, off-shift or malingering.

Most were unarmed. Alicia dodged blows and spun as she ran, grabbing the arm of an assailant and flinging him full circle without breaking pace, using his body as a battering ram to fling at the crowd ahead. Bodies flew left and right. She leaped onto another's back, springing off and high into the air, kicking two in the face as she came down to land and digging her elbow into the skull of a third. Russo was the deadly weapon at her side, shooting without let-up, a gun in each hand. Alicia saw two men converging from two directions in front of her, dropped and slid on her knees beneath their combined lunges. Still in her slide, she spun around and fired her own guns, blasting at their bodies.

She holstered her weapons as the knee-spin reached full-circle, rising to her feet and racing hard at Healey's cell. Another man came in fast from behind and this time she leaped above his attack, saw him slide by below and came down hard on his exposed neck. The movement unbalanced her and she fell, rolling hard into the metal bars.

Russo smashed hard into the cell door, a crag attacking a mountain, but the bars held. Russo shuddered in pain.

"Fuck!"

"What the hell did you expect?" Alicia coughed in disbelief.

"That they would break!"

"Christ, and I thought Healey was the immature one."

Alicia fired from the hip, downing another two runners so that they impeded those that came after. Healey stepped away and Russo shot out the lock. The young man accepted the gift of a shiny Heckler and Koch, unable to keep the grin from his face.

"Knew you guys would do something stupid like this."

"You can count on us!" Russo ducked and fired as bullets slammed into the wall behind his head. The added firepower was from some new arrivals entering through the hole Alicia had blown into the far end of the building.

"Down!"

Alicia exposed the next part of their plan as she threw and detonated a brick of C4 just as it hit the wall to their left. Another blast destroyed part of the wall. Russo grabbed Healey and the pair hightailed it back out into the open, Alicia crabwalking and using her semi-auto for the first time.

Ducking out through the newly opened hole she threw the empty weapon back inside. "Ain't worth getting yourselves killed for, boys," she said and set off the explosive she'd attached to it.

"Boom."

Outside, she wished they'd had time to neutralize the guard towers. Men hid in the shadows up there, taking pot shots, their only disadvantage having to duck as Russo and Healey emptied their clips at them.

Alicia opened fire with her second machine gun. With a precise lob she slung a grenade so that it landed under the nearest tower, detonated, and destroyed its moorings. Bullets struck the soil all around her feet. Dancing from side to side, she raced after Russo and Healey as the guard tower smashed into the forest floor, timbers shattering amongst the rocks and trees. Russo put paid to another tower as they changed the angle of their run, heading not for the main gate but back toward the HQ.

Mercenaries gathered around the entrance, weapons trained and bristling, stood up in surprise.

Alicia pounded the dirt, breath flowing easily, fighting in her element, the life that she lived a testament to almost all that she loved. Only with thwarting death could she send cloying old, desperate memories back to the darkness where they belonged. By risking her life she chose to go on living.

Head down, shooting to left and right, bloody and bruised and loving it, her attention was suddenly captured by a booming voice.

"Look, they are there, you idiots! Take them!"

The man stood on the roof of the HQ, peering down at her. Philip Solomon, the monster, stared down as if he had every right to take her life, to choose whether she saw another tomorrow. His furrowed, loveless face was stretched with hate and arrogance, lit by the fires of hell. With a gesture of disdain he shook both fists at the air.

"Do not let them escape!"

Alicia veered at the last moment, as did Russo and Healey. A quick glance back showed them that the mercs that had gathered at the entrance were now pounding toward them as if taking part in the bad-guys' hundred-meter sprint, guns waving. Alicia opened the door of the lead Jeep and shouted at Healey to get behind the wheel.

"Move!"

The keys were already in the ignition, as Russo had determined earlier. Healey started the engine and gave it chance to roar. Alicia and Russo clambered into the open back, ducking beneath the ridged metal sides.

"Which way?" Healey cried.

Alicia shook her head at Russo. "Through the front fucking gate! Which way do you think?"

"Just checking." Healey floored the gas pedal. The Jeep sprang forward, wheels spinning, gravel spraying from beneath its tires. The initial acceleration sent it hard into the running men before they could bring their guns to bear. Faces slammed into the windshield and bodies smashed off the bodywork.

Alicia blinked in shock at what she saw nestled beneath the vehicle's tailgate. "Oh, look. A rocket launcher."

Russo gawped. "I guess such discoveries are just normal to you."

Alicia picked it up. "Assholes love their big weapons." She grinned. "I'm just a teacher, showing them the error of their ways."

With that the Englishwoman hefted the RPG over one shoulder and took aim at the only target that really merited a rocket launcher's full attention. When Solomon saw the weapon and its intended goal his face lost all of its conceited bravado and fell no doubt at least as fast as his heart.

"Goodnight . . ." Alicia depressed the trigger. "Motherfucker."

THIRTY SIX

The roof exploded, the blast firing blocks and wreckage in a wave off the far side. Flames spurted at the skies and ignited the nearby trees. Solomon and his closest men vanished in a blaze of fire and a deadly surge of rubble, their side of the roof completely collapsing.

Alicia discarded the RPG as Jeeps started up and sped after them. She shouted at Healey to hold the vehicle as straight as he could and picked up her machine gun.

Russo slid to her side. Together they kicked the tailgate off its hinges.

Healey picked up speed as he smashed through the gates. Chain-link fencing swarmed to the sides and rolled wire coiled above the roof of the vehicle. Metal struts bent and shattered. The Jeep bounced across a double-dip, momentarily out of control but quickly reined in by the young soldier. As the last obstacle tore around the Jeep's hood and a heavy crossbeam soared away, Healey swerved them back onto the main track, heading between the first trees of the forest.

Alicia lay half on her back, alongside Russo, watching the pursuing Jeeps speed ever closer. She smiled when Russo held out a hand.

"Pleasure working with you, Myles."

"Likewise, Russo."

As one, they opened fire, their bullets strafing the first Jeep, making it veer madly to the side. Its wheels rode up a rise at the side of the track, sending it up and over, suddenly landing on its roof, smashing and scraping into the surrounding trees.

Instantly, a second Jeep took its place.

Men leaned out of the windows, firing madly, crazily. Alicia and Russo climbed to their knees, machine guns pouring bullets off the back of the Jeep. A tire blew on the chasing vehicle, sent it spinning to the side.

A third took its place.

"Shit, how many more do they have?"

Healey flung the truck around the meandering track, upsetting both Alicia and Russo's aim more often than not, shouting sorry but assuring them they'd rather be *on* the track than off it. Alicia fell into Russo more than once, and he into her, but the pair silently agreed to speak nothing of it. Bullets clattered against the rusted side of their truck as one of their assailants scored a lucky hit. The Jeep at their rear came in close, its occupants' faces visible through the dirty glass that separated them.

Healey swerved hard. The pursuing truck didn't stand a chance. It plowed on through the forest, hitting trees and plummeting down a vertical slope. Alicia moaned as a fourth vehicle took its place.

"Last clip." She rammed the mag home.

"Make 'em count."

Caitlyn's voice hollered at them through the comms. "Y junction ahead. Take the right-hand fork."

Healey listened as Russo relayed the information, but missed the turn because of the hard camber.

"Idiot!" Caitlyn cried. "There's another fork three minutes ahead. Go left there, for fuck's sake."

"Jesus," Alicia murmured, firing again. "It's like having an abusive satnav in my head."

"I wish it was in mine!" Healey cried.

"Yeah, I bet you do." Alicia listened to Caitlyn's highly-strung voice, knowing at least half the nerves were due to Healey's predicament.

Healey made the turn this time, pitching them back on track. Alicia stood up in the rear of the Jeep, keeping her footing amongst the rusting metal ledges that made up its bed, and squeezed her trigger. Instantly, their pursuer's windshield shattered and blood fountained into the air as both driver and passenger died. With nobody to give it momentum the Jeep came to a standstill, a blockage to those still behind.

As one more tried to squeeze by, Alicia lobbed her final grenade at it. The explosion took out the front end, leaving it a twisted mass of metal and iron, innards smoldering. The road was now well and truly blocked.

Healey threw their vehicle from corner to corner, allowing the tires to slew around the bends, drifting from one to the next. The young man even appeared to be enjoying himself.

"I guess they didn't hurt you then." Alicia bent through the window at the back of the cab.

"Nah. Told them exactly what you'd do to 'em if they did."

"Good boy." Alicia grinned. "Now you're learning."

Healey chanced a look at her. "You said . . . you said you had Caitlyn in your head?"

Alicia sighed heavily and took out the implant. "Here you go. Keep it clean." She turned to Russo.

"I guess tonight we're soldiers and we'll get drunk together."

"That we will," Russo agreed. "Because we're still alive."

Alicia grinned. "Cheers to that."

THIRTY SEVEN

Two days later the team were assembled back in Las Vegas, just another group taking in the sights.

They found that if they walked out in the open, down the Strip itself, there was more space and it was easier to talk than if they squeezed into any of the local restaurants or bars. The night was pitch black above them, Vegas' multimillion lights holding it at bay.

Cruz was back, and so was Lex, complaining about bruised ribs and elbows. Even Kate Stanton had joined them and Armand Argento was louder than life through a mobile link.

"We believe Solomon died in the explosion," Argento confirmed. "Though the South Africans have not found his body. It has to stay as unconfirmed, do you see? Interpol does not make guesses and rightly so. Stay safe, my friend."

"Understood." Crouch led them all past the New York, New York rollercoaster, staring up as it thundered overhead. "What of Coker's family?"

"They're well, Michael, they're well. The FBI apprehended a team of men that were spying on them. Unfortunately they will have to go into the WITSEC program with Solomon's threat not yet defused. Not a hair from Coker's head has been seen."

Crouch exhaled. "He's a fool. He'd do better to come out and face the music."

"He's humiliated. Maybe he can't even face his family anymore."

Crouch let it go. Argento could be right. He signed off with a hearty thanks and a promise to get together soon. Then he turned to Cruz.

"And the lowdown on the treasure, Jose?"

"Our Aztec gold is safe and being documented as we speak.

The finding was immediately made official, the locale safe, the location undisclosed to the public. Experts are on site and I believe the Nahua elders are being flown out to the area. We're out of the internal and external wranglings now. We can only hope the governments don't get too greedy."

"I believe our benefactor might help with that." Crouch reminded them of Rolland Sadler. "He has enough clout to move mountains, believe me."

"Good."

The group stopped near the Luxor hotel, its enormous Sphinx head before them, the great black pyramid to their right, its magnificent beam of light seeming to penetrate the very heavens, visible for miles around.

Crouch drew their attention. "A grand job well done," he said. "Our first outing wasn't so bad, and every person here played a part. I can't thank you enough."

"Maybe they'll hand you the head of operations position now." Alicia smiled. "Head of eleven countries. Something like that. You deserve it."

Crouch smiled back, but included every one of them. "I wouldn't take it," he said. "This is what I've waited for my whole life. I wouldn't squander this chance I've been handed to live my dream."

"And what do I get out of all this?" Kate spoke up, the seemingly permanent leathers creaking.

"Like we said," Alicia stepped in. "Next time we're in Vegas . . . oh and you can still have Lex here, if you like."

"Thanks," the raven-headed woman said drily and made to leave. "And when I say Vegas I also mean Reno, of course. And San Diego. Los Angeles."

"Of course."

The team watched her depart, thankful for her help. A moment of perfect relaxation fell over them like a soft, gentle curtain of satin falling from the skies. The aftermath was seldom easy, but at least meant that the team could start to unwind.

It was Alicia who broke the peace, predictably so, looking toward the road ahead. "Where to next?" she wondered.

Michael Crouch's cellphone rang.

Crouch glanced at the caller ID, said, "Oh no, this can't be good," and answered immediately, jabbing at the speaker button. "Yes? Crouch here."

The quiet voice spoke in highly stressed tones. "Are you free? Are you finished?"

Crouch sent a worried glance toward Alicia. "We are."

"Then we need you. I mean, all of you, and more. This Pandora thing's gone intercontinental; we're fighting a war in four countries now."

"*What?*"

"Drake?" Alicia felt the onset of an approaching doom. "You're not making any sense."

"It's the end of the world, Alicia. The plagues of Pandora. The Pythians are everywhere. We're losing. This is going to take every single resource, every ounce of brainpower, every grain of courage. We're all going to get bloody or dead on this one, Alicia."

"We've faced Armageddon before, and recently. More than once."

"Not like this." Drake sounded as troubled as ever she'd heard him. "Something this big comes along just once in a lifetime. Survival isn't even on the bloody menu. Saving our society, that's all that matters."

Alicia swallowed heavily, never one to be lost for words, but now standing back and staring at her boss, Michael Crouch. "We have to help them."

He nodded quickly, his own face taut with strain. "My team is all yours, Matt. What do you need?"

"First of all head to Europe. You'll be our response team there. We're in the process of appointing others."

"Europe's a big place, mate," Russo put in, shrugging.

"I realize that. We don't have the right Intel yet, it's a fluid operation. Start with Rome. I want you on the mainland."

"Done." Crouch took a last wistful glance around the city of a million lights. "I'll be in touch when we've landed."

"Thank you. Oh, and guys?"

"Yes?"

"If you have loved ones and relatives, I'd call them before you land."

THE END

Aztec Gold is the first book of the Alicia Myles series. Part two should be released toward the end of 2015. The ending of this book leads us into Matt Drake 9—*The Plagues of Pandora*— a crossover novel, which will be released in early March 2015. The SPEAR team are joining the Disavowed and Alicia's new crew to take on the Pythians in an epic archaeological mystery action adventure.

As ever, e-mails are always welcomed and replied to within a few days. If you have any questions just drop me a line.

Check my website for all the latest updates— www.davidleadbeater.com

Word of mouth is essential for any author to succeed. If you enjoyed this book, please consider leaving a review at Amazon, even if it's only a line or two; it makes all the difference and would be very much appreciated.

Made in the USA
San Bernardino, CA
15 December 2016